Winter Shadows

Winter

Shadows

A Novel by

MARGARET BUFFIE

Tundra Books

First paperback edition published by Tundra Books, 2012
Text copyright © 2010 by Margaret Buffie

Published by Tundra Books, a division of Random House of Canada Limited,
One Toronto Street, Toronto, Ontario M5C 2V6

Published in the United States by Tundra Books of Northern New York,
P.O. Box 1030, Plattsburgh, New York 12901

Library of Congress Control Number: 2009938091

Library and Archives Canada Cataloguing in Publication

Buffie, Margaret
Winter shadows : a novel / by Margaret Buffie.

ISBN 978-1-77049-358-2

1. Métis – Juvenile fiction. I. Title.

PS8553.U453W56 2012   jC813'.54   C2011-906510-X

We acknowledge the financial support of the Government of Canada through
the Canada Book Fund and that of the Government of Ontario through the
Ontario Media Development Corporation's Ontario Book Initiative. We further
acknowledge the support of the Canada Council for the Arts and the Ontario
Arts Council for our publishing program.

ONTARIO ARTS COUNCIL
CONSEIL DES ARTS DE L'ONTARIO

Cover images:
Footprints diverging on snow © Chip Forelli / Getty Images
Old open book © Vladimir Voronin / Dreamstime.com
Sash: Métis Nation of Ontario

Design: Terri Nimmo

Printed and bound in Canada

1 2 3 4 5 6   17 16 15 14 13 12

To all the women of my family tree who lived their lives before me. Aren't I glad they did! I wish, with all my heart, I could sit down and talk with each and every one of you.

And to my daughter Christine and nôsisim Emily McGregor – my own ôhômisîsis.

∾

BEATRICE

1856

The sleigh's runners hissed over the snow, leather harness creaking in the frigid air, the horse's hooves muffled, clods of snow flying. Beatrice Alexander sat huddled under a pile of buffalo robes, the reins loose in her mittened hands. She was warm, except for her cheeks growing numb in the icy wind. She pulled her scarf higher and her fur bonnet lower, longing for a cup of hot spruce tea.

As Tupper followed the snow-packed track along the narrow river road, another conveyance suddenly appeared ahead – a strange bright yellow thing with many shiny windows, like a small house on fat bulging wheels.

As it drew closer, Beatrice sat up. That thing *couldn't* be real. It was moving under its own power – no horse in sight. Instinctively, she pulled hard on the reins. Tupper lurched to the left and stopped, his breath frosting the air in white gusts.

The apparition moved quickly and silently toward them, snow frothing behind. The great horse trembled, muscles twitching. He saw it, too.

Beatrice held tight to the reins. As the conveyance passed, a girl with a halo of red hair stared down at Beatrice through one of the windows. Her eyes widened, and she lifted a red mittened hand in salute. Then she and the strange device were gone . . . vanished . . . fallen from view, into the blowing snow.

CASS

My stepmother, Jean, was sitting at the kitchen table when I got home from school, chin in hand, looking out the window toward the river.

"I've been waiting for you," she said. "You were way out of line this morning, Cassandra. Overreacting, as usual, by storming out of the house and not listening to me. You *like* pushing Daisy's buttons. Well, you can't push mine. Just remember this, Cassandra: one day it will be too late to put the toothpaste back in the tube."

She just *can't* stop herself from offering up one of her stupid clichés, so I said, "For the hundredth time, it's Cass. That's what I want to be called. It's my name. I don't need a different take on it from you. As for this toothpaste, it's already out of the tube, so who cares if it goes back in or not? It's just toothpaste." The already edgy look on her face tightened, and that was good enough for me. Don't tell me I can't push her buttons.

"I don't want another shouting match. Just apologize to Daisy, okay? And you might think about apologizing to me as well, Cassandra." She stood up and walked away, her back stiff, shoulders high.

Stiff should be Jean's middle name. She told me often enough that she was "bending over backwards" to make a home for all of us, but if she ever actually did bend over backwards, she'd snap like a Popsicle stick. With her angular face, straight black hair, bony hands, thick legs, unvarying twin sweater sets and droopy skirts, she was no match for Mom. It should have made me feel better. It didn't.

As her footsteps retreated down the hall, I mimicked her way of walking, then stood for a second or two thinking. *Did I win that one?* No idea. We both knew I wouldn't apologize to Daisy. Or her. It was her daughter who took my favorite CD, stuck gum on it, then lied about it. The kid was a thief and a bald-faced liar. So why should I apologize?

There was a tea tray laid out on the table with a gloating Santa-head teapot and cups shaped like demented elves on it – for Jean and Dad's usual cozy little after-school schmooze. Christmas was less than two weeks away – the third since we'd moved out here from Selkirk and the second Christmas since Mom died. Hanging on a peg by the stove was her old red apron, splashed with white snowflakes. Last week, Dad gave it to Jean. She wore it every day now. She figured it was hers. Across the bodice, *Merry Christmas!* was stitched in white.

Merry? Huh. Not likely. Jean was removing all traces of Mom stitch by stitch. She called it *putting away keepsakes for Cassandra.* Pieces of furniture quietly vanished into our barn across the road. Jean said Mom's stuff was too old-fashioned for her "decorating plan." Luckily, before she started grabbing other stuff, like Mom's collection of antique pastel paintings, I packed it up and took most of it to Aunt Blair's for safekeeping. My favorite things I kept in our old blanket box, at the foot of my bed.

Thinking about all this made my blood steam. I snagged the apron off the peg and tucked it under my arm. It would go in my box. When Jean asked, she'd get the truth – it wasn't hers; it was Mom's and mine.

I was glad Daisy had to stay late at school. Dad was picking her up on his way home. I'd be free from the little rat for another hour at least. I turned around, automatically reached for the fridge door to get a juice box, and grabbed air. I kept forgetting the fridge was on the other side of the room now. The big kitchen was only half usable – the other half torn apart. Whenever I saw the workers, they were sitting around with coffee mugs in their hands. But, clearly, they'd earned their money today. The far plaster wall was gone, exposing a huge stone-slab fireplace, its deep hearth black with soot. The faint scent of ashes hung in the air. The broad wooden mantel was big enough to crush ten men, if it fell. The yawning mouth of the hearth was packed with fire tools, blackened pots and pans, and other murky things. Down one side were two cast-iron oven doors.

Jean would probably replace the whole thing with cupboards. I sighed. Mom would have been so excited, making sure the fireplace was restored to its former glory. *Me?* I couldn't let myself care. I used to argue every time Jean and Dad changed Mom's plans, but I wasn't up for a new fight. I was as burned-out as the silt that sifted down from that ancient chimney.

The sun suddenly streaked through the window, slanted across the opening of the hearth, and glinted off something deep inside. I reached in and touched the faint glitter with my fingertip, surprised to feel it move. I pulled it out and was shoving it into my pocket when Jean's head poked around the door. She frowned and vanished again. *Yes, I am still here, Jean.* Dad would be home soon. She didn't want me getting to him first.

Something I'd refused to admit until that moment hit me with a swift and painful stab. I'd lost not only Mom, but, slowly and surely, I was losing Dad too. I ran up the back staircase that led off the kitchen and came out next to my room. Locking my bedroom door behind me, I fell on the bed and stared at the old beamed ceiling without really seeing it.

I tried to take a deep breath, but it stuck in my throat. I wouldn't think about Dad. Or Jean. I slid a new CD called *Wintersong* into my machine and put on my earphones. Sarah McLachlan's sweet voice floated into my head. Just like last year, I couldn't listen to our old Christmas music collection because the memories hurt too much, but maybe this one of Sarah's wouldn't make me sad.

When Mom was still with us, on the dot of December 1st, in the midst of loud, fake complaints from Dad, our house was always filled with carols, jazz, and Christmas ballads – everything from Frank Sinatra, Nat King Cole, and Mel Tormé to the Vienna Boys Choir and even strange ones – like Yoolis carols and medieval motets, which I quite liked. My best friends, Tina and Crystal, didn't know a single old Christmas song when we were in grade school until Mom made them drink eggnog and listen. They'd giggled a lot at first, but they liked Mom, and soon the eggnog thing became a tradition. They even started buying their own oldies and bringing them over.

I hadn't really talked to either of them since early September, when Dad married Jean. Both live about ten miles away, in Selkirk. I had to change high schools when I moved, and at first we kept in close touch. Until Mom got sick. Now they may as well be a thousand miles away. I still got a few E-mails asking what was wrong, but how could I tell them I hated Jean and her kid, hated my life, and that I just didn't want to talk to anyone? I wrote back that I wasn't mad or anything – I just needed time to get used to things here.

Sarah's gentle voice flooded my ears. She sang about seeing someone standing in the snow on Christmas morning and how she'd keep that memory alive. All the times Mom and I made angels in the snow together flashed into my head. I pushed them away. But other memories rose up in their place – the ones that are always nearby . . . the ones that never go away. Mom's final few days.

Her skin looked translucent the last Christmas Day we shared, as if she were vanishing into the light. In less than two weeks, the cancer took her away. Now, in less than two weeks, it would be Christmas again – the second one without her and the first with Them. How would I ever get through it?

Why didn't you wait for me, Mom? Why aren't you here, so I can beg you to forgive me? I swallowed hard. I wouldn't cry. I couldn't cry – hadn't been able to since she died. *Where are you, Mom? Where have you gone?*

When I woke again, Sarah's voice was silent, the room filled with a dark blue light spinning spidery branch-shadows across the walls. Night meant I didn't have to see or talk to anyone. On the weekends, I slept a lot – even during the day. No reason to get up. I checked my watch: almost six o'clock. Only a few minutes left before facing Them at dinner. For the first time, I included Dad in that group.

Shifting my position, I felt something poke me in the hip. I dug it out of my pocket and rubbed some of the soot off with my thumb. A small brooch, shaped like a star. *How long has it been hiding in the fireplace? Who put it there?* I should tell Dad. No, Jean would take it for herself. I walked into the bathroom and carefully washed it with toothpaste and an old toothbrush I found under the sink. It came up nicely. Aunt Blair taught me that.

Back in my room, I stood by a window and examined

the little star while gently polishing it with an old cloth. Each gold point was filled with tiny pearls, the center crusted with bits of . . . *glass? Diamonds?*

All at once, the floor softened and heaved under my feet, the room lurching in staggered shifts, like a rusty merry-go-round. Nausea washed through me. I groped my way to bed. At the same time, I was sure I heard two muffled voices near me – an old woman's and a younger one answering. When they stopped, the room anchored itself again.

My heart pounded. The wind was whistling through the cracks in the old window frames. *Is that where the "voices" came from? Did my dizziness and nausea come from not eating much all day?* I closed my eyes, took deep breaths, and forced myself to think about something else – something that would get me back on track.

Like the fact that my room wasn't my room anymore.

When Mom inherited the house from her great-uncle, Barton Andrews, I was allowed to pick my own room. I chose this one because it overlooks the river. After the cheap siding was stripped off to reveal thick stone walls, we used electric baseboard heaters to keep the deep cold at bay. Even so, pockets of icy air still floated in all the corners of the room. Mom and the restorer had worked out a plan for insulating it and putting up original-style paneling. So far, not done. Facing the river were four deep-ledged windows. I would tuck myself into one on warm summer days and watch the tawny Red River flow slowly past, but in winter the ledges were rimed with ice.

The next job in line for this room was the removal of the stained and crumbling wallboard around a square bump in the wall – a small fireplace for sure. You could see one tiny edge of pale stone. I'd been looking forward to a fire in the grate on a midwinter's night. I stupidly said this to Dad a few days ago – with Jean hovering nearby.

"For safety reasons, we won't open the flue," she'd said firmly. "So there will be no fires, Cassandra. The fireplace, *if* we keep it, will be purely decorative." And she'd looked at me as if I were holding unlit matches behind my back and biding my time.

Maybe she thought I'd push her pest of a daughter into the roaring flames. Maybe she was right. I'd never had the heart be cruel to anyone, especially those who didn't fit in like other kids at school. And I'd never been a stray-dog kicker. But when Jean and Daisy moved in, Jean's condescending and Daisy's obnoxious attitudes toward me, Mom, and the house triggered this horrible coiled thing inside me that flung itself around and blurted out malevolent comebacks. At first, I got a lousy torn feeling after mouthing off. Not anymore.

The wind howled past the window beside me. Beyond its thick icicles was a big maple, snow flying off the heavy branches. Past that was a white slope down to the river, edged by more trees. Mom said the old house had faced winds off the river for well over a hundred and fifty years. This room was my haven after she died.

No more.

Now, across the floor was a second bed, piled with

clothes, Barbie dolls, and kid-junk. Daisy's bed. My stuff had been crammed into a much smaller space. How I hated the sight of it!

Before the wedding, Dad and Jean decided we'd all live in our place, and her divorce settlement would help pay for the restoration. She'd owned a market garden on her family farm nearby until she and her husband split. Now she taught piano to locals.

The third bedroom should have been Daisy's, but Jean had grabbed it as her music room, moved in a baby grand piano, and put our old upright one in the living room, which she kept telling me to use whenever I wanted – like it wasn't mine in the first place. She also hinted she wanted to help me with my grade-ten music exams, so I made sure all my music books were packed away. Like I'd let her anywhere near my love of music.

Dad said that, one day, this house would belong to me because that's what Mom wanted. But as far as Jean was concerned, it was hers now. There was no way she'd ever give it up. Seeing her swanning around Mom's house made me sick.

Last week, after another fight with Daisy, I told Dad I wanted to live with Aunt Blair. He and my aunt had a bad falling out after Mom's funeral, and they still weren't talking.

"No, Cass," he'd said. "You're staying right here with us. Give it time. Your mom would not want you leaving Old Maples." He was right, so I stayed. Very reluctantly.

When she was a kid, the minute Mom saw the house where Great-Uncle Bart lived, she fell in love with it and the little parish of St. Cuthbert's. She, Aunt Blair, and I used to come and visit Uncle Bart, and he'd tell us stories – like how, when his father inherited the place from his grand-father, there was a set of turbulent rapids upriver. It was drowned out when a large bridge with power locks was built to control flooding downriver to Winnipeg.

Old Maples was one of the few stone farmhouses remaining from those belonging to retired officers of the Hudson's Bay Company in the mid-1800s, all built on strip farms dotted along the banks of the Red River. There were lots of smaller farms, too, given to retired workers called servants of the company, set in long rows like two-mile ribbons, running from the river road's edge to shared pastureland far in the distance. Except for a few like ours, and a few more cared for by Parks Canada as historic sites, almost all of them were gone now, replaced by modern houses.

Old Maples was set well back from the steep river-bank – two stories high, with tall chimneys, but still managing to look wide and low at the same time. Its roof was slate, smeared with green moss in the summer. A stone wall stretched across the yard facing the road. It ended at a low wood fence, which sloped past a large stand of trees and staggered down to a wide flat river shelf, where it encircled a huge vegetable and flower garden. The house was surrounded on three sides with wide lawns ringed by pines, oaks, and maples. Old Maples' actual farmland lay across the road. Uncle Bart's family worked it from the late 1800s right up to the 1970s.

Since then, a local farmer rented it for growing hay.

Dad used the old barn for Jean's car, our truck, and things like sleighs, gardening tools, firewood, and now our old furniture.

I slid off the bed and stood looking out the half-frosted window. Maybe it was time to visit Aunt Blair. Sometimes, after school, I'd catch a lift to her place and have supper there. Sometimes I'd spend the night.

When Mom was told that, as the eldest, she would inherit Old Maples, my grandfather, Duncan Andrews, willed his house and antique business near Selkirk to Aunt Blair. He'd died seven years ago of a heart attack in Scotland, and that's where he was buried. Most of his final years were spent in Scotland, in a cottage he'd inherited from his family, so I didn't really know him. Blair had been running the shop on her own for years, anyway.

Usually I felt a bit better after seeing Aunt Blair, but sometimes the opposite happened. Blair didn't like Jean any more than I did, but she never talked about her – or Dad. So I couldn't really let her in on what was going on at Old Maples. Besides, I figured she might do or say something that would only make things worse.

When Dad married Jean this fall, I felt a lot like I did after Mom died – restless, with an irritable exhaustion that never let up. Except for school, where the work was pretty easy and distracting, I just couldn't focus on anything for long. All my favorite books lay unread. I couldn't even watch TV. I was either twitchy and on edge or plain dog-tired – no in-betweens. Old Maples felt alien, not like home anymore. I didn't tell Dad. He would've gone all defensive on me or insisted I take the antidepressants I was given after Mom died – which, by the way, I secretly threw away because they made me even more tired.

Before Jean and Daisy moved in, all I wanted was to keep my own room, but Dad sat me down and said, "Can't do it, honey."

"But there *is* a spare bedroom. Dad . . . please?"

I could see he was struggling. He knew that Jean snagging that third bedroom was wrong. For just a moment, he looked right at me. He knew what was going on. When he sighed, I felt a surge of sad tenderness for my tall thin father, with his receding hairline, small paunch straining against his gray flannel pants, and boring blue school shirt. Mom always bought him greens and rusty oranges and bright checks that suited his pale freckled skin and dark red hair. But Jean liked him in what she called a more classic look. He seemed washed-out and old now.

Dad looked down at his hands. "Jean needs the smaller one for her music lessons. That's a big room you girls will be sharing. Takes up almost the entire front of the house. I don't want to divide it into two rooms. We're all going to have to try and shake down together the best way we can, Cass. Even if it means making compromises."

"But compromises that never include Jean, right?"

He couldn't look at me this time. Any warmth I'd felt shriveled up. He was betraying Mom in the worst possible way. By forgetting her. *How could he live with stiff, unfunny Jean after the bright quick warmth of Mom?* Of course, he didn't really *love* Jean. *How could he? But what made him bring her and her demented twelve-year-old kid into Mom's house?* Beats me.

The day of the wedding – I don't know why – I'd blurted this out to my dad's sister, June, from Toronto. She'd looked at me witheringly from under the brim of her huge hat and said, "You want him to be happy, don't you? Your father's had a tough time, Cass. Accept the rules of good behavior today, and don't look so annoyingly miserable."

Aunt Blair, who to my shock turned up that day, gave June a scowl and put a hand on my arm, but I shook it off. *Why couldn't she have stayed at home? Why was she here with Mom's clear blue eyes and her own tight concerned face?*

As I walked away from both of them, I thought, *Who but the annoyingly miserable would ever want to do anything else but break the rules?*

So, after that, I just kept on breaking them.

Now, Christmas was looming, and I still had no privacy, no life, no old friends, no new friends and . . . I jumped when someone turned the door handle. I put the star brooch in my pocket.

"Let me in!" Daisy shrieked, kicking the heavy slat door.

"Hang on!"

"Mommeeee! Cass locked me out agaaain!"

I swung the door open and glared at the oversized glasses and elongated Pippi Longstocking braids. "See? Open. You can come in now."

"You – you did that on purpose!"

"Of course I did," I said. "Anything to get five minutes of privacy from you!"

"That's enough!" Dad was there to do Jean's dirty work again. "Daisy, go wash for dinner. I want to talk to Cass."

"Nooo," she whined. "I want you to be really mad at her. I want you to *spank* her!"

You'd think she was five years old, not twelve. Dad gave her a gentle push, which she shrugged off, but then decided to let it propel her down the stairs so she could cry to her mommy that Jonathan had pushed her.

"Don't lock the door again, Cass."

"I opened it right away. Gawd."

"Look, just *try* to be nice. She only wants to be friends." I looked at him steadily. "Yeah, okay. She's giving me a hard time as well, but this is all new to her – and it's new to Jean too, remember that. Just try, okay?"

"Do I have a choice?"

"That girl of mine who got me through the last two years seems to have gone completely AWOL. Do you know where she is? 'Cause I don't."

"Just leave it, okay, Dad? We both know there's no point in going over it all again."

"I'll try harder to understand if you will. Come on. Dinner. And please don't bait Jean tonight."

I opened my mouth, but he held up one hand. "If you can't be nice, at least be quiet." Then he tried to put his arm around my neck like he used to do, but I ducked quickly past him. I could hear him moving slowly down the stairs behind me. I didn't look back.

3

BEATRICE

I wasn't going to keep a diary on returning to the parish, in case my father's new wife, Ivy, got her grasping hands on it, but I have found a perfect hiding place. Not even she will find it. On the inside, I've written Meditations of a St. Cuthbert's Parish Daughter, *December 8th, 1856, Old Maples.*

I won't keep day-to-day notations – just the things that compel me to write. I hope that recording my musings will help me get through the long winter months ahead, with Ivy as mistress of the house. After Mama's death, caring for the house and Papa had been nôhkom's and my job. But now my grandmother is too old and frail, and I have once more become the daughter of the house, not its mistress.

As I look out into the dark night, my spirits drift down like the ragged snow falling thick and fast past my bedroom window. I will soon be a woman of eighteen, yet I can't seem to stop these feelings of despair and sadness. I become angry at myself for allowing them.

The rush of the rapids sound to my left in the distance, while directly in front of the house, the Red River is silent, smoothed to a blanket of muted blue-white. Beautiful. Cold. Remote.

The winters in St. Cuthbert's, encased in ice and snow, are endlessly long. How I yearn for summer, even with its torment of mosquitoes and black flies. For then the river will be busy with York boats, canoes, and other craft plying the waters between the Upper and Lower forts, some on their way to northern places, others delivering goods to parishes like ours, dotted along its banks.

Summer brings with it picnics, visits to the settlement down the river, and social calls to Papa's friends at the Lower Fort, where I can buy much-needed thread, beads, and luxuries like sugar or tea. The post is more reliable in summer, too, with the possibilities of new books to read and family letters to answer from England and Scotland.

When the lilacs against the house are in full bud and the days grow longer and warmer, some of nôhkom's kin will once again arrive on their yearly visit, dragging their canoes into the tall grass and setting up camp under the maple trees along the riverbank. I will hear the crackle of their fires at night through my bedroom window. Each day, they will quietly climb up the trail to take sage tea with nôhkom. I learned Cree as a child, and I love listening to their stories. Unlike so many in our staid parish, Grandmother's wîtisâna find much to laugh about despite their hard life – the women covering their mouths with their fingertips, their eyes filled with easy enjoyment. After offerings of smoked fish, beaded moccasins, and other things to nôhkom, Papa, and me, they will leave as silently as they came.

I sigh as I write this. Last summer is but a distant memory, and in this icy heart of winter, I see no glimmer of warm light ahead. In a month, we'll have a brief exciting week when the dog team, horse, and carriole races take place on the frozen river. But then, the short cold days and long dark nights will close around us once again. Christmas used to offer a short happy time as well, but I don't hold out much hope for it this year with my stepmother, Ivy, and her puritanical Presbyterianism at the helm.

Earlier this morning, I dressed in a similar darkness to this. To brighten my spirits, I pinned Mama's star brooch on my collar for the first time this year. Having it close always takes me back to happy Christmases with my tall and cheerful mother, Anne, who died the Christmas Eve I turned ten. But as I tied my moccasins, I knew Christmas this year would be anything but cheerful.

A soft cough from nôhkom reminded me there was no time to indulge in worries or sad memories. I tightened my resolve not to give in to the shadows hovering nearby.

Wrapped in a goose-down comforter by the lowering fire, she spoke in her raspy voice, "The sun is rising, nôsisim. You will be late for your teaching." She had coughed often during the night. I had to make sure she had plenty of rosehip syrup and hot spruce tea beside her before I left.

"I still have time," I said. "I'll be right back."

Downstairs, the kitchen was unusually warm. My stepmother stood by the fire, ladling porridge into a bowl. Our little maid, Dilly, a girl of twelve years or so who had recently joined the household, glanced shyly at me and left the room with a broom and dustpan. She was the daughter of a poor farmer and his deceased Indian wife. The farmer had left St. Cuthbert's when Dilly was five, taking his two sons with him and leaving the girl child with a neighbor, who had allowed Dilly to go to school until she was ten. After that, she demanded the child leave in order to help on the farm, training Dilly as a scullery maid and letting her out to people who needed cleaning or outside work done – for a price. Papa had heard from others that the girl was being treated badly and asked the farm wife if she might come to us on a full-time basis. The neighbor received money from Papa, of course – how much, I do not know – to release Dilly. As I looked at Ivy's stiff disapproving back, I wondered if poor Dilly had leapt from one sizzling pan right into another. I decided to watch over her and make sure Ivy didn't take advantage.

A man sat, arms on the table, waiting to be served. Ah, I thought, so that explains the large fire snapping in the grate. The Big Fellow has come for his breakfast. Ivy's son, Duncan Kilgour, glanced at me, then peered into his thick mug with an irritating half-smile.

While I was away at school in Upper Canada, Kilgour had arrived from Scotland to visit his widowed mother. He now lived on his mother's farm – the small Comper place, farther along the river road. A coarse fellow, with black curly hair hanging in greasy coils around his thickly bearded face, he wore a woolen jerkin over a flannel shirt, rough wool pants, and knee-length moccasins. His arms and shoulders were heavy with muscle – like one of the broad pale oxen in our barn. Boorish in his manners, he was either rudely silent or talked too much, with a loud laugh that grated horribly on my nerves.

He and some of the local farmers had been away hunting when I arrived home. Papa said the October hunt was late getting started because early snow slowed their progress. They returned a few weeks back, with buffalo meat and hides as well as deer and smaller game. Of course, trapping will continue all winter in the bush around the village.

I could see Ivy was making another pot of her venison stew for dinner tonight, sparsely dotted, as usual, with exhausted vegetables from the root cellar. Out of necessity, the best of the meat, already stored in the ice house, must be sold off. I cannot abide her thin and greasy stew, so I eat little of it. I suspect Ivy deliberately makes these miserly meals to show her displeasure at Papa for holding the best cuts back from her.

As for Kilgour, he has barely said two words directly to me since I arrived home. Not that I care, as I am still adjusting to finding his widowed mother installed in our house as my father's wife!

"Good morning," I said. "My grandmother needs more wood placed on her fire." I looked at Kilgour. "I wonder if you would –?"

Ivy pushed the bowl of porridge at her son, and he sprinkled it, not with precious sugar, but with lake sîwîhtâkan, the brown salt sold to us by Indians every fall. He nodded at my request, the spoon moving back and forth.

Ivy's eyes narrowed when she spotted the brooch on my dress collar. She had followed me to my room when I unpacked from my long trip home and saw the pin when I placed it on my table. She'd asked me if it had once belonged to my mother. When I'd said yes, to my shock, she snatched it up and darted off to Papa – with me, outraged, following behind.

"As your wife, it should rightly be mine!" I'd heard her cry through the door of Papa's study.

On entering, I could see him teetering on the edge of giving the small jewel to her, but I said, "That brooch was given to me on my mother's deathbed. I shall never part with it, Papa. Never."

He nodded, returned the brooch to me, and left the room, Ivy skittering after him, talking all the while. Her shrill voice was cut off by the loud bang of the kitchen door. She ran up the stairs, gasping and huffing with indignation. Later that evening, Papa asked Kilgour to help him move a truckle bed into his study. Ivy now slept alone in their room upstairs. The next morning, she had claimed it was all her idea, as she was tired of hauling that man upstairs every night, but we all knew the truth of it.

"I'll get the wood." Kilgour pushed away his empty bowl, filled a basket from the wood bin, and left the room.

I began to count . . . one, two, three. . . . With perfect timing, my stepmother snarled in her thick Scottish accent, "No reason why you can't fix the old squaw's fire yourself." She held the bread knife in front of my face. "If I had my way, she'd be living in that Indian town of St. Anthony's with her own kind. It's bad enough I have your ailing father to attend to."

I finally threw the gauntlet down after three weeks of holding my tongue. "My grandmother is with her own kind, right here. Do not speak of her this way again!"

She bridled, sucking in a sharp breath. Up to that moment, I'd steadfastly refused to rise to her bait, although I often felt as if I'd swallowed its sharp hook. I knew if I fought back, Ivy would only make things miserable for nôhkom when I wasn't around. But let her try her worst now! With trembling hands, I piled a bowl with porridge for Grandmother. As I reached for the bannock, the flat of Ivy's knife slapped hard across my knuckles. I let out a yelp.

"What's this, what's this?" Papa stood in the doorway, gripping his pronged walking sticks.

Ivy ran to help him into the kitchen, simpering, "Goodness, can you believe it, Gordon? My knife accidentally tapped Beatrice's hand. No harm done."

She settled him into a chair at the table, picked up her weapon, and handed it to me, handle first. With unsteady hands, I took it and cut slabs of cheese and Ivy's hard bannock for Grandmother's midday dinner, covering them with a damp cloth. I then filled a heavy jug with fresh cold water and a stone foot warmer with boiling, which I slid into a fur cover. Ivy served Papa his breakfast, chatting cheerfully. I knew Papa wanted me to get along with Ivy, so to keep the peace and protect nôhkom, I kept my anger to myself.

As I left with the tray, she returned my cold stare with one of sneering satisfaction.

When I reached the upstairs hall, I heard nôhkom's tittering giggle and Duncan Kilgour's deep chuckle. He was stoking the fire in our room. "And will you tell me more if I come again, nôhkom?"

How dare that oaf call her Grandmother in Cree! And what was so funny?

"I will," Grandmother replied, "for I have many to share."

He grinned at her and, with a quick nod toward me, walked out.

"What will you share with him?" I asked.

Grandmother's dusky crumpled face peered out from under her gathered bonnet. "Can I have no secrets? You will be late, nôsisim. Go to your teaching. It will help you be content away from this unhappy house."

I'd accepted the teaching position at Miss Cameron's School for Girls a few days after returning home. Following the incident with the brooch and other unhappy events, I knew I could not stay in the house with Ivy every day. I now have a plan for the small wage I earn. I hope to save enough so that one day nôhkom and I can go to the settlement at the forks of the Red and Assiniboine rivers and find a small house or a few rooms to live in. I've heard that teachers are needed more and more in the growing center. We must get away from here!

Although she is up here all hours of the day, Grandmother knows what is happening below stairs. She also knows my shadows are back. But I say nothing. I keep my plans to myself. Aggathas Alexander is too old and frail to take her granddaughter's worries into her weary heart.

"As long as I have you, nôhkom, I'm happy." I kissed her soft cheek. "I wish I could stay and care for you all day."

"Do not worry about me. I can stand up to that skinny mac-âya below stairs."

"She is wicked. And with you feeling so much stronger, she'd better watch out!" We laughed, but we both knew she was no match for Ivy. I threw my pinafore on the bed, straightening everything quickly. "I'll try and come home midday."

"No! No! I will use the chamber pot. I need only fire, food, and my memories. I will see you tonight." She lowered her voice. "Little Dilly comes up and talks to me, and I can send her to fetch things. She is homesick and finds comfort with me. I get to talk in my own tongue, and I find comfort with her."

That made me feel a bit better. I'd have to keep that little secret from Ivy, though, or the poor child, Dilly, would suffer for it.

Before leaving for the Upper Canada school five months earlier, I had shown Papa and our daytime help, Mrs. MacRay, how to care for nôhkom. Papa was busy then as the main builder of stone houses for the entire Red River area and one of the leaders of our community. Why he suddenly up and married Ivy, the Widow Comper, a month after I left, is a mystery to me. Ivy brought to their union her late husband's poor farm, a sour disposition, and a close-fisted, yet grasping hand. One of her first acts as mistress of the house was to release kind Mrs. MacRay from her duties.

Farmer Comper had been known as a grim, short-tempered man living with his Indian wife and two small sons in virtual isolation on his small farm. Five years after his country marriage took place, his young wife suddenly died. He had never been involved in our community and, *clearly, no parish woman would marry him, so one day he up and left, returning two months later with a thin dark Scottish widow by the name of Ivy Kilgour. Not long after Farmer Comper's death from a heart seizure, my father became Ivy's third husband.*

Soon after he and Ivy wed, Papa fell off a scaffold in the church, whilst hanging a wrought-iron chandelier. The doctor from the Lower Fort told him that his spine was damaged – perhaps permanently – and although Papa has hopes for a return to full health, his new and leaner financial situation forced my return home.

I was shocked to find nôhkom so weak, with running bedsores on her narrow back and thin shanks. I pressed her to tell me about Ivy's treatment of her, but she refused to say anything.

I immediately called in our local healer, Mrs. McBride. Ivy had objected at first, but I told her that Papa would soon know about nôhkom's condition. She'd blustered her ignorance of any "condition" at first, but soon grew very quiet on the subject. No doubt, working out her defense. I was angry with Papa for accepting Ivy's lies, but I also knew he had been distracted by the loss of his work and his own physical pain. I made sure, however, that he saw his mother's scarred back.

I could tell, like me, Mrs. McBride was aghast, but she quietly set to work on nôhkom. I so love this plain, unfussy woman. The last time she came, she was satisfied that nôhkom's open sores had finally healed, thanks to her hot poultices of alumroot and my turning nôhkom regularly when she was in bed.

Mary McBride came as Mary Macfarlane from the island of Islay in Scotland, where she had been a healer and midwife. A short, broad, cheerful body with rusty flyaway hair and red cheeks, she had just turned thirty when she'd married a widower with five children – James McBride – a kindly Rupert's Lander and a great friend of my papa's. At the time, she was working in the settlement as a midwife. She moved to St. Cuthbert's with Mr. McBride and became a willing student of the Indian shaman who visits our village. We have one English doctor for the entire settlement, and as he must tend to all families, from the river forks seventeen miles away to the Lower Fort six miles past us, he has come to rely on Mrs. McBride for much of our parish health concerns.

Note to myself: Call by her farm soon and buy more winsikis – which she calls snakeroot – for nôhkom's persistent cough.

When I'd helped Mrs. McBride put the final steaming poultice on my grandmother's back a week ago, she'd looked at me intently. "Can I help you, lass? Are you no' sleeping well? You need a tonic, I think. Do you no' have some Laborador tea around?" When I shook my head, she added, "Well, I'll leave you a mixture of that and dried birch leaves – makes a good all-round tonic, that does. If that doesna help, I'll make you a tincture of valerian. I used that a lot back home. I think you might need it." She chucked me under the chin and left.

Her concoction of leaves helped give me a bit more energy, but the shadows remained. I couldn't ask for the other medicine. We owed her enough for nôhkom's treatments as well as the massages and specially prepared mixture for Papa's constant pain – and Mrs. McBride deserves every penny of the small amount she charges. Besides, what could possibly help disperse this darkness in my mind? I must find my own way out of the shadows.

As I settled nôhkom, making sure she had everything at hand, the guilt I still felt for having left her to go to school in Upper Canada flooded me again. I couldn't talk to Papa, who was dealing with too many dark things of his own. What does the future hold for us all? For me? I wondered.

"Go, child, or you will be late for sure!" nôhkom called.

Unable to speak, I gave her a hug, gathered up my books and papers, shoved them into my pouch, and ran down the stairs. I heard Ivy's and Papa's voices in the kitchen. Suddenly Ivy's grew shrill and Papa's silent. A dark wing fluttered across my vision. Dressing quickly in my outer clothing, I grabbed my snowshoes, wrapped a warm scarf over my fur bonnet, and escaped into the snow.

4

CASS

With Daisy asleep in her bed, I sat against my pillows in the dark, letting Debussy's *Clair de Lune* flow through my earphones. I'd learned to play it on the piano because Mom loved it so much. Suddenly, on a swell of music, I knew my heart was about to burst. I shut the music off, picked up the little star brooch, and, holding it tight, fell asleep, only to be woken up by raspy murmuring followed by heavy coughing. Daisy must be getting a cold. That's all I needed – a snottier than usual roommate.

I lay there, groggy and dry-throated. The room was freezing. *Have the electric baseboards gone off again?* Outside my window, snow was falling heavily and silently, the moon's light glowing dimly behind it. I could see Daisy's fat little mound in the middle of her bed. *Have I been talking in my sleep and woken myself up?* I used to do that a lot when Mom was sick. Dad would always appear and stroke my sweating forehead until I fell back to sleep. Neither of us ever spoke. We knew why it was happening.

I was about to sit up when my bed tilted, and the room started to lurch around me. Then, just as quickly, it stopped. I was dragging in a shaky breath of relief when I realized that a small table stood where my desk should be. Daisy's bed looked different too – bigger, chunkier. Low flutters of red and orange bounced off the spot where the wall jutted out. *The fireplace? With a fire in it? How could that be?*

I pushed away the heavy comforter and stepped down, stumbling over a fur rug. I could hear a distant sound of rushing water outside. A book lay open on the table. I felt no heat from the flames as I moved closer to the fire. *A dream. That's what this is!* I touched the book with a fingertip. Cold and damp. A page covered in handwriting shimmered in the dim light.

I scuttled back to bed with it under my arm. The comforter was not mine, and a fur rug was piled on top of it. *Don't panic, Cass. It's just a dream!* I climbed onto the lumpy mattress and reached over to turn on my lamp. There was only a candle stuck in a metal holder, a rough tin cup beside it bristling with long wooden matches. I scraped one against the cup. It fizzed into a pale flame, and I touched it to the wick. The book was a journal of some sort. On the first page, in small scripted writing, was *Meditations of a St. Cuthbert's Parish Daughter, December 8th, 1856, Old Maples.* The writing was tight and hard to read in places, but I caught the gist of it quickly.

A hundred and fifty-four years ago, the writer – a girl a bit older than me – lived in this very house! The diary had been started a few weeks after she returned home from a private school in Upper Canada. She described her life with her father, grandmother, and horrible stepmother. She also described something called her shadows.

Is that what you have in your head, Cass? Shadows? Is that why you're so down all the time? Where did this diary come from? How did I –

"I've been watching you," a voice called. "You're acting weird!"

I quickly slid the book under my covers. Daisy was sitting up, pointing an accusing finger. My bedside lamp was on, the candle gone.

"You acted like you were reading a book, turning pages that weren't there. You looked really crazy!" Daisy's mop of dark hair stood on end, her cheeks flushed.

I was chilled right through to my bones, even though the air was much warmer than before. All my furniture was back in place, the fireplace covered in its cheap siding. *Nothing's changed, Cass. It never did change; it never really happened.*

"See, you're still acting weird," she cried. "All googly-eyed!"

"Go back to sleep." I turned off the light and burrowed deep under my covers.

"I'm going to tell Mo-om," she sang. "I'm going to tell her your craaazy!"

After a few more threats, she shut down. When I

heard soft snoring, I searched for the diary. It was gone. *Okay . . . if I wasn't dreaming, what else could have happened? Was I seeing things that weren't there? Hallucinating? Doesn't that usually mean a person is going crazy? I'm pretty sure I'm not nuts. Not yet, anyway. No. Had to be a dream. Definitely.*

The next morning, I woke up surprised that I'd actually slept with no new dreams at all. I searched the bed thoroughly. Still no diary. *Confirmed. It was all a dream. Wicked stepmothers are even in my dreams now. Soon I'll turn into Cinderella.*

I got ready for school and clumped downstairs to the kitchen. Jean was sipping tea while Daisy whispered furiously at her. I grabbed a cheese scone, nuked it, and sat down.

"That's enough, Daisy, thank you," Jean said, her eyes on me. I blinked right back at her, then bit into my jam-smeared biscuit. "What are you up to, Cassandra?" she asked, as if genuinely puzzled.

"Eating breakfast, thank you, Jeanette May." I'd learned her full name when the minister announced it at their wedding.

"You know, Cassandra, you don't pull the wool over my eyes. You may be able to pull it over your dad's eyes, but I know what you're up to."

"Yeah!" cried Daisy. "We know what you're up to!" But she suddenly looked confused. I wanted to laugh, but didn't have the energy.

I swallowed my mouthful. "I wouldn't know what wool to pull over your eyes, Jeanette May. I don't even knit. And by the way, when you figure out exactly what I'm up to, let me know, okay? I bet it's far more interesting than I think it is!"

I grabbed my jacket, hat, and scarf; stuck my feet into my boots; threw my backpack over my shoulder; and walked out the door to wait for the school bus.

5

⌒

BEATRICE

I cannot sleep. I am sitting in bed, writing by candlelight. The fire is crackling in the hearth, but I also indulged in a few wedges of pine in the corner Carron stove. Grandmother woke in the middle of the night with deep-chest coughing. I gave her some of the snakeroot mixture Mrs. McBride had stopped by with. It calmed her enough that she was finally able to sleep. I sigh. Soon it will be time to get up again.

Yesterday morning, after leaving Papa and Ivy arguing in the kitchen, I walked outside to find the snow no longer falling. The pink haze drifting across the horizon promised more to come. A path had been cleared to our barn across the cart track. When I pulled the barn door open, our pair of oxen snorted and lowed in their stalls. I was pleased to see Tupper already hitched to the little sleigh inside the dark odorous space. I am always thankful for this invention of Papa's, with its strong runners and buffalo skin stretched like stiff yellow parchment over the wooden frame. With moccasins, fur hat, mittens, and a thick buffalo robe, I can tolerate the coldest weather.

Minty Comper, Ivy's stepson and our stable hand, moved from the shadows and opened the side door, followed by Papa's mongrel hounds, Brutus and Caesar. Ivy no longer allows them in the house. She claims they will knock Papa off his sticks, but it's really because she hates dogs. Minty is a slender boy of fourteen, with the dark skin, sooty hair, and black eyes of his Cree mother. He wore his usual thick coat, moccasins, and round buffalo hat.

I climbed into the sled. "Thank you for getting Tupper ready, Minty."

"Not me." He smiled shyly, then looked away, opening the door wider.

Tupper stepped forward, and the sleigh scraped across manure and hay to the snow trail outside. Duncan Kilgour appeared around the corner, carrying a shovel. I nodded my thanks. He raised a hand. I made a promise to keep my eyes and ears open on Minty's behalf — just in case Kilgour or his mother decide to take advantage of the boy. While he eats supper with us now and again, I see no affection between Ivy and Minty, although she's known him since he was a child.

Tupper pulled the carriole over the crisp whiteness toward the river track, his hooves tossing up clumps of snow, his mane and tail whipped by the wind. Soft puffs hit my face, decorating my bonnet with snow flour. Soon he found his rhythm along the tamped-down road. Our neighbors are always busy on the track, hauling wood or keeping river holes open for water and fishing.

I sucked in a deep breath of sharp air, and the remains of my early shadows fluttered away. For now, a small voice inside me warned, only for now. I wouldn't listen to it. I would be brave today. And, if not happy, then resolute.

Farmyards flashed by, with their small whitewashed houses of squared logs. Their barns crouched nearby, piles of new manure steaming into the icy air. I waved at James MacDonald as he came out of his barn. He and his wife, Amelia, had lost their new baby to croup last week. There are now six tiny crosses in a row in the church graveyard marked BABY MACDONALD. Not one of their children has survived. James walks with a stooped shuffle, although he is still a young man. Many children are buried alongside their mothers in that graveyard, but this poor couple lives in a state of unending grief.

The St. Cuthbert's church steeple appeared just over the rise. Our long-term bishop, Mr. Gaskell, is retiring to England this week. Whether the new minister, Robert Dalhousie, and his sister, Henrietta, will bring some life to the parish remains to be seen. Miss Dalhousie, a sickly young woman, automatically became the new headmistress of the parish school. I can't help but wonder how she copes with farm children every day with only two young girls as helpers. Or how long it will be before she begs off her duties.

I would like to have taught in the parish school upon my return, but the only work I was offered came from Miss Cameron's School for Girls. I was grateful to take it.

Until Bishop Gaskell and his domineering wife take their leave, the Gaskells and the Dalhousies are living together in the vicarage across from the church. I was asked by Reverend Dalhousie to become the new choir mistress, one of Mrs. Gaskell's *former duties, taken over by determined force and ruled by an iron fist for many years. Even so, Mrs. Gaskell is quite incapable of holding a single note in pitch. I can at least carry a tune and play the piano quite well, so I can surely do no worse than her.*

As I drove past the church, I wondered if this new duty would help dispel some of my shadows. Ah, the voice whispered, you know they will never leave you.

Something heavy dropped inside me. I pulled on the reins and Tupper stopped, looking back at me, puzzled. The sky above his head was a sweep of blue-gray; the rising sun a brilliant arc. I knew I should be feeling joy at such splendor. This small village along the banks of the Red River is my home – and yet, I see it so differently now, with altered, more critical eyes. Like those that had so recently judged me in Upper Canada.

It was Papa's idea to send me for advanced schooling at Miss Peacock's Ladies Academy, far away in Upper Canada. He wanted me to find stimulation and new interests in a more sophisticated society and secretly hoped, I think, that I would find a husband to offer me a better life.

My childhood had been a lonely one. Miss Cameron's school had not yet been built, and Papa didn't want me taught my lessons by Mrs. Gaskell, so he tutored me at home. When I turned fifteen, social visits were arranged with a handful of the daughters and nieces of retired factors in the parishes of St. Cuthbert's and St. John's, but not one had the same interests as me. Now these daughters of retired officers are focused on their own husbands and children or planning visits to members of their family in the settlement, in order to enjoy a more exciting social life. Finding a husband is a matter of great importance to them.

I don't want a husband. I agreed to go to Upper Canada because Miss Peacock's academy offered lessons on teaching children, but more importantly, it stressed the reading and comprehension of literature, music, and art. I hoped these would help with my writing, so that, one day, I might become a published author like Jane Austen or Charlotte Brontë or Mrs. Gaskell – no relation to our bishop! While at the school, I read Charles Dickens's Oliver Twist and David Copperfield, and I knew the author had based them on his knowledge of London. I was shocked by the plight of the downtrodden in his stories. Before that, I had received Jane Eyre from one of my mother's sisters in England and had read it over and over, until its pages curled.

At the academy, I soon learned that my dream of intellectual freedom had been just that – a dream.

One day, a girl with large red carbuncles on her chin asked questions about my distant home with seemingly casual interest. I told her about my parish in Rupert's Land and about my family. The girl, whose father is an archbishop in York, glanced slyly at her friends. "See? I told you so. Beatrice is country born, à la façon du pays, as my papa calls it. That's French, not Indian." She sniffed with such disdain, it was a wonder to me her nose didn't turn inside out. I suppressed a smile, which only inflamed her. She snapped, "Your father's mother is a savage, Beatrice. Which makes him one as well – and you!"

"What does 'country born' mean?" asked an English girl, whose parents were recent immigrants to the Red River settlement some twenty miles from St. Cuthbert's.

"Don't be such a simpleton, Penelope. It means Beatrice is a half-breed. Her grandparents weren't married in a Christian church! They lived in sin – breeding like animals." The carbuncle girl looked as if she were sucking on a mouthful of chokecherries.

I didn't say a word, though my heart was pounding, but I looked long and steadily at her. She blushed an ugly purple and turned away, calling to her friends.

As a number of other daughters of Hudson's Bay officials were at the school, we soon split into two groups. To be fair, a few of the English girls were kind, if not openly friendly. For this I was grateful, yet I found myself suspicious of their motives. Only Penelope kept trying to be friends, and, as time went on, our interests in music and literature bound us in quiet companionship. But there was still much reserve between us.

When I think about it now, of course, I shouldn't have been surprised by the archbishop's daughter's nasty comments. I had always felt quite distanced from local gossip, but the scandal concerning the Company's chief officer's country-born wife and a young English captain only a few years ago had torn the Red River settlement apart. The rumors of this so-called affair, having been started by vicious tittle-tattle from people like our bishop's wife and her friends at the Upper Fort, soon grew in strength and ugliness. The rumors were so ferocious and widespread that even I, tucked away in Old Maples, heard them. Although a court case proved the young woman innocent, the gossips considered the results a travesty of justice. The young wife's friends thought them fair and true. But societal pressure caused many of her friends to move quietly away from her and her now-depressed and devastated young husband. Either way, it changed the settlement for good. The new English residents became very cautious about befriending anyone with Indian blood.

Papa told me recently that many mixed-blood people like himself, who were educated in good Scottish public schools and who held high positions in the Company or in the settlement's new political establishment, were denying their Indian blood. I realize now that the archbishop's daughter was simply giving me a taste of more ugly things to come.

When I was called home by Papa, Penelope promised to write and has been true to her word. Since she was also summoned back to the settlement not long ago to look after her sick mother, we exchange letters regularly, usually about books or the weather. But never anything of a private nature. She has not invited me to her home and has refused all invitations I have sent to her. I must try not to read too much into this. But it is hard.

Her father opened a provisions store for the droves of new English arriving in the Upper Fort area. Last week, Penelope sent me a jar of marmalade from a Scottish shipment. I felt, ungratefully, that she might be showing off a little. As oranges are almost unknown in our parish, the golden jelly, thick with orange peel, was a special treat for Papa, who had enjoyed it many times in Scotland. It is a rare event for him to smile with such pleasure. Afterward, I was weighed down by its brief sweetness.

———

I stared across the white expanse of the Red River. Tupper whinnied, but I held fast. Did that horrible girl in the academy succeed in making me ashamed of my family? Of Aggathas, my beloved grandmother? Of my papa? No. It couldn't be true.

Are you telling the truth, Beatrice? the voice asked. Are you?

To Tupper's startled ears, I cried, "I won't be ashamed of those I love! Or ashamed of myself for being their child. I won't!" The shadows once again slid around me with the swish of ravens' wings.

Why does it feel at times as if my mind and body will suddenly shatter into thousands of pieces and never join into me again? Sometimes, when I look into the future, I see only a terrifying black nothingness. I have to keep these thoughts a secret from everyone — especially Ivy and her ox of a son. Papa is battling his own shadows; I can't ask him to suffer mine as well. And I cannot burden my sick grandmother.

I am alone.

Everything inside me changed during my stay at that faraway school. Even my faith. Now, after only a few weeks of teaching, my once-steadfast beliefs in the missionary and its so-called good work throughout the parish are being tested. Perhaps Dickens's books and those of the Brontës have awaked something in me, for I've become convinced that the church's purpose here is not just to preach the word of God to us "half-breed savages." It's to break the tie between the English mixed bloods and their Indian families; to make the Company servants into English farmers and citizens; and to turn the young daughters of Company officers — who will

run the homes of the men their fathers choose for them – into
perfect little English ladies. A passage in Jane Eyre *says:*

> . . . they [women] suffer from too rigid a restraint, too
> absolute a stagnation, precisely as men would suffer;
> and it is narrow-minded in their more privileged
> fellow-creatures to say that they ought to confine
> themselves to making puddings and knitting stock-
> ings, to playing on the piano and embroidering bags.

When I first read it, I felt it had been written just for me.
I wouldn't spend my life making puddings and embroider-
ing bags – there had to be more for me than that! I fumed
with indignation and a strange kind of hope that I might be
able to make something wonderful happen.

But not a single thing in my life has changed for the better
since reading any of those books. Somehow, I feel even more
stifled. How can I possibly make changes while I live in this
closed community, with its religious patriarchal rules? And
if I develop ideas of my own, how will I ever find the courage
to act on them?

I do feel better after I write my thoughts down, but I often
wish I was writing to a friend who could advise me. One
who understands. One who feels as I do.

Sometimes the shadows come at me from nowhere, like
an unexpected low branch slapping my face on a summer
walk in the woods. Sometimes they spiral slowly, like thick
dark clouds, for days on end. Do they come from somewhere
outside of me? Or are they bits of my soul turning to dust?

When I think of the God who lives in that church, I cannot feel Him near. I am still told every Sunday that, although He watches over me, I cannot expect to understand His ways. I am told that He promises everything good. But, to me, He seems obscure, disinterested, even cruel, especially to people like the MacDonalds and their lost babies.

I try hard to remember spring afternoons as a child, when I sat under the budding trees along the shore and watched for silver flashings of fish; when I created wondrous images in the sweep of clouds over the far shore; when I listened to the distant rush of rapids. I try to remember, in winter, how I loved the scattered glitter of snow in the sun; how I breathed the scent of frozen balsam needles in my hand; how I felt the warmth of the sun on my woolen arm. How, then, I felt brief moments of His presence.

But I can't feel, see, or hear anything that gives me such peace anymore. I see nothing ahead except endless murky days and sinister nights stretching before me. Only one small glimmer now and then flashes in my peripheral vision – a little light blinking like a tiny star. But I am afraid to look at it. Is it offering me a safe harbor, if only I would look? Or will it vanish forever, if I dare to turn my head?

This morning, sitting in the carriole, I knew I had to face the busy day ahead. I couldn't stop to rail at Fate or the Furies or whatever was making my thoughts so bleak. At least for a few hours of every day, when I teach at Miss Cameron's School for Girls, I am free of these dark thoughts. And, I remind myself, I also have Dilly as a quiet ally at home. Blessings, too, must be remembered.

I should be wearing a sackcloth and ashes, I decided, for I am Gloom itself today.

"Miss Alexander!" someone called. "Are you all right? I thought I heard you talking to someone."

My sleigh was blocking the narrow church road. Ten feet away, Reverend Dalhousie sat astride a horse with a dour expression, rather like his master.

"Still miles away, Miss Alexander, in the cosmopolitan world of Upper Canada?" he asked.

I laughed to hide my fluster. "I'm still recovering from my long days of travel, Reverend. I was practicing a lesson for my pupils. I must go. I am already late."

"Will you be attending our little gathering for the Gaskells?"

"Indeed, I will," I said, hoping it would be more cheerful than Mrs. Gaskell's other dismal events over the years.

"I am pleased with the new hymns you included for the Christmas Eve service, Miss Alexander, considering I gave you such short notice about taking over the church choir. I am looking forward to hearing them and, of course, your school choir as well. I won't keep you. Mr. Campbell is failing and wishes to say his final farewells to God and his family."

I couldn't help smiling. "Not again! Mr. Campbell has been dying for forty years."

He looked shocked. "Now, Miss Alexander, you mustn't poke fun. Mr. Campbell is old and convinced of his looming demise. Perhaps this is indeed his final day."

I tried to look contrite. "If it is, please say good-bye for me. But do please remind him that our next choir practice is Friday at seven o'clock."

He was clearly disconcerted by my flippancy. I flushed, stammered out an apology, and sent my sincerest best wishes to Mr. Campbell.

Sometimes words fly out of my mouth. It can be strangely satisfying to be slightly reckless, but it is not wise. Women are not allowed to be offhanded or opinionated in our bishop's community. Perhaps that will change with the Dalhousies. Hope rises, but often its bubble is quickly pierced.

Reverend Dalhousie lifted one hand, and his horse high-stepped away. I turned to watch him. He sat well, slim and tall, his fair hair covered with a woolen scarf topped by a narrow fur hat, his upper body in a heavy coat with a thick fur collar. But his feet in those knee-length riding boots would grow cold. A few episodes of painful frostbite and he would soon learn to wear the moccasins of our people.

Robert Dalhousie is like no other man in the parish at present – a prize to be won at all costs by hopeful mamas in the other stone houses. He is English, pleasant-looking, in his late twenties, if somewhat stiff and formal. The mothers of marriageable daughters have issued a long list of dinner invitations well into February.

Is he a little interested in me, *I wondered,* in his detached, cautious way? *Perhaps I was reading too much into his pleasant manner. Perhaps not.*

Feeling suddenly better, I flicked Tupper's reins, clicked my tongue, and we were off.

6

CASS

A scratchy throat started on the way to school. By the time math came around, it was really sore, my eyes watery, and my nose full. As I finished a pop quiz and waited for the final bell to ring, I played with the star brooch pinned to my sweater and wondered how bad this cold was going to get. Suddenly a young woman in a long dark dress appeared right beside Mr. Weizer's desk, looking bewildered. Weizer just sat there, sipping coffee and picking his nose, like he always did during a test.

The girl had a narrow dusky face, with high cheekbones and dark eyes, her black hair pulled back from her forehead into a braided knot. She wore no jewelry except a small brooch in the middle of her collar, which glinted in the strange light around her. I sat up. The brooch was identical to the one pinned to my sweater!

I knew, when Weizer kept sipping and picking, that he didn't see her. A few of the other kids were waiting for him to notice that they were finished their tests, so clearly they didn't see her either. I lifted one hand to wave at her, but just as she looked my way, she stepped back and . . . *vanished*. To keep myself from crying out, I put my head down on my arms. My head whirled. *Was I hallucinating? Was I dreaming while awake?*

Someone touched my elbow. "You okay, Cass?" I peered over my arm at Martin Pelly. "You just went the color of Elmer's glue."

"I – uh – I'm gedding a cold, I think," I said.

The bell rang. I threw my paper onto Weizer's desk, lunged for my locker, then ran out into the cold fresh air. My throat was swollen by then. I pulled my woolen hat down over my aching ears. *Could a fever make you see things that weren't there?* I wiped away beads of sweat from my upper lip. My stomach tightened. *Please don't let me throw up!*

I ran through huge floating snowflakes toward the school bus. For once, I was glad to be returning to Old Maples. I even waved at Daisy in one of the backseats. For some reason, seeing her made me feel better. She stared at me, mouth open, glasses still frosted from the cold.

I sat beside a girl I didn't know, so I wouldn't have to talk. Kids crowded onto the bus. There's not supposed to be anyone standing in it, but once the dust settled, Martin Pelly and two other boys were left over.

Gus Thompson, the bus driver, looked in his mirror, his expression grim. Clearly some kids were taking friends home with them. "Hang on tight, you three," he shouted. "I'm not takin' the blame if you go ass over teakettle!" We knew he was a good driver, but he was taking a big chance.

He put his foot on the gas, and the yellow box rumbled slowly forward.

Before I knew it, Martin was staring down at me, one hand holding the rail above, the other gripping the tubing on the back of my seat. "Hey, partner, feeling better?" he asked.

The girl beside me shifted her attention to listen.

"Yeah," I said, but it came out a squeak. My hands were clammy in my mitts.

"You look like a sick puppy."

"Thanks for that," I said. The girl glanced at me, but I frowned and she turned away.

"So, Cass, you sure got worked up about group assignments in English class today," Martin said. "I think partnered assignments are a good idea. I figure it'll be –"

"– less work for you?" I croaked. "I'll be the one who ends up doing it all. I prefer completing assignments *by myself* – not with someone who serves up chips and dogs every night, ignoring the whole thing."

Martin's parents owned a fast-food restaurant called Pelly's, just behind the locks that span the river as a bridge. Pelly's was known for its foot-long dogs and homemade fries. I'd heard Martin worked there on weekends. I glared at him, then sneezed into my sleeve – three times.

"Triple blessings, my child," he intoned, and the girl giggled. I ignored them, searching in my pocket for a tissue. "We could get together during winter break and get most of it done."

"Whatever," I said, mopping my nose and wondering if my throat was actually on fire.

"Don't worry, Cass. I'll do my share." I could hear the smile in his voice.

"Yeah, well, if we *do* end up working together, you'd better."

The bus stopped and a bunch of kids got off, freeing up seats. Martin stayed where he was.

"Or else, huh?" he asked, grinning. "*Ooh,* scared."

The girl was darting interested glances at him now. I decided he was okay-looking – a bit taller than me, with straight black hair, dark eyes, and an angular face. His teeth had a space between the two front ones, and there was a small black mole on his upper lip. He always looked like he was ready to laugh. He was in my home-room, but we'd never really talked before.

My throat burned too much to talk anymore, so he chatted to the girl beside me. She told him her name – Tricia – and he told her his. She'd just moved into a new development, not far from where I lived. He suggested she drop by Pelly's, and he'd give her a free order of fries. *Aah, young love.* She left her seat, laughing at one of his lame jokes.

Afterwards, I could feel him looking down at me as the bus trundled along the road, but I just looked steadily out at the snow. Finally Gus shouted at him to sit down, which he did, right in front of me. I noticed how thick and shiny his hair was.

Soon the bus swung a hard right, into Pelly's parking

lot. The restaurant stood above the locks, and you could hear the sound of rushing water as the bus rolled up in front. A huge wooden cutout of a pelican, its beak full of giant fries, decorated the front entrance of the long low building, along with cutouts of mustard-smeared hot dogs, hamburgers, and plates of pale onion rings.

Martin hoisted his pack onto his shoulder. "Okay, tough girl. See ya in class." He and about ten other kids got off the bus and headed into the restaurant.

The bus's brakes let out a hiss and we were off again. There were fewer than a dozen kids left. Daisy scuttled to an empty seat behind me and began to kick the back of mine. "Cassandra's got a boyfriend. Cassandra's got a boyfriend," she sang.

A group of girls across the aisle giggled and whispered, eyes glinting knowingly at me.

"Who'd wanna hook up with her?" one said. "She never talks to anyone, and I heard . . ."

I tuned her out and gave Daisy my most evil *I'll-take-you-down* look. She stopped singing, but kept up the boot work. My head was pounding along with it. I stared down the aisle and out the front window of the bus, anxious to get home and crash on my bed. Suddenly a horse and sleigh appeared on the road, just around the curve before the old stone church.

As it approached, Gus Thompson kept up the same speed. He was a good driver, but what if he spooked the horse? I lunged sideways to look out my window. The sleigh's single passenger looked up at me, and everything went into slow motion. It was the strange girl from math class, covered in furs. Snow blew everywhere. I held up a mittened hand. I saw her eyes widen, and then she was gone. I ran to the back of the bus, frantic to see if she was okay. But there was no sign of her or the horse and sleigh.

"Oh, no! Where are they? Stop! Stop!" I shouted.

Gus slammed on the brakes, and I lurched backward, falling onto an empty seat. We must have hit an icy patch because the bus spun halfway around. A back wheel went deep into a snowbank.

"What the devil!" Gus shouted, throwing the bus into gear and charging down the aisle. "Is everyone okay?" All hands went up.

I jumped to my feet. "Didn't you see that horse and sleigh?" I cried. "What's the matter with you!"

He ran to the front of the bus, and the door wheezed open. A few kids followed him off. When he came back, his chubby face was red. "What horse? What sleigh?"

I ran outside, the rest of the kids crowding behind me. There were no tracks in the new snow. It was obvious there'd been no horse. No sleigh. No girl.

"I – I –"

Gus looked at me closely, his face softening. "Fell asleep, maybe?" He felt my forehead. "Hey, kiddo, you're hot as a griddle. Better get your ma to check you out when you get home. You're Cass Cullen, aren't you?"

"I feel sick. I'm *really* sorry."

"Never mind, never mind. Sure everyone's okay?"

he called. Then he pointed at three of the older boys. "You, you, and you. Climb into that snowbank and push."

Throwing disgusted looks at me, they did as they were told. The rest of us waited on the side of the road. A few of the kids were snickering and doing finger whirls around their ears. I didn't care.

A few minutes later, the bus was on the road again. Gus stood at the front and said, "Okay, there's no need to take this any further. Cass fell asleep and woke up disoriented. No one's hurt. It's over."

When the bus stopped outside our place, I thanked Gus. He waved me away. "You just get to bed and take care of yourself there, Cass."

As I got up to leave, someone shouted, "Watch out! You might get run over by Santa and his reindeer!" Hoots of laughter followed me out.

Daisy bolted past me, no doubt to blab to Jean about what happened. When I walked through the gate, I saw she'd slipped and landed sideways in a pile of fresh snow. Only her bright pink boots, jeaned legs, and thrashing pink mitts were visible. Then she was upright, shaking snow everywhere and wailing loudly. I tried to help her up, but she pushed me away.

Jean's horsey face peered out the front door. "I have a student in here! What on *earth* is going on?"

"Cass pushed me hard into the snow and left me here!" Daisy howled.

"You little liar!" I shouted.

"You did! And, Mommy, she made Mr. Thompson stop the bus – just to play a trick on him – and we drove off the road. We coulda been killed!"

"That's enough!" cried Jean. "Get in the house, both of you. I'll be talking to you when Mrs. Carter's lesson is over." She slammed the door.

My throat felt like the skin had been stripped right off it. Daisy ran ahead and was trying to lock the side door from the inside when I thrust it open. The kitchen counter was covered with racks of cooling shortbread. Even through a clogged nose, I could smell the browned sugar that always meant Christmas in Aunt Blair's house. Mom hadn't been much of a baker.

I was taking off my boots, ignoring Daisy's whining about snow up her sleeves, when Jean walked in. She wore her teaching outfit – twin sweater set, baggy skirt, round-toed shoes, and grim face.

Daisy perked right up – someone to listen! She whimpered about how wet she was from being pushed in the snow, but her performance was cut off in mid-gripe when Jean put her hand up. "Not now, Daisy. I'll listen to what Cassandra has to say first."

"But, Mommy, she made Gus Thompson –"

"Quiet, Daisy!" Jean ordered. "What happened, Cassandra? I saw you leaning right over Daisy."

"I have nothing to say, Jeannette May."

"She pushed me!" Daisy cried. "And before that –"

"According to you, someone is *always* pushing you,

Daisy," I said. "I did *not* push you. You slipped. I was nowhere near you."

"Did too!" she bellowed. Then she told Jean her version of the accident. "She was playing a trick on Gus! We coulda been killed!"

Jean stared at me, hands on hips.

"I didn't do it on purpose," I said. "I fell asleep and dreamed I saw a horse-drawn sleigh. I didn't sleep much last night and –"

She shook her finger at me. "You are pushing your luck, my girl, and that luck is running out fast. I know Gus. I'll call him and check this out. Meanwhile, you had better watch your p's and q's."

"Wow! Two clichés for the price of one today, Jeannette May. If I knew what my p's and q's *were*, I might decide to mind them. And as for pushing my luck, I don't have any! If I did, you'd still be living in your own house and not in mine!" I grabbed my backpack, ran upstairs, stumbled into the bedroom, and fell on the bed, my whole body shaking. I closed my eyes and took long deep breaths. When I opened them again, everything had changed.

The room was cold, even though flames flickered in the small fireplace. I pulled the covers over my head and curled into a tight ball. *What was happening to me?* I lay there for a while, heart pounding. Soon suffocated by the heat of my own body, I peeked over the top of my comforter.

The fire still fluttered in the open fireplace. The small shelves on either side of it were filled with rocks, pieces of wood, and books. The room looked cozy . . . peaceful. I sat up slowly. An ancient woman wrapped in shawls sat on a bizarre chair, with moose antlers for arms, in front of the fire. She turned her head and looked right at me. My panic subsided when I saw her sweet smile. She pointed at the small table. On it lay a book. I recognized Beatrice Alexander's journal.

∽

7

BEATRICE

Something happened in school that has deeply alarmed me.

My students were already there, looking like the bright-eyed birds we call kîhkwîsiw, *in their gray woolen dresses and white pinafores. I greeted them and was untying my bonnet while they chanted, "Good morning, Miss Alexander!" Once I put on my "Miss Alexander" face, I can often ignore the shadows.*

Two students have recently arrived from an officer's home at York Factory. Another five will be coming in the spring. Only last week, Miss Cameron asked if I would be interested in taking on the post of full-time teacher. Her assistant, the frog-eyed Miss Stiles who keeps one bulging eye permanently on her watch pin, is forever complaining about too much work and too little time. Will teaching and fussing about time like Miss Stiles be enough to keep the shadows at bay? I don't know.

I looked at my girls and sighed. Their thick hair, usually glistening with grease and strung with ribbon, was now carefully washed and brushed. Only moccasins were allowed in the school for warmth in winter, as long as the trimmings didn't go beyond simple bead rosettes. Most of these girls would be married before they are my age.

"Have you all learned your parts?" I asked. "At church on Christmas Eve, we must show everyone what fine singers we have in our school!"

They all nodded eagerly, except for one near the piano. I didn't recognize this pale girl, with her soft pile of dark red hair. Was she a new pupil that Miss Cameron forgot to tell me about? Although red hair in this half-Scottish community appears now and again, she didn't look like a mixed-blood child. She stared at me, bewildered. Something about her was oddly familiar and made me uneasy.

I was about to ask her name when Miss Cameron walked through the door wearing a gray taffeta dress, her chestnut hair bound tightly to her head as always. She is a slim plain woman, just past thirty years, but her skin and eyes are lovely.

"You made it, my dear. So much snow. How is your grandmother?"

"Her croup is a little better today, thank you, Headmistress," I said.

She put her hand on my arm. "I'm glad." Then she turned to the girls. "Good morning, ladies!" They curtsied and spoke their greeting as one.

Suddenly I realized the red-haired girl was no longer in the room — neither seated nor standing.

"Did anyone see where the new girl went?" I asked.

The pupils looked around. One said, "What new girl, Miss?"

The floor tipped under my feet. Miss Cameron grasped my arm firmly. "Miss Alexander . . . Beatrice . . . what is it?"

"I didn't eat breakfast. I-I'm a little light-headed. I thought a new girl was arriving for lessons today."

"Come to my office when this class is over," she said in a low voice. "Cook will leave you scones and a pot of tea. You must not neglect your health, Beatrice."

"I have to go straight to the library," I said. "My watercolor class is preparing seasonal greetings for their families, which must be ready for Mr. McQuaker tomorrow. Right afterward, I have piano and violin students to tutor."

"Then I will have the tea sent to the library. You must eat, Beatrice," she said firmly as she left the room.

I turned to the girls and my next words stuck in my throat, for the red-haired girl was back in the same place, sitting behind a low desk. She wore a garment with a finely knit bodice, a high neckline, and narrow sleeves. Even more shocking, it was the dark red of moss berries. She was holding a book. It looked like – it couldn't be – my private journal! My heart lurched. The light surrounding her dimmed. She faded away, leaving only murky vapor.

The schoolroom revolved slowly around me. Ivy's smug face flashed into my mind. I couldn't remember if I'd put my diary back in its hiding place. How did this girl get hold of it? Where had she gone? In the distance, someone cried "Miss!" just as the floor rose to greet me. A flurry of hands lifted me onto a chair. One pushed my head toward my knees. When I was able, I sat up, bracing myself to see the wild-haired girl again, but she was not among the concerned faces.

One student thrust something at me. "Lump birch sugar, Miss," she said. "Nikâwiy sent it. It will help you. It helps me when ê-nôhtêhtâmoyân."

"Thank you," I whispered. I took it from the child's damp palm and put it in my mouth. It was sweet and melted on my tongue. I felt better instantly. I took the other piece she offered, along with a glass of water, and, after a moment, regained my balance. I forced any thoughts of the red-haired girl away. A few deep breaths and a slow walk around the room and the Christmas concert rehearsal finally got started. I played the piano and the girls warbled away, backs straight and faces keen.

Last night, I ate nothing but one slice of dark bread – the sight of Ivy's pot of stew, floating in globules of fat, was too revolting – and I had only tea for breakfast. This vision was surely the result of having too little in my stomach and being kept awake by Grandmother's persistent coughing.

I'm trying to be rational about what happened. People can have visions when they are starving. I know this from Grandmother's experiences as a child living in the triangular mîkowâhp of her people. When it turned brutally cold, or when snow fell too heavily, game would become scarce. Many of nôhkom's kin were plagued by visions and died, including two of her sisters and a number of the elders. One winter, when nôhkom was older, the tribe was forced to take shelter near the fort at Norway House, where they were allowed to camp nearby and trade furs for food. This was where Aggathas met her future husband, John Alexander, who became my Scottish grandfather, a writer at the fort.

They became husband and wife in the country way. A canny man with many skills, John Alexander rose to chief factor of the fort. Aggathas's status climbed with him. Years later, they sent their only surviving son – my father, Gordon – to be educated in Scotland. He met my mother there after she arrived from Devon to take care of an elderly aunt.

But this morning, as I finished the last few chords of the choir's final song, I chided myself. I was not starving as my grandmother's family had starved. I was merely hungry and tired. So why was I seeing a girl that didn't exist?

"Miss! Are you feeling faint again?" a small voice called out.

I shook my head and smiled. "Well done, girls. Off you go!"

In the small library, I gave directions to my next set of pupils, then, a few minutes later, I tried to eat one of the scones left for me. But my stomach rebelled. I did, however, drink the large teapot dry, and, although I was anxious to get home to make sure my diary was safe from Ivy's prying eyes, I felt more settled.

The girls worked on their Yule greetings with ribbons, dried wildflowers, scissors, and paste. I wrapped a small watercolor portrait, pressed between pieces of heavy card, with brown paper. It was of my friend Penelope – I'd finished it from memory after I came home. Once I'd completed my task, I turned to the girls and hastened them along. I'd tried to have them emphasize the birth of Jesus in their cards as Miss Cameron is a deeply religious woman. The resulting manger scenes and starry grass plains filled with long-legged lambs – looking more like white-tailed deer – were finally ready. I gathered them up, along with my own package, and put them aside to give to Mr. McQuaker, who would take them north with the dog teams while the *weather held. I waited for the red-haired girl to return, but she did not appear.*

As Tupper pulled me home in the waning light, I gazed across the river, striped with lengthening blue shadows. We passed a group of men and two massive workhorses draped in chains, pulling titanic slabs of ice from the river onto a sharply angled dock. I was certain that one of the men was Duncan Kilgour by his height and bulk. There was loud laughing when one of the men slipped and fell.

On my long journey home from Upper Canada, I'd worked hard at fighting the suffocating thought of another winter in St. Cuthbert's. The bishop's wife, a former housemaid from England, had for years used her narrow ignorance of the world to ban anything that smacked of higher education or a social nature in our parish. There had rarely been musical, poetry, or dramatic evenings to look forward to.

Mrs. Gaskell had suffered the nearest thing to an apoplectic seizure when I once had the temerity to suggest we start a literary society. I may as well have murdered one of my students in front of her, the way she went on about it! When she heard of an evening poetry-reading at one of our neighbor's, her husband's reproachful sermon blew over the congregation the next Sunday like the cold wind of doom.

Thinking of the long days ahead and the strange girl, I suddenly found it hard to breathe. Tupper, sensing my tension through the reins, slowed and stopped. I closed my eyes. Like a swift phantom, a yellow vehicle rose behind my eyelids. As it flew toward my mind's eye, I saw once again the flash of red hair and the small startled face. I have had this same vision three times since returning from Upper Canada.

Was the girl in the yellow carriage the same one I saw in my classroom today? It was, I'm sure of it. Did she recognize me? Was it really my journal she held in her hands? Did she read it? I realize how kakêpâtis I must sound as I write this. Papa might say I was having a nervous breakdown. Am I? I am sure Grandmother would say that these visions have a purpose.

Grandmother told me once how she was visited by a spirit woman. It was the last time she and her family faced starvation. Her younger sister had just died, and Aggathas was breathing her last, when the spirit appeared to her. It told nôhkom to be strong, for there were still many things to do in her life and her family would need her. She recovered to marry John Alexander and give birth to my papa.

But, unlike me, nôhkom is spiritually strong and filled with an inner calmness that radiates off her. I feel no such tranquility, for I must constantly battle my black cakâstêsimowina.

This afternoon, as I sat in the carriole, Tupper's breath puffing small clouds from his nostrils, I wondered if the girl had been sent as a warning to me . . . if my diary had somehow been left out and been found by Ivy. I clicked my tongue, and Tupper moved forward. In the distance, smoke rose from Old Maples's chimney like a coiled gray snake. As we turned into the barnyard, I wondered how long it would be before I saw the spirit girl again. . . .

The only good thing (and yet one that keeps me wondering) about this frightening day was that I found my diary still in its hiding place.

8

CASS

I sneezed hard and the book dissolved in my hands. The old woman was gone. My room was back. My fingertips tingled where they'd touched the leather. *It's all just your fevered imagination, Cass,* my inner voice called out. *You're sick! Forget it!* Even that niggling voice sounded panicked this time. *How could I forget?* I didn't want to think about imaginary old women . . . about a fire that couldn't possibly be lit . . . or a book that appeared and disappeared out of nowhere.

I paced the room. Okay. I'd held the diary in my hands. It *felt* real. *Think logically, Cass. Think clearly. What was really happening? Was this another life I was seeing? Another time? A ghost? Could a book be a ghost? What about Beatrice's story?* Even I couldn't make up something as real as that. If I accepted that I'd somehow time-slipped into her life or she had time-slipped into mine, then what?

I couldn't escape downstairs; Jean and Daisy were there. I scrambled onto my bed and flopped back on my pillows, dragging the comforter up to my chin, ready to fling it over my face. I thought about Beatrice's life as described in her journal and realized that she was a nice person. The old woman (her grandmother?) looked kind. *So, what did I have to be afraid of?* Beatrice wrote things about her feelings that I felt too. I wanted to go over them again in my head, but I couldn't think anymore. The soft swish of snow against my windows lulled me to sleep.

I woke up when my cell phone rang. Aunt Blair bought it for me so she didn't have to talk to Dad or Jean unless it was absolutely necessary.

"Hi, babe," she said. "Still on for Christmas shopping next weekend?"

"Not sure. I gotta cold," I croaked.

"Cass, you sound *awful*. Is she giving you something for it?"

"She doesn't know about it yet. I came home from school and went straight to bed."

"How are your ears?"

"Aching."

"You always get an ear infection with a cold. I'm calling their phone."

"No – wait. Dad will be home soon. I'll tell him. Promise."

She sighed. "I wasn't going to yell at them, Cass. Okay. I'll let it alone for now, but I'm calling later. If you haven't told them you're sick, I will."

Aunt Blair is Mom's fraternal twin. They didn't look much alike, except they were both slim. Mom had pale floaty hair, kind of like her personality. Blair's hair is shoulder-length, thick, and black, with strands of silver. But the lilt in her voice, the way she laughs, and a lot of her expressions are exactly the same as Mom's. Hearing her speak is the only time I remember what Mom sounded like. And it always hurts.

I'd tried wearing Mom's old faux fur coat, with its big amber buttons that looked like barley-sugar candies, but every time I put it on, I remembered. And I couldn't let myself remember. There were things I just didn't want to look closely at when it came to Mom – memories that made my head fill with darkness and shame. Knowing Blair was only fifteen miles away – and the only person completely on my side – made me feel protected. *But could I reveal to her – to anyone – what happened on Mom's last day?*

After we hung up, I lay there unable to move, my mind ticking down into the silence. Soon I fell asleep.

"Get up! Dinner's ready!" someone shouted in my ear.

"Go away!"

"No. Jonathan says you *have* to get up."

I opened my eyes. Enormous smudged glasses leered down at me. "You're red," Daisy said. "You been holding your breath or something?"

"Get lost."

She left muttering, no doubt working out some big fib to tell Jean.

In the darkening afternoon light, a new sleety wind

moaned past my window, icy bits clicking on the panes. I dragged the comforter higher. I guess I drifted off again, for the next thing I knew, a cool hand touched my forehead. A dark-haired woman was leaning over me. *Beatrice?* I flung one arm out to ward her off.

"She's got a temp, all right." It was Jean. I blinked up at her.

Dad's face hovered over her shoulder. "We should ask Peter to drop by."

"Give her two Tylenol, and if her temperature doesn't go down in an hour, I'll call him. Or we could bundle her up, and you could take her to the emergency room in Selkirk."

"I'm not driving her twenty miles in this weather, Jean. Peter's our GP and just half a mile away. I'll get her a hot drink. Here, take her temp."

She fiddled with the thermometer, then thrust it at me. When it beeped, I took it out and read it.

"What's it say?" Dad appeared behind Jean again, holding a steaming mug.

"Almost a hundred and two," I said.

Dad handed me pills and a cup of chamomile tea with lemon honey – our family cold remedy. I took the pills and lay back, whispering, "I just wanna sleep."

"Why did Daisy say Cass was too lazy to come down for dinner?" Dad said to Jean. "Anyone can tell she's sick. And how come *you* didn't notice earlier?"

"Because she came in from school as her usual obnoxious self, that's why! I told you about the bus!"

"Who came in obnoxious?" he asked. "Cass? Or Daisy?"

"Oh, ha-ha, Jonathan!"

They hardly ever argued. *And why was I too sick to enjoy it?* Jean had blabbed to Dad about the bus. Typical. "Go away," I croaked.

Dad's voice softened. "I'm sorry, Jean. I'm just worried."

"She'll be fine. Don't fuss." She put her palm on my forehead. I rolled away from her. She stepped back. "See? It will never change, will it?"

"Jeez, she's got a hundred and two temperature. Give her a break, okay?" Then he said to me, "About this incident in the school bus. Want to tell me about it?"

"I fell asleep. I woke up calling out something. I can't even remember what it was. I guess I was dreaming. Gus stopped the bus kind of fast. One wheel got stuck in a snowbank. Kids pushed it out. We came home. He said to forget it. End of story."

"Okay. We'll let it go for now."

"Thanks, Dad."

"You're not even going to phone Gus?" Jean asked him.

"If Gus wasn't upset about it, we'll let it go, Jean. And you can tell Daisy not to go on about it. Cass was obviously running a fever," he said and left the room.

Jean walked out right behind him. I could hear them arguing down the hall. I sighed. I had a good dad – okay, a dad who'd say or do anything for peace and quiet, even ignore his daughter's need for her own room back, but a pretty good dad all the same. As for Jean, not so good. And not getting any better.

The night after he and Jean announced their engagement, when she'd looked around our house with this flushed look of ownership and made a list of things to change, I knew trouble had just begun.

"This place is a pit! It really needs a woman's touch," she'd said.

Dad and I had done our best to keep things under control, but – I admit it – the house was pretty lived-in and the kitchen could have been cleaner. We also owned a miserable old cat named Tardy, who shed everywhere. Turned out Jean was allergic to cats. Of course. After a huge argument, I handed him over to Aunt Blair. It felt like I was handing her my old life with Mom at the same time.

Not long after, Jean started her "trimming-down" process, saying there was just too much junk in the house and that she needed room for her and Daisy's things too.

"I want that dollhouse and these old Barbies," Daisy had announced, holding one of my Barbie dolls to her chest and gazing greedily at my three-story dollhouse.

After crocodile tears from Daisy and pleading looks from Dad, I gave up my Barbies, which were stored in organized coded bags in my closet. But I dug my heels in on the dollhouse. "Mom and I made that together, and we collected or made all the stuff for it bit by bit. It's mine. Mom said it's a family heirloom."

Jean looked at it doubtfully. "I don't think it's quite *that* caliber. You could at least let Daisy play with it. You don't have to actually give it to her."

"No. I don't want it wrecked."

"Don't you think you're being just a bit selfish? Daisy is a careful child."

"She's already ripped two of my best Barbie dresses by yanking them on the dolls." I stared meaningfully at Dad, who was hovering around uselessly while my stuff was being ransacked.

Finally, he said, "The dollhouse is Cass's. She can decide what happens to it."

"I'll pack it up, and Aunt Blair will store it for me."

Jean pursed her lips and looked at me with a deep frown. Probably wondering why I couldn't be stored away with the dollhouse.

That night, I asked Aunt Blair to take some of Mom's stuff that I was afraid might get thrown out. When she agreed, I lined everything up on the floor to decide what to keep.

Jean walked in and laughed. "Goodness, Cassandra, you're not taking all that old junk to Blair's, are you? I doubt she would want it, even if she is an antique dealer."

I looked her right in the eye. "She won't sell it. She'll keep it until this house is mine again. You've wanted rid of Mom's stuff since you got here. Clearly, you don't know good antiques when you see them. These are special . . . unique. Like Mom."

Her cheeks went a dull red, but she turned on her heel and left. A few minutes later, I heard her playing a thundering piano piece in her music room. She did that a lot after I'd ticked her off. I grinned.

Daisy, who'd been watching everything from her bed, said, "You hate my mom, don't you?"

"Well, she hates *my* mom."

"But your mom is dead."

I stared at her until she looked down at her hands, shrugged, got off the bed, and slid out of the room.

Now, as the late-afternoon light crept across my bed, the cold medicine finally kicked in, dulling the pain and relaxing me a bit. My nose felt less stuffed, although my head was still floating slightly above my pillow. I finally let it drift away into the night's soft blackness.

Sometime later, I sat up wide-awake and clicked on my light. Daisy wasn't in bed. It was only 6:30 P.M. As I lay back on my pillows, my light suddenly went out. When it flickered on again, I was no longer in my bedroom, but sitting on a wooden chair, looking at the back of a line of gray dresses and white apron straps, edged in a hazy glow. One of the dresses turned around. It belonged to a young girl with a round face and dark skin, her black hair held back with a blue ribbon. She whispered something to a girl behind her. I could tell they didn't see me. There were more than a dozen girls in three rows. Facing them, wearing a long dress with full sleeves and a pleated bodice, was a tall young teacher. My star brooch rested in the center of her plain collar. It was definitely the young woman from math class – the same one we'd almost hit with the bus!

Where was I? Slowly everything came into focus. In front of each girl was a music stand. Small wooden tables ringed the space. A classroom. The young teacher was talking to the girls, but I heard only a soft, windlike sound. Her smooth hair was parted in the middle and pulled back into a braided knot. Her mouth was small and curved, her cheekbones sharp, and her black eyebrows tipped up at the ends like a blackbird's wings above dark eyes. She had skin as smooth as caffe latte. *Would she see me this time?*

It was like looking at one of those scratchy old movies on TV, but in pale muted colors. Suddenly the teacher looked right into my eyes, then at the brooch pinned to my sweater. Her face went a chalky gray, and her hand flew up to her own pin. She looked like she was about to faint.

Dad stood over me with a tray. I closed my eyes and breathed slowly in and out to calm my racing heart. Struggling into a half-sitting position, I made sure the pin was covered by my comforter. I didn't want any questions. On the tray was a bowl of chicken noodle soup, two red pills, and a glass of orange juice. I was so sticky, hot, and disoriented, I could hardly focus.

"Better get into your pajamas, honey," he said. "How are you feeling?"

"Both ears hurt," I mumbled around the first spoonful of soup. I wasn't sure I could manage a second.

"You always get an ear infection with a cold. Peter Graham says he'll drop by on his way to the hospital tomorrow."

"You can head downstairs, Dad. I'll take the pills and go back to sleep."

"Daisy will stay in our room. We don't want her getting sick with the holidays starting."

"Oh, no, *we* wouldn't want *that*."

He gave me a look of weary sadness and left. The soup was salty and felt good on my throat, so I ate a few more mouthfuls. *Why did I keep dreaming about a time so long ago – a time I knew nothing about?* I wished the diary would appear again. In it, Beatrice said she was getting ready to teach at a nearby school, and clearly I'd just dreamed my own version of that very place. *What was really going on in my head? Or in this house?*

BEATRICE

I *stepped inside fresh footsteps in the snow to find Minty, a buffalo cape over his shoulders, standing by our back door.*

"What are you doing out here in the cold? Come into the house."

"Waiting for the mister to take me home on his horse. Mine is sick."

"Mr. Kilgour? Where is he?" The boy shrugged. "Come in and wait by the hearth," I said. "At least you'll be warm."

He shook his head. "Mister's mother don't like me."

"Doesn't like you," I corrected, then added quickly, "but she must like you. She's been your mother for years."

He looked away. "I am ininiw. Missus hates Indians. Even âpihtawikosisânak."

Like me – I am a half-breed, too, I thought. But she doesn't hate Papa. Not that I can see, in any case.

I looked at the lad, his fur hat topped with snow. How could any woman not feel affection for such a gentle boy? But this is Ivy, remember, my inner voice murmured.

Minty had received some schooling in St. Anthony's, but

he needed more now that the settlement's society was changing so quickly.

Note to myself: Begin to tutor Minty right after Christmas. Ask Papa why he hasn't done it before this, although I think I already know the answer.

I smiled at the boy huddling under his buffalo cape. "I won't leave you alone with her until Mr. Kilgour arrives. Do come inside. I insist."

He allowed himself to be pulled through the door. I prayed Ivy was busy elsewhere in the house. But she was there – scrabbling furtively in a wooden crate on the kitchen table. As she swung around, startled, Duncan Kilgour walked in behind us.

"There you are, Minty. What have you got there, Mother?"

Ivy glared at me and then at a box. "I thought it was for Gordon, so I opened it. And I don't feel bad about doing that! I don't!!"

"Mother, it clearly says MISS BEATRICE ALEXANDER, OLD MAPLES, on the outside of the crate!" I was surprised Kilgour was chastising his mother in front of me, but then it struck me that Ivy had opened something addressed to me. How could she!

"What's hers is her father's," she cried, "and what's her father's is mine!"

"Don't be ridiculous," Kilgour growled. "You've even opened one of the gifts."

I looked at him surprised. Why was he supporting me?

Inside the box were cloth-wrapped bundles of dried fruits, peels, raisins, and unshelled nuts, tagged with paper markers. A tin of tea, small glass vials filled with spices, a crock of

Stilton cheese, and a box of sugared confections, whose wrapping was in tatters, lay alongside them.

I lifted up the broken lid. "I can't see a note of any kind. Who is this from?"

Ivy threw a small white card on the table. On one side was a little deer, with a red ribbon around its neck. On the other was written TO DEAR BEATRICE, FROM HER FRIEND PENELOPE. HAPPY CHRISTMAS!

"How lovely!" I said. "I didn't think I'd ever be able to make a fruitcake again. But now I can!"

Dilly walked into the kitchen at that moment, mop and pail in hand. "What is fruitcake, Miss?" she asked.

"Never you mind! Get back to work!" Ivy snarled.

"It's a special cake for Christmas, Dilly," I said, ignoring my stepmother. "Come and see what my friend Penelope from the settlement has sent me from her father's store." I held open a bag of translucent glacé cherries for the girl to smell.

"Mmm," she said, smiling nervously at Ivy. "Smells good."

"Such an uncommon treat to look forward to, Miss Alexander," Kilgour said. "Mother, I know you have eggs layered in salt. Give Miss Alexander as many as she needs. I'll make it up to you."

"No. Those eggs are mine. My kitchen. My eggs. And I don't hold with rich foods for the Lord's birth. I won't allow it."

"Mother, you will give Miss Alexander the eggs."

I frowned. Why did he continue to argue? Surely not for my sake.

"I will not," she said.

"It's of no consequence," I said. "My mother showed me how to use crystallized snow in place of eggs. It works quite well."

"You will get eggs," Kilgour said, giving his mother a stare of such intense disdain that it solidified my thought that this had nothing to do with me.

"I can give her only a few," she muttered.

"That will do, thank you, Mother. Miss Alexander, you wouldn't also consider making shortbread, would you?"

I hesitated, then decided to play my part.

"Indeed, I would! And there might be enough fruit for a small plum pudding. I've kept all my mother's receipts."

Ivy bristled, Dilly smiled, and Duncan Kilgour smacked his lips deep inside his beard. Minty, who still wore his buffalo cape, studied the box with interest.

"I've got a good-sized goose to kill," Kilgour said, eyeing his mother. "That will be my contribution – and I will catch you a whitefish as well, Miss Alexander. Do you need anything else? A Yule log, perhaps?"

Ivy stood, arms crossed, face red with anger.

"We had a decorated balsam tree when I was a child," I said in a subdued tone. "Mama took the idea from her friend in the settlement. Even Queen Victoria has one during the Yule season. Penelope's gift brings back so many memories, and . . ."

"Why haven't you continued with these traditions?" Kilgour asked. "Wouldn't your mother have wanted that?"

I shrugged, not wanting to explain how painful our Christmases had become without Mama's lively presence. Besides, I didn't want this charade with Ivy to continue any longer.

"That first wife was a Church of England worshipper," Ivy spat out. "Presbyterians like Gordon and me don't care two pins for their papist ways. You'll soon see a decent kirk built down the road. We're forced to worship in the only one we have, but we don't have to like it!"

The woman was her own worst enemy! I smiled bitterly. It was my father who had designed and built St. Cuthbert's Church for the Missionary Society ten years ago, and he has worshipped in it faithfully every Sunday since.

Ivy snapped, "Don't you snigger at me, missy! You didn't have any Christmas nonsense after your mother died because your father could finally – gratefully – return to his true roots. You mother's death freed him."

I turned my back on her and lifted the wooden crate. I'd had enough of both of them! It was heavier than I thought, and I lurched to one side before finding my balance. "I will take this away and ask my grandmother to watch over it so nothing else goes missing. We'll all share what is left of the bonbons on Christmas Eve."

A sharp intake of breath from Ivy told me the barb had struck home.

Even as I write this, I ask myself again why I didn't just ignore her. I know she will get even somehow.

Note to myself: Keep a sharp eye out, so Dilly or Grandmother do not become scapegoats for me.

I refused Duncan Kilgour's help, staggered out of the room, and stomped up the stairs, wishing my moccasins had military cleats on them. When I banged into my bedroom, I called out to Grandmother, but there was no response.

For a moment, the floor tilted under me. This wasn't my room, and yet I knew it had to be. Disoriented, I called out again, "Grandmother? Nôhkom?"

A new moon glinted its thin light through the windows. The hearth was shrouded in something pale, and the room was very warm. Where was Grandmother?

Someone was in my bed. Had Grandmother become confused and climbed into the wrong one? I reached toward my night table for matches, but found, instead, a strange porcelain lamp with a cloth-covered shade and beaded trimming. Where was my candle? The figure in the bed stirred, and a long pale arm stretched out and pulled the tassel on the lamp. Light flowed across the bedcovers.

I stared at the young face looking back at me and could only register, somewhere in my mind, that the dark red hair flowing over the slim shoulders belonged to the girl from the yellow vehicle – the same girl who had vanished from my classroom. She looked ill. How did she get here? Why was she here? How had she made the lamp into instant light by simply pulling a short tassel cord? She said something to me, but it was only a low murmur in the growing darkness. I couldn't think, I couldn't hear, I couldn't – the box dropped from my hands with a distant rumbling crash. I heard faint shouting – nôhkom calling my name – and then silence.

10

CASS

I woke to the sounds of wind whistling through cracks in the windows, along with distant hammering from the workmen in the kitchen. My nose was still stuffed, my ears still ached. It was dark out, but my light was on.

That's when I remembered the dreams – the classroom full of girls and the young teacher appearing in this very room, staring down at me lying in bed. *Was she Beatrice? Was this her room?*

I know she recognized me both times – I could see it in her eyes. I groaned. *Recognized me?* She was a dream ghost! My inner voice murmured, *But think, Cass. Were you possibly awake and seeing a ghost?*

I caught my breath, coughed, then sneezed loudly just as the door opened and a man walked in. My heart stopped, until I realized he was dressed in a modern coat, carrying a doctor's bag. It was our new GP, Dr. Graham – a friend of Jean's. I'd met him only a few times, but he seemed nice. Mom's longtime family doctor, who'd looked after her when she was sick, retired soon after she died. I was glad. Seeing him only reminded me of that awful time.

Dr. Graham grinned. "Hi, Cass. How's it going?" His deep voice didn't match the soft jowly face. Jean walked in behind him.

"I'm okay, I guess," I croaked.

"You don't look it." He felt my head, snapped open his case, thrust a thermometer in my mouth, then peered in my ears with a lit instrument. He smelled of spicy soap.

"It's just a cold, Peter," Jean said. "But as her father scrapes and bows to her every whim, she's playing it up for all it's worth."

Dr. Graham looked at her for a moment before taking the beeping thermometer out of my mouth. He told me to open wide and, using a flat stick, gazed down my throat.

"My dad scrapes, huh? Scrapes what?" I said, as he straightened up. "As for whims, I didn't think I was allowed any whims in this house."

"That's what I have to put up with, Peter," she said. "She fights me tooth and nail."

"Well, Jean, she's not playing it up this time." He threw the plastic stick into the garbage. "You've got strep, Cass. I suspect the infection has gone into your ears. I don't want it heading to your chest. So I'm going to give you a dose of antibiotics now and a prescription that someone can pick up for you."

Jean sighed heavily. "I hope Daisy doesn't get this before Christmas. That's all I need." She frowned at me like getting sick was *my* idea.

"I'm sorry I'm under the weather, Jeannette May," I said. "I'll rise above it soon and try not to rub you the wrong way while I work on it."

Dr. Graham tried hard not to smile. "The meds will begin as soon as you take them, Cass. You'll be better soon. And, Jean, this illness is serious – not something *to be sneezed at.*" I snorted, and he winked at me.

"Oh, very droll, Peter," she said. "I've got to get Daisy ready for school. Thanks so much for coming, though." And she marched out of the room.

"I think *you* may have rubbed her the wrong way," I said, swallowing the pills.

He laughed. "I've known Jean a long time, Cass. She has trouble with change. She loves your dad. I can see that. I bet you see it, too."

"I don't see anything, except someone who doesn't want me around."

He snapped his bag shut. "She's focused on your dad and Daisy right now, I bet. Jean's one of those people who is almost too easy to tease, though. Like shooting fish in a barrel." He grinned at his own wit. "She's a good person. She'll figure it all out eventually."

I closed my eyes. It was too much effort to explain about Mom, the dollhouse, the cat, having to put Mom's treasures out of sight, Jean hating me – and I could never talk about the other thing, the one I kept locked away and didn't think about. *What would this nice doctor think if he knew about the guilt that sat like a shard of glass in my chest, ready to stab me whenever I thought of Mom's last day?*

"Remember, Cass, Rome wasn't built in a day. Give Jean time."

"Rome went belly-up, didn't it?" I murmured. "Are you trying to help me get better or just rubbing salt in my wounds?"

He laughed. "You're so sharp, one day you'll cut yourself."

"If I do, at least I'll be taking enough meds to cut off the infections!" Despite his need to defend Jean, I liked him.

He handed me a big red sucker on his way out. He'd made me feel better. For about fifteen minutes – until Jean brought me a tray. Tea, a poached egg, and a muffin.

"Peter says you can't go to school yet. He's phoned in the prescription. How much further behind will you get by missing school?"

"I'm not behind."

She looked unconvinced. "I never see you do any homework."

"That's 'cause I do it up here, when Daisy's downstairs watching TV and not doing hers."

"Well . . . I'll get someone to bring work home for you anyway."

"Everything's up to date for the holidays, except the English assignment due after Christmas. Martin Pelly's my study partner. I'll call him when I feel better."

"So you aren't behind in anything?"

I slid the tray to one side of the bed. "I'm not hungry. I'll eat this in a bit."

"Your tea and egg will get cold."

"I like cold tea." I turned over on my side. "And hate poached eggs."

I could feel her standing there looking at me. "If you're up to date in school, maybe you could get back to your piano lessons again. I could work out a plan for you."

"Not interested."

Silence for twenty counts, then a huge exaggerated sigh. "I'll get that prescription filled." The door closed behind her with a quiet click.

My stomach was tight. I should just leave, go and live with Aunt Blair. The idea had been floating through my mind a lot lately. Maybe it was the only way to be free of Jean. She would never let up on me. Take the piano lessons, for instance. One day, I heard her telling Dad that by not playing the piano anymore, I was cutting off my nose to spite my face.

"She has a piano teacher in the house, for heaven's sake, Jonathan. I could do a lot for her, but she refuses to play. Just to get at me, I'm sure."

I heard Dad try to say how losing Mom had been hard on me, but she cut him off. "She can't *always* use her mother as an excuse for not doing something that would benefit her future. You've spoiled her, Jon! Made her impossible to deal with."

I hadn't stopped playing because of Jean – I just didn't have the heart to do it anymore. Having her around made it easier to avoid.

Dad had let her dismantle our real home and change it into some kind of sterile hotel space. Jean's new furniture was modern and plain – all brown or cream. The walls were coffee-colored. Mom's mahogany dining-room furniture had been replaced by a plain oak table and chairs. The only decorations in the living room were three stoneware pots on the hearth and some generic modern art on the walls. It was all safe and all boring. Like Jean.

A few days before I got sick, I'd looked through the living-room door and realized, with a jolt, just how changed everything was, and something had clicked inside me. *This was my house, too!* Maybe I'd feel closer to Mom again – feel her near me – with a few of her things back where they belonged. I went upstairs and filled a cardboard box with the stuff I'd kept aside in the blanket box, then staggered back down. I put two of Mom's Art Nouveau candlesticks at one end of the mantel and a matching vase, covered in swirling silver irises, at the other. In the middle, I placed her figurine of a skater in a long dress, tiny fur hat, and muff. Perfect for Christmas.

The coffee table was bare except for a few magazines, so I put Mom's favorite mint green bowl, streaked with curving black lines, in the middle. With great care, I'd put ten family treasures back into the room.

The antiques glinted in the afternoon light. A big framed picture of Mom and Dad remained in the box. I would have loved to rub Jean's nose in their happy marriage, but I just couldn't use Mom like that. Looking down at her smiling face, the shard of glass in my chest slid deeper. One day I'd put the picture out. Not yet.

I looked around the room and shook my head. Mom's things didn't belong. Not in Jean's beige world. Jean had won. She'd finally got rid of Mom. I would not cry.

I'd just decided to remove everything when Jean walked in. Her eyes narrowed.

"I put some of our special things out," I muttered. "I didn't think you'd mind. But you don't need to –"

"I do mind, actually, Cassandra. This sort of outdated stuff clutters the place. I don't like clutter. And these things are yours now. Keep them for your own future home."

My ears grew hot. "This will always be my home. Long after you're gone."

"I'm not going anywhere fast. And, meanwhile, it is my home – and your dad's. I can do whatever I like with it."

"These are Dad's things, too! They stay."

She walked around the room. I could tell she was thinking hard. "Of course it's your home, Cassandra," she said with a tight smile. "Let's live with these knick-knacks for a little while and see. Okay?"

"They belong here," I said, knowing they didn't fit at all.

"Fine. Leave them for a bit then. We may have to move things around later on, though, as Christmas is coming and there are decorations to go up."

Of course, I knew what she'd do. She didn't even wait until the Christmas things were put out. Each day, when I returned home from school, something was gone. The vase and green bowl were stuck in one of the built-in corner cabinets in the dining room. Mom's figurine was given a place in another, hidden by the silver candlesticks. I gathered everything up and packed them away. I didn't want her touching them ever again.

One day, to my surprise, Dad asked why the skater figurine wasn't out on the mantel anymore for Christmas. I told him why. He called Jean and me into the kitchen.

Jean said, "Cassandra is more than welcome to display these things. We'll have shelves built in her room for them. What I'm trying to do with the house is . . ." I tuned out of her desire for a "fresh updated" (i.e., dreary and beige) look for the house and watched Dad's reaction.

He seemed harassed and defeated at the same time. *How could I tell him I couldn't feel Mom in the house anymore, and that's why I'd put her things around?* As it happened, putting them out hadn't made a bit of difference.

"You don't want them around because you're jealous," I said to Jean.

"Don't be ridiculous. I'm not jealous of *you*."

"No, you're jealous of *Mom*. Her things remind you that if she was still alive, she'd be here with Dad, not *you*! He still loves her, and you can't stand that. Look in his wallet. There's a picture of them dating in high school and another one of Mom and me –"

"Cass, stop it," Dad said.

"But it's true. You still love Mom. And Jean acts like she never existed. And if I even mention Mom, she gets all tight-mouthed and sneery."

"Of course I still love your mom. But I also love Jean, and I've started a new life with her. Jean knows all about my marriage with your mom."

"What's that supposed to mean?" I demanded.

"Your mom was a wonderful person, Cass. But she wasn't perfect, was she? You've put her on some kind of pedestal. She wouldn't like it there. And it stops you from allowing Jean in and –"

"How can you say anything negative about Mom? You were crazy about her. You told her all the time! And now you're pretending to love Jean. But I don't have to pretend – not even for you."

"That's right. You don't," Jean said. "Okay, maybe I was a bit unfair. If you'd like to choose one special thing of your mom's, we'll put it in the living room. There's that nice piece of turn-of-the-century pottery that might look good on the coffee table."

"Forget it," I said, scraping my chair back. "Daisy would deliberately break it. When I finally get this place to myself, I'll put everything back where it belongs." I looked at Dad. "You don't want them. You don't care about them anymore."

As I walked out, I heard Jean say, "You didn't deserve that, Jonathan. Do you see what I mean now?"

From that moment on, I made it my mission to get good and deep under her skin.

Listening to the workmen banging around downstairs, I removed the star brooch from my sweater and pinned it to the waistband of my pajamas. My fingers tingled. The hammering sounds grew muffled, and the light in the room softened. *Was something about to happen?* I waited.

Nothing.

My throat was still raw, but the pain in my ears was easing a bit. The half-light blurred around me. Something fluttered past – the pale figure of someone leaning over beside my bed. *A workman?* I sat up with a jolt. He was large, with a bushy beard, and when he stood up, he was holding a woman in his arms! Behind them, I saw the old native woman in her antler chair, speaking to him. I couldn't hear her, but the young man nodded in response. The girl struggled to her feet and pushed the man away. *It was Beatrice!*

Hard as I tried to keep them in my sight, they faded. I hovered above a gulf of gray nothingness, then let myself slide into safe, empty darkness.

11

BEATRICE

*O*n my way home from Miss Cameron's this afternoon, there was much to think about. School was over until well into January. A few of the girls not in the choir were already on their way north to their families, but the main group was staying with relatives at the settlement. Six of the youngest choir members were to be billeted at the governor's house at the Lower Fort, eight miles away, while Miss Cameron found billets for five others on our more prosperous farms. By teatime, we were left with ten of the oldest choir members to place.

As we sat down over our final cup of tea of the year, Miss Cameron said, "I can manage five girls on my own, despite the fact that the cook, all but one of the servants, and Miss Stiles have gone to the settlement at the Upper Fort. That still leaves five girls to sort out."

Without thinking, I said, "I could offer to have three, but that would still leave two." I knew Ivy would be furious, but I'd face that later.

Miss Cameron was delighted. "Are you sure your grandmother is well enough?"

"Oh, yes, and she will enjoy the girls." Ivy wouldn't, however.

We were sorting out when my three girls would arrive at Old Maples the next day and what to do with the last two when Reverend Dalhousie was ushered into the room by a pupil.

When we offered tea, he accepted and settled into a chair by the fire. *"I have come to see if all is set for the Christmas Eve service."* On hearing of our situation, he said, *"I could welcome the remaining two girls, but Bishop Gaskell and his wife are taking their servants when they leave, including the cook. Mrs. Gaskell informed me of this just yesterday. After their farewell party, Henrietta and I will be without domestic help, and although I am working hard to find replacements, I must admit we are totally inept at caring for ourselves, not to mention two young girls as well."*

Miss Cameron cried, *"Problem solved! The remaining two are my oldest students, well-trained in running a household. They would certainly earn their keep until you find replacements."*

"Then I shall do my best for them as my thanks – with enlightening books and a few social gatherings to which both of you and your temporary wards shall be invited."

My heart lifted. But then I wondered if Robert Dalhousie would actually allow more socializing in St. Cuthbert's. He did seem somewhat aloof, and his sister rather pale and listless, but perhaps it was because the Gaskells had simply worn them down. Those two would wear anyone down – even the most lighthearted of folk.

On closer examination, I saw deep lines beside the minister's narrow mouth. His hair was neatly combed, the sideburns *curving just above his jawline. His eyes were the palest of blues behind sandy lashes. But his black vestments were slightly wrinkled, and there was a small stain on his white collar and cravat.*

He glanced at me with a puzzled expression.

My teacup clattered onto the small table. "I must go," I said. "I will expect my three charges around two o'clock tomorrow, then, Miss Cameron." On impulse, I added, "I would like to extend an invitation to you both to dine at Old Maples on Christmas Day, following the afternoon service . . . including your charges and, of course, your sister as well, Reverend."

Miss Cameron's face lit up. "But how kind, Miss Alexander! My girls and I should love to come. I'll bring — let me see — seedcake, gingerbread, and a large dish of winter squash, of which I have many. You will have quite a crowd of people!"

"It will be wonderful to have a full house!" I said, counting heads quickly in my mind. It seemed an alarming number!

Reverend Dalhousie said, "My sister will be delighted to come, but I must consult her before offering anything."

"Please, don't worry about that, Reverend. We will have a large goose, a fine haunch of venison, fish, pudding, and cakes. I can't promise a high culinary standard, but we will have enough to fill us."

I was babbling. I stopped at once, said my good-byes quickly, and gathered myself together before scuttling down the hall, where I pulled on my outdoor clothing. As I reached for the door handle, I hesitated. Once I walked through that door, I would be under obligation to follow through with what I'd promised Miss Cameron and Reverend Dalhousie. To have three young girls stay with us for a fortnight was going to be hard enough to explain to Ivy, but adding ten students and three adults for Christmas dinner was madness.

"What on earth have I done?" I whispered.

Only last night, I fainted dead away after imagining a sick young girl lying in my bed. What makes me think I can manage the huge task of Christmas dinner on my own? What if I see the phantom girl when my three young guests are crowded into Grandmother and my room? What if I forget myself and try to speak to the spirit girl while people are nearby — for I could easily do that, she is so real to me. And what if she tries to talk to me again — what if I actually hear her voice? If I do, does it mean I've lost my mind? Will everyone find out about the shadows and think that I am crazy?

I backed quickly away from the door and stumbled into Reverend Dalhousie. As he tucked an old scarf around his neck, I noticed his wool coat had frayed cuffs. Someone needs to take care of him, *I thought wildly.* How can his sister let him out looking so neglected? *Knowing my thoughts were out of control, I staggered to one side, apologizing.*

He caught my arm to steady me. "Miss Alexander, are you ill?"

I almost blurted out my fears, but noticed a slight withdrawal in his pale eyes. "I am fine, Sir. Just momentarily dizzy."

"Does this happen often, Miss Alexander? Perhaps you should see Doctor Wilson when he returns to the parish."

"I'm so busy getting my grandmother settled in the mornings that I forget my own breakfast sometimes." I tried to laugh. "Only when I am halfway through my lessons do my rumblings remind me I haven't eaten."

"You must take care of yourself."

"I will have more time now that school has broken for the holiday. Will you attend choir practice this week, Sir?"

"Yes. I should tell you that Mr. Campbell is indeed ill with bronchitis – but not seriously so – and I have asked your brother, Duncan, to step in. I hear he is a good fiddler and an excellent singer."

"He is? Are there musical gatherings in the parish? Since when?"

"Mr. Kilgour started them when he arrived. I don't go, of course, as I can't make any decisions about them until I am in charge. I don't condone drinking or wild dancing, however."

I wanted to say, as opposed to sedate dancing? But, instead, I said, "I didn't know about them. And he is not my brother. He is the grown son of my father's wife, the Widow Comper."

"I do beg your pardon. Of course. But I'm sure he will be a fine addition to our choir. It will do him good to think on God's lessons and less of his own pleasures. Good-bye for the present, Miss Alexander."

As Tupper trotted through freshly fallen snow in the afternoon gloaming, I tried to take in what Robert Dalhousie had just told me. Clearly the young reverend disapproved of parties or community ceilidhs. And I could only imagine how rowdy they would get with Kilgour in charge. Still, it must surely do the farmers and their families good to have some enjoyment like that.

But enough – I must prepare myself for this new battle with Ivy over Christmas dinner. Perhaps Kilgour would stay away for a few days after that awful episode over Penelope's Christmas box.

I couldn't help but wonder why he came all the way from Scotland to stay with his mother. It was obvious they were not comfortable in each other's company. She was often strangely fussed and excited around him, and he seemed cold toward her, even deliberately unkind, as he'd been yesterday. Yet he continued to come by each day to see her. Why? It is all very curious.

His dark eyes always seem to be laughing at me. Yet he has been almost solicitous over the Christmas box from Penelope. My inner voice chided, But, surely, that was because he wanted to annoy his mother more than help you, wasn't it? And don't forget the humiliation of waking from your faint in Duncan Kilgour's arms and how you reacted with such revulsion.

After he'd left the room, Grandmother had scolded me. "I called for help, nôsisim," she said. "Mr. Kilgour came running. He was kind, and you were rude to him."

She was right. But the smoky closeness of him had angered and confused me. Must I apologize? No . . . I couldn't.

I thought about both the minister and Kilgour – one reserved and temperate, the other rough and coarse – and knew which man I preferred. Not that I would ever be offered a choice! I shook my head. How pathetic you are, Beatrice. Pathetic. As well as half-mad.

As Tupper pulled me homeward, down the final slope to Old Maples, the little voice whispered, Find courage, Beatrice – and some wits. For you are about to face the dragon in her lair below.

12

CASS

I slept all morning and woke up to see Aunt Blair leaning around the door frame. "How ya doing, honey?"

"Aunt Blair! Hi! Be careful around me. I have the plague."

She threw her sheepskin jacket on Daisy's bed and sat cross-legged on the foot of mine. "I'll only stay a few minutes." She pulled magazines and candy out of her bag, then two books and a plastic box filled with my favorite cookies – peanut butter.

"Thanks. Hey, you haven't been here since Dad got married, have you?"

She nodded and looked around. Her hair was in a spiky ponytail. As usual, she wore no makeup except lip gloss. "I see Jean's still chopping away at the house. I caught a glimpse of the living room. Where's all your furniture gone?"

"In the barn, where else?"

"It should be in proper storage. It'll get wrecked out

there. Listen, do you want to come to my place for a day or two?"

"I'm okay. They've got the devil child sleeping with them, so at least I have the room to myself for now."

She laughed. "When you feel like a break, come on over. I don't think your dad would fight that, would he?"

We both knew that the rupture between her and Dad was serious. The only time they talked was when I stayed with her and he was forced to phone her house.

"I'd like to come for sure. But when I feel less like dying," I said. "We'll go shopping, right? How did you get past Jean, anyway?"

She smiled. "Just walked in. I told her I came to see you. She seemed surprised as all get out. You look terrible, kiddo."

"I feel terrible, believe me. But I'm glad to see you. You better go before you get sick." She squeezed my foot under the covers.

"Okay. You know where to find me – just call."

As soon as she left, Jean brought me homemade chicken noodle soup and raspberry Jello – the sort of lunch Mom would've made, except Mom always used canned soup.

Jean looked out the window. "I wanted to do some Christmas shopping, but it's snowing buckets out there."

I couldn't be bothered with even one tiny jibe about buckets clanking down from the sky. I *must* be sick.

"Have you decided what to get your dad?" she asked. "I could buy it for you. I know he needs socks."

"One rule in our house is that Dad doesn't get socks for Christmas. Or ties," I said. "The other rule is, everyone does their own shopping. Dad and I bought for Mom together, though. He liked getting her custom-made jewelry. He said she looked like Branwen – goddess of the north seas – so he gave her a lot of pearls. I have them all put away."

She looked at me. "I don't care for pearls. And I'm not competing with your mother. Or your aunt."

"Really? I'd call getting rid of everything that even hints of my mom trying to destroy the competition. And you've never bothered to get to know Blair."

"That's not true. You might ask Blair why she hasn't been here since last summer."

I shrugged. I knew why.

"It's possible to love more than one person in a lifetime, Cassandra. Your dad loves me now. Blair doesn't want to accept that. She won't listen. That's your biggest problem, too, and it's why we don't get along. You –"

"Oh, but I do listen, even to your thoughts, Jean. And that's my biggest problem."

Before she could answer, the door flew open. Daisy cried, "They sent us home early! Tracy's mom gave me a ride. I'm hungry!"

Jean left, guiding Daisy ahead of her, her back stiff as usual.

I forced some of the soup down, then slid under the covers and drifted off. By the time darkness fell, my throat felt a bit better. I couldn't eat the slice of meatloaf

Dad brought upstairs, but I managed a few mashed pota-toes. The dessert – yogurt – went down easily and filled the hole in my stomach.

Dad said casually, "I hear Blair dropped by. What did she want?" I looked at him as if he'd said something stupid. Which he had. "Yeah, okay, she came to see how you were. But what else?"

I knew what he meant. Was Blair filling my head with stuff he didn't like? Like how she felt Dad had been rushed into marriage by Jean, who had secretly and slyly courted him even before Mom died. That was Blair's theory anyway. Mine, too.

Jean had been one of a small group of neighbors from the local Women's Institute Mom belonged to who helped us in her final few weeks. Jean had spent a lot of time here. I was so focused on Mom, I hadn't noticed her much. She and the other women were usually gone when I got home from school anyway. Blair wanted to be the only caregiver during the day, but Mom said Blair had to make a living and shouldn't shut down her shop. She insisted her sister come only in the evenings.

"Did your aunt say anything about the changes in the house?" Dad asked.

"Just that the old furniture should be in proper storage, not in the barn."

He looked sour. "She'd probably like to sell it in her shop. She was always jealous that your mom got this house and the antiques in it."

"You have *never* said that before, Dad! Because you know it's not true. Blair got Grandpa's business and house when he died. Mom got this house. It was worked out between them ahead of time. That's sick, Dad. You must really hate Blair."

"I didn't mean it the way it sounded. And I don't *hate* her," he said quickly.

"I bet it was Jean's idea that Aunt Blair hasn't come around because she's jealous. You both know why Blair doesn't come. She's not welcome here."

He shrugged and looked away.

"Look, Dad, she just stopped by to see how I was. She said I could come and stay with her when I feel better. I'll go there during the holidays for a few days."

I saw him bristle. "Of course. She's your aunt. However, Jean did say Blair was very brusque with her."

"Aunt Blair didn't come to see Jean. What are you going to do? Ban Mom's sister from the house?"

"Don't be silly. It was her choice to cut herself off from the rest of us. I'm glad she stopped by to see you. But if she's going to be difficult . . ."

I was done. I heard Dad sigh, then the door clicked shut. I rolled onto my side. I knew he was still hurt by Aunt Blair not accepting Jean into the family. But he hadn't done anything to fix it.

Around midnight, I woke up and thought about Beatrice. I touched the star brooch. My skin prickled and, almost instantly, the diary appeared on my bed. It felt warmer this time, the brown leather oily soft. I quickly turned the pages until I reached the spot where she'd ended the last time.

Something had been added! The ink was fresh, dark. I read avidly. She *had* seen me in the school bus and in her classroom, too, her brooch pinned to my bright red top.

I kept reading. I loved it when she caught Ivy stealing from the wooden crate and Duncan witnessing the whole thing. I especially liked Duncan for telling his mother off. Beatrice thought he was doing it to get back at his mother, but I think he likes Beatrice. After the fight with Ivy, Beatrice saw me lying sick in my bed, and the shock of it all, plus the lack of food, had made her faint. It was clear from her writing that she was totally bewildered. *Was I only adding to her already fragile state?*

After agreeing to spend Christmas with Miss Cameron and Reverend Dalhousie, I wondered if Beatrice would get a chance to know Robert better. So far, I wasn't all that impressed with him. He seemed stiff, with almost no sense of humor, but oddly enough, of the two guys, Beatrice seemed more interested in Dalhousie than Duncan. *Was she really interested in either?*

There was one thing I was sure of, though: Ivy would get even with Beatrice somehow for catching her stealing from that gift box.

I closed the book. Suddenly it hit me. I was definitely seeing three people from this house – Beatrice, her grandmother, and now Duncan, even if it was only a quick blurred view. I wish I'd caught a glimpse of his face when he picked her up. It might have told me how he really felt about her.

What was happening to me? I could feel the chill of the room on my shoulders and the smoothness of the sheets on my toes. I knew for certain I wasn't sleeping. I could smell the scented oil from the leather diary on my fingertips, along with banana-strawberry sweetness from the empty yogurt tub. I had an 1856 journal resting in my hands. I put it down and watched it slowly fade away, then fell back on my pillows. *If Beatrice was really living in this house in 1856, why was the journal passing through time and appearing to me?*

And if all of this was about ghosts, or time travel, or about seeing people from the past who weren't alive anymore, why didn't Mom come to see me? Where was she? Was she angry at me? Was she gone forever?

I hadn't really cried for her yet – I was still too angry at the unfairness . . . the awfulness of it all. I longed for her, and yet I couldn't think about her too often because the glass shard inside my chest would stab me again. When she was sick, I knew I was losing her bit by bit. But then, suddenly one night, she was gone, and I couldn't say sorry.

After that, I had only Dad and Aunt Blair to lean on. And then Jean came and Blair left. And Dad let her go.

I didn't choose to have Jean or her kid in my life. Yet here they were. They say you can't choose your family, but you can choose your friends. I have news for you. Sometimes you can't choose either.

I *hated* it here now. Every day, I got up. I went to

school. I came home. I lay in bed until dinner was called. Afterward, I did my homework and went back to bed. That was my life.

Was I becoming a ghost in my own house?

I stared into the darkness, too tired to think. The sun was just rising when the door opened and Jean entered with a tray. Tea, toast, jam.

"No coffee?" I asked.

"Your dad said lemon herbal tea. He made it."

Dad walked in. "I'm off, girls." He kissed my forehead, testing my temperature like Mom used to do. "Fever's down. How're ya doing?"

What should I say? My ears and throat feel a bit better, but my brain has strep, and it's eating away at my brain cells and making me imagine all sort of weird things? And, oh yeah, I still hate your new wife?

"Better," I muttered.

"Good." He grinned. "Holidays start in less than a week. You'll be fine by then. Man, I'm looking forward to the break."

"Our first Christmas together, Jon," Jean simpered. "The first of many."

As they murmured to each other, I pretended to go to sleep. When the door shut behind them, I looked out the window. Great-Uncle Bart told us how the rapids once stretched a long way downriver, causing problems for the traders. After the locks were built, they flooded the rapids with so much water, they vanished. That's how I felt. Flooded. Unable to see the surface.

I spent the day sleeping until the door opened and Daisy shouted, "You awake?"

"No."

Someone plopped down on the foot of the bed, then bounced up and down. I kept my eyes closed. "Go away, you horrible child!"

A strange voice said, "News from the outside world has arrived."

I pulled the cover over my head. "What are *you* doing here?" I croaked from inside my dark cave.

Martin Pelly laughed. "Greetings from Grand Rapids High. Your mom called the school, and, as I am your brand-new English partner, Mr. Bruin told me to bring you the assignment and two poetry books. It's worth thirty percent of our final mark. Victorian poets – comparing the romantics with the pastoral ones, whatever that means. We're to choose two female and two male writers. Fun, huh?"

"I don't care. I'll never feel better again," I croaked. "And FYI, Jean's not my mother. And also FYI, I don't want to do schoolwork. Go away."

He pulled the cover off my head. The static made my hair crackle. I could actually feel it floating in the air. I smeared my hand with lotion and tried to hold my hair down.

"Red nose, red hair, green top. Very Christmasy. You know, I seem to recall someone telling me to make sure I pulled my weight in this project. So who's backing out now, huh?"

I glowered at him. Jean came in with two mugs and a plate of shortbread.

"I made you some hot chocolate," she said to Martin. "I'm assuming you came on the school bus. That snow is building up out there."

He shrugged. "Yeah. But I'll be fine walking home."

"You can get a ride with me." She handed us each a mug. "I'll stop in and say hi to Donna, if she's on afternoon shift. Haven't seen her in a while."

"Who's Donna?" I asked.

"Our restaurant manager," Martin said.

I looked at Jean. "You're friends with her?"

"I did have a life before I met your dad, you know."

I frowned. I sometimes forgot she grew up in St. Cuthbert's.

"Next time, I'll go home and get my truck first," Martin said.

As she left, Jean called over her shoulder, "She's sick, Martin. Half an hour."

He ate two cookies while checking out my room. "You share, huh? With that weird kid – what's her name – Dizzy? Maisy?"

"Daisy. And I *have* to share this room. But as long as I'm sick, she's in with my dad and Jean. That's fine by me."

"Your parents divorced?"

"No. My mom died."

"Oh, right. I've heard that. Forgot. I'm sorry."

"Not your fault. Why do people say they're sorry when you know they really aren't? How could they be

when they didn't know her? But thanks for the books."
I pretended to begin reading.

"I'd miss my mom something awful. That's why I said it."

I glanced at him. He was wearing a denim shirt over a yellow T-shirt and jeans. His hair was glossy and almost touched his shoulders. His eyebrows and eyes were nearly as black. The mole by his mouth was flat and smooth.

"Okay. Sorry I snarked," I murmured.

"Been pretty sick, huh?"

Tears pricked my eyes, but I pretended to sneeze to cover it up.

"Look, first we have to sort out the four writers we're going to focus on. I used the Internet to see who might be the most interesting. My list is on a sheet inside one of the books."

"Thanks. I'll be better soon, and I'll take a look."

"Bet you're glad you've got a partner now!" he said.

"Maybe. We'll see."

He crunched his way through another cookie. I sipped my hot chocolate, but I could hardly taste it.

"This house is really old," Martin said.

"Yeah."

"What's it like living inside history?"

"What do you mean?"

"Well, you know – this place is one of the oldest in the area."

"Built over a hundred and fifty years ago," I said.

"Pretty amazing when you think about it – I mean, who built it? People who have been dead for a long time."

"You may think they're dead," I blurted out. "But I'm not so sure!"

∾

13

BEATRICE

The dragon was waiting in the kitchen. Before announcing my Christmas plans, I decided to ignore her and make bannock and a batch of molasses gingerbread for Papa. He was working on a leather harness at a side table and looked pleased to see me assembling my ingredients, though his glance slid uneasily toward Ivy. We both knew her bannock was like chewing thick leather, her gingerbread dry as dust. She was reheating the inevitable stew, giving me looks of cold malice whenever she caught my eye. I rarely cook anymore, except to prepare Grandmother's meals. I wonder how much pleasure I'll have preparing our holiday feast with Ivy hovering nearby like a thin shadow of gloom.

Why does she hate me so? I tried hard to be pleasant after my return from the east, despite the incident with the brooch. But she refused to offer anything in return. I finally settled for the barest of civilities until our recent arguments. This week has been difficult, strange, and even frightening, as her anger seems to come from deep inside her. I dreaded telling her and Papa about Christmas Day and the number of people coming for dinner!

While the bannock cooked on the griddle, I mixed spices from Penelope's Christmas box for the gingerbread, inhaling the scents of cinnamon, mace, allspice, and ginger. There was plenty of buttermilk and molasses to work with, although no doubt Ivy would keep an account of every missing spoonful.

When the bannock was browned, I slid the round off the griddle. The smell of toasted oatmeal reminded me of winter mornings helping Mama. Sadly, instead of soothing me, it heightened my anxiety. I ate little, my insides balking at the greasy stew, but I managed a piece of gingerbread to settle my stomach.

"I have some news," I said brightly, my heart in my throat.

Papa lowered his spoon, looking interested. Ivy kept eating.

"Miss Cameron has asked people to host some of our choir members for the festive season . . . and I have agreed to take in three. They will be no trouble and will sleep in Grandmother and my room."

Fortunately, Papa spoke before Ivy, who was huffing like a rooster ready to crow. "A fine and charitable thing to do, Beatrice. I look forward to hearing young voices in the house. However, it will mean more work for Ivy."

"No, Papa! I will do all the work with the help of Dilly and the three girls. For Christmas dinner, I have asked Miss Cameron to come, as well as her pupils and . . . and Reverend Dalhousie, his sister, and the girls they have agreed to take in."

"How dare you invite strangers into my home without asking me first!" Ivy screeched, mop cap askew. "Well, you can tell them it's off!"

Dilly kept her head close to her plate, hands in her lap.

"It will all be done for you, Ivy," I repeated. "You won't have to do a thing."

"No! I forbid it! I forbid it!"

Papa took her hands in his. "Christmas is a time of peace and good will, Ivy; of giving and sharing. Yes, Beatrice should have asked you first. But it will be pleasant to have the new vicar and his sister here. We should have had them long before this."

"I don't care about that papist minister and his spoiled sister! She's had two tea parties and hasn't invited me to one. Because I speak my mind about her brother's namby-pamby services! At least Bishop Gaskell gave a good rousing sermon."

Papa said, "We can't unask them now, and remember, Ivy, these young girls from Miss Cameron's are without their own families the whole year long."

"And where will the food come from to feed all these people?" she cried. "Here I am, making do with bits and pieces of scrag end of buffalo and venison and —"

"We have more than enough for this special night," he answered. "I will choose a large haunch of venison. I told you this very morning to start using the remaining better cuts as I have made good money on the rest. We will allow Beatrice to do this, Ivy."

I tried to soften things a little by saying, "Miss Cameron is bringing a number of dishes as well. And your son, Ivy, is going to add a goose and a whitefish for our table. Remember?"

At that moment, the door flew open and Duncan Kilgour

burst in, beard and hat thick with frost, a large burlap bag slung over his shoulder. Why does he always fill a room to overflowing with his presence? But I was glad to see him, for once, despite the embarrassment of last night.

Papa laughed a little too heartily. "What have you got there, Father Christmas?"

"When I was at Charlie Dibbott's farm, I heard that a crowd was coming for our Yule dinner, so I'm going to add my last maple-sugar-cured ham. And Minty just trapped these rabbits this morning." He lifted a huge crusted ham out of his bag, then flopped two jackrabbits softly down beside it. "The jacks will hold you until the big day!"

Ivy ground her chair back. "We've been eating scrag-end stew while you've been hoarding a ham and rabbits? And how did Mr. Dibbott know about all this before I did?"

"One of Miss Cameron's students is living with them, Mother. The hares are fresh killed. I'll skin them and put them in your ice house if you don't need them right away. As for my ham, you've had plenty of cured meat, hocks, and smoked chops off this beast even before Miss Alexander came home. I'm also pickling three buffalo tongues. No doubt, you will have one of those to hoard soon."

Ivy's scrawny neck flushed purple. She was having a terrible day and knew who to blame for it. Me.

I prepared a tray for Grandmother. "That ham will be most welcome come Christmas Day, Mr. Kilgour," I said.

"Duncan, please. Now, Mother, I'm hungry."

Ivy banged a thick bowl on the table before dishing up her gray stew. Kilgour peered into it, his nose wrinkling. As

Dilly and I cleared away our dishes, he said, "Mother, you've outdone yourself with this bannock. And the tenderness of the gingerbread is a wonder."

"Miss Beatrice made them," Dilly said.

Duncan glanced at his mother, then at me, with a sly smile. "I can hardly wait for the rest of the special baking then. I hope you have all the ingredients, Miss Alexander."

He seemed to take pleasure in teasing Ivy. There was definitely something not right between this mother and son – not right at all.

But Ivy, by then, was standing by her store cupboard like the queen's guard, arms crossed over her chest. I'd wondered for some time what she had in that cupboard, as she kept it locked, but suspected that if any of us approached her at that moment, she would cry, "You will have to kill me to get anything out from here!"

I cleared my throat to keep from laughing. "Yes, I have all I need except the eggs. I'll use the kitchen now and tomorrow, if I may, Ivy. Tonight Dilly and I will stone the raisins, shell the nuts, and line the cake pans with brown paper."

"And you will have those eggs," Duncan said, looking at his mother.

"You take a day off, my dear Ivy, and let Beatrice go to it," Papa said. The look she gave him should have turned him to cold stone.

I escaped with nôhkom's tray. After giving her supper, I brought the cloth bags of nuts and dried fruits to the kitchen.

Dilly was wiping the last plate clean. She smiled. "We will begin?"

Ivy guarded the table, as if daring me to try and get past her. Papa was working on his harness with exaggerated concentration. Duncan Kilgour was gone.

As I edged past Ivy, she snarled at Papa, "And how am I supposed to make our meals tomorrow with those two all over my kitchen? It won't do, Gordon, I tell you!"

"I'll make rabbit pies for tomorrow's dinner," I said. "Minty and your son will cut wood for the ovens."

Faced with solutions for all her complaints, Ivy stalked out of the room, banging the door behind her.

"Ach, she's still getting used to life in this house, Beatrice," Papa said. "'Tis hard having another grown female around."

"Do you want me to cancel the Christmas plans?" I asked curtly.

"Of course not, dear girl. This is your home, too. I just wish Ivy could accept . . ." I knew what he was trying to say.

Kilgour brought in a pile of firewood. "I've loaded the outside clay oven with dry wood and kindling. You only have to light it tomorrow and keep feeding it."

I was suddenly happy at the prospect of baking for our Yule gathering. "You really do want that shortbread, Mr. Kilgour!"

"Aye, that I do, lass!" he said in a broad Scottish accent.

We smiled at each other. Suddenly unsettled, I turned to Dilly and began to show her how to stone the raisins for the cakes.

Kilgour asked, "Would you like me to carry your grandmother downstairs to help or to watch? She gets so little company."

"Would you, Mr. Kilgour? She'd like that."

"I haven't the legs to do it yet," Papa said sadly.

After my smiling grandmother was tucked into an upholstered chair from the parlor, she started to sort out the less-perfect raisins to be used in scones and soda bread on another day.

Duncan lifted the rabbits to the butchering table.

Even Papa helped, cracking nuts and sifting wheat flour to create a finer blend.

"I wish there were apples for the pudding," I said, "but grated old carrots will have to do."

"What about a jar of crab apples? Would that work?" Papa asked. "I saw some in Ivy's store cupboard a few months ago, and they've never passed my lips!"

Ivy's store cupboard had a lock on it. I knew the key hung on a string around her waist, but Papa reached into his vest pocket and handed me a single key. I hesitated.

"Take it, child!"

Curiosity won out over guilt. When I swung the doors of Ivy's fortress open, I marveled at the sight. There were rows and rows of jars packed with raspberries, saskatoons, crab apples, and wild plums.

"She did all this?"

"She got most from Annie Druce, who sells them for a bit of extra money," Papa said. "I didn't realize how many were in there. Take out a jar of apples, Bea."

"I couldn't, Papa –"

"Don't be ridiculous, girl, my brass bought those! Take one, I tell you!"

I opened a jar, poured off the juice, and gave it to nôhkom as a restorative drink. She smacked her lips with pleasure after each sip. Dilly and I chopped the fruit, throwing the tiny cores into a pail for the pigs. The room smelled of apples, spices, and the sharp scent of dried lemon and orange peel set in the warm oven to soften. Memories of doing the same thing with Mama washed over me.

I said to Duncan, "If your mother gives me a few eggs, I would be most grateful. But what if she –?"

Duncan was staring at the locked store cupboard. "My mother will give you the eggs. She's not as bad as she seems, you know. Is she?"

At those words, the rest of us looked at each other, then Dilly got the giggles, followed by Grandmother. They were so infectious, even Papa snorted while I bit my lip. With Duncan grinning and protesting weakly, the mood lightened. Soon we were busily working together.

As Duncan gutted and skinned the rabbits, asking which of us would like warm mittens after he'd dried and cured the skins, Ivy strode into the kitchen. He quickly moved in front of the empty crab-apple jar. "We are almost done, Mother."

"You'd better clean up before you leave, for it won't be me who does it!"

Why were we so afraid to let her know about the apples? Did we expect her to take up arms? The thought of Ivy in a helmet, brandishing swords, was almost too much to imagine. I turned away to swallow a bubble of laughter. Was I becoming giddy? It was as if part of me had broken free.

Someone tapped on the door, distracting Ivy long enough for Duncan to grab the empty jar and push it deep into the pile of kindling beside the fireplace. He winked at me, and I grinned back. Dilly ran to open the door, and Reverend Dalhousie walked in, looking pinched with cold. He bowed to Ivy, who sneered and left the room. He nodded at Papa, then at the young giant with rabbit blood on his hands, the old woman in her blankets and shawl, the little maid who fumbled a small curtsy, and me breaking sugar with a mortar and pestle.

"I see I have come at a busy time. How snug it all looks in here. I should leave you to it."

"No, Reverend," Duncan said. "You came just in time. In fact, you could say you saved us from a right good rollicking."

And everyone laughed as the minister stood, hat in hand, looking startled.

14

CASS

"What's that supposed to mean?" Martin asked. "You have ghosts?"

I shrugged. "Forget it. It's nothing."

He moved closer. "Your face says it's not nothing."

"I had a high fever. I thought I saw things," I muttered. I probably looked completely mental with my hair on end.

"I heard about the bus incident."

"Yes, the Alarming Incident on the School Bus," I sneered. "Crazy Cass making Gus stall the bus in a snowbank. I fell asleep, woke up with a jerk, and called out. Gus stopped the bus. Its back wheel got stuck for all of five minutes."

"So who was the jerk you woke up with? I wasn't even on the bus!"

I had to laugh. His hand came up and touched the brooch on my green top. "Hey. Diamonds on pj's? Where'd you get that? Looks old. And expensive."

He was examining it, his head close to mine, when Jean walked in. I slapped his hand away and pulled the covers up over my brooch. Martin slid back, his face flushed.

"I came to see if you needed anything, but Martin's leaving. Now," Jean said.

I sneezed. "We still have work to discuss. Go away, Jean."

"*Excuse* me?" she said, hands on hips.

"Yes. I *do* excuse you."

It was Jean's turn to go red. "I will not ask twice, Cassandra."

"We were doing nothing wrong."

"I'm sure your father will be interested –"

"It's okay, Mrs. Cullen," Martin said. "I was just looking at –"

I stared at him, eyes wide with warning.

He stood up. "We'll get together as soon as school is over and set up a plan, Cass. After you've read about some of the poets, we'll decide who to write about."

"Sit down," I said. "We have other stuff to discuss."

"Nah, I gotta get going. I'm taking that girl I met on the bus to a movie tonight."

I was stunned. Jean looked confused. I kept the covers up over my brooch.

"Nice you can date on a school night," I snapped. "No need to do research."

"I'll drop by after school tomorrow, Cass, okay?"

"Don't exert yourself or anything. I'll be busy reading these books for you."

He grinned, and I made a face at him while Jean watched us through narrowed eyes.

"You can go, Jean. I don't think we'll be having sex today," I said. "We don't want Martin getting this cold, right?" She slammed out of the room.

"So you two get along great, I see," Martin said, but I threw the books on the floor, turned on my side, and pulled the covers over my head.

"You can go too," I said from my cave. When I didn't hear him leave, I peeked. He was looking out the window.

"Do you ever hear anything up here?" he asked suddenly.

"Like what?" I sat up.

"Music. Faraway sounding."

"My ears are blocked. But that would be my lovely stepmother. She's at the piano all the time. Drives me nuts."

"But I heard it when she was in here, too."

The door opened and Daisy bustled in. She pointed at Martin. "Hey, you live behind Pelly's in that blue house. My mom knows you, right?"

He smiled. "Yeah. I'm Martin."

"Are you coming to the Christmas party on Sunday night with Cass?"

"What Christmas party?" I asked.

"Mom has one every year. She asks some friends and her old-age music students. Some teachers are coming from Jonathan's school, too."

"She didn't tell me," I said. "When was this all decided?"

"I don't know. It just was."

"Is your mom giving a piano lesson right now, Daisy?" Martin asked.

"Why?"

"No reason. You were playing, though, right?"

She shook her head. "Not me. I hate practicing." She plunked on her bed, looking ready for a long visit.

"Go away, Daisy. Jean doesn't want you to get sick," I said.

She slid off the bed. "Mom's on the phone with your dad, you know. She's mad. She said you were driving her around the bend." She closed the door behind her with a satisfied click.

"I hope you're not in trouble because of me. There! Hear it? Music."

I waved at him. "I'm always in trouble." I strained to hear his so-called music. "I don't hear anything." Then I grinned. "Hey – good one. Thought I'd fall for ghostly music, huh?" Suddenly a trill of oddly metallic notes echoed from below us.

"That! Hear that?" He stared at me.

I laughed. "*That* must be Jean on the living-room piano. It's badly out of tune."

He was gone and back in a flash. "Still hearing it?" he asked. I nodded.

"Well, Jean and Daisy are in the kitchen. No one is near the piano downstairs. But yet, when I went in there, it was silent." We stared at each other. "Too weird. Must be a radio playing somewhere." He checked his watch and grabbed his backpack. "Anyway, I'll see you tomorrow."

"Yeah, have a wonderful date with Blondie," I said. "Don't get caught checking out her brooch, okay?"

He waved at me and left. I lay there thinking about the piano music. I couldn't hear it anymore, but who else could have been playing it *but* Jean? The thing was, the only image that kept flashing in my mind was Martin sitting in a movie with that Barbie doll from the bus. *Had I expected him to ask me out?* Yes, I had. I sighed. So much for pretending I didn't like the guy.

I fell asleep watching the moon hanging like a smoky glass orb outside my window. Dad woke me with a plate of chicken, peas, and mashed potatoes.

"Did Jean tattle to you?" I asked.

"About what?"

"About anything."

"No. I just got home. Why? Have you and she had another set-to?"

To distract him, I said, "I hear Jean's having a Christmas party on Sunday night."

"The whole family is having a Christmas party. You included."

"No one told me."

He looked guilty. "Jean wasn't sure she was going to bother this year, with the kitchen renovations going on right now. We only decided yesterday and made some phone calls. Turned out most people were free. You've been so ill, I didn't think to mention it. Anyone you'd like to ask?"

I shook my head.

He said heartily, "I'm sure it's not too late."

"I don't want to ask anyone, okay? I may not bother coming anyway."

"I want you there. So don't get any ideas about skipping it."

I didn't say anything, just picked up my fork and poked at the smooth brown gravy. It ticked me off that Jean was a way better cook than Mom.

"I mean it, Cass. It's important to Jean." He probably saw my eye-roll because he added, "But especially important to me. Okay?"

I nodded and pointed at my food. "Getting cold."

As he left, he said, "I'll expect you there. No arguments."

After I ate half my meal, I pushed the rest aside and leafed through one of the poetry books Martin had brought. Soon my eyelids were drooping. I hauled myself out of bed and had a quick shower, but this time I pinned the brooch inside my pajama pocket. I fell asleep quickly.

When I woke up, music was filling the room. I recognized an old Christmas carol that was on one of Mom's albums. I'd learned it when I was a kid – "Drive the Cold Winter Away." It had a light airiness about it on that recording, yet I always felt there was a sadness beneath its melody. Right now, it was being played in a slow sad way. I remembered some of the words.

> All hail to the days that merit more praise
> Than all the rest of the year,
> And welcome the nights that double delights
> As well for the poor as the peer!

I pulled on my housecoat and woolly socks and tiptoed down the stairs. The walls were bumpy and cold under my fingertips. I couldn't find the light switch. I understood why. My heart picked up speed as I neared the bottom.

Moonlight shone from two small windows across the main-floor foyer, sliding softly over dark green walls, a fur rug, and a hat rack made of deer antlers. The closer I got to the heavy oak doors of the main room, the stronger the music grew, becoming complex, sweet, and melancholy. Then it stopped.

As I swung the doors open, I smelled wood smoke. A low black stove, with a big smokestack curling around the ceiling and out through one wall, glowed in the corner of the room. A dark-haired girl sat beside a tiny piano, her candle wavering shadows around the walls. She was writing in a book on the table beside her. I watched her put down her pen, cover her face with her hands, and rock back and forth.

"Beatrice?" I called softly.

She became still. Then carefully, slowly, she turned to look at me.

15

BEATRICE

I gave Reverend Dalhousie a wedge of bannock with last summer's honey. He sat beside Papa and accepted a cup of tea from Dilly.

"I've come to tell you that the party for the bishop and his wife will be tomorrow evening," he said. "Mrs. Gaskell wants to stay with friends at the settlement for Christmas, before moving on. I'll take over both parishes once they leave, of course."

"You don't seem happy about it, Reverend," Papa said.

"Oh, no, I'm not unhappy, Mr. Alexander. I mean, if I'm honest – I expected something quite different coming to this wilderness area . . . to what I thought would be wilderness. Something really worth my . . . not this. . . ." He looked around uncomfortably.

I compared Duncan's full beard, wide arched nose, and thick body to the minister's delicate features and narrow shoulders. His chin barely showed signs of blond whiskers, even late in the day. Duncan's eyes were dark, often sparking with mischief, alive, while Robert Dalhousie's pale eyes were calm, until this odd moment, when he had become clearly uncomfortable. I realized I'd never seen him laugh.

Duncan asked, "You expected savages and found reasonably civilized people, is that it?" His tone was challenging.

"That's an unwarranted thing to say, Mr. Kilgour!" I said sharply.

"I should explain," Reverend Dalhousie replied. "Since a young student, I've felt a calling to take God's word to those who do not know Him."

Duncan's accent deepened as he spoke: "I was a young student once, too. But my aunt made me read many writers, including freethinkers, and their views on the church and on missionary work. I found myself agreeing with the freethinkers more and more, especially after traveling around this globe and seeing the multitude of religions and ways of living that people like you insist on changing to suit your version of what is the right way to live."

My jaw tightened. The air was thick with tension.

Robert Dalhousie turned to Papa. "Here, in St. Cuthbert's, the Indians and half-breeds have been well integrated into our more complex society. I have little to do, even ministering to my second congregation at St. Anthony's, where most fullbloods are Christians."

Duncan slapped a hand on the table. I held my breath. "Half-breeds, eh? My mother would approve of your implied prejudices, Minister, but I'm not sure Mrs. Alexander would. Or her son. I believe country-born is less inflammatory, Sir!"

Grandmother sat quietly, an unreadable smile on her face. Papa held up a hand. "This is not something I wish to discuss, Duncan." But I could see the light had not dimmed in Kilgour's eyes.

Robert Dalhousie's face colored. "Please understand, I do not judge. We're all God's children. It's my duty to go where He is not known — to teach His word and to show, by example, the way to live a more enlightened, devout, civilized life. The freethinkers, to whom you refer, I know little about. What I do know is, they say and write things that will never change my church or my God."

"Showing the way to a more tolerant and cultured life sounds an admirable thing, Sir. But you would change other people's churches and gods to accomplish it, would you not? Surely there are less insidious ways of enlightening people."

"It is our duty to help others find our Lord. We embrace people who have lived in ignorance through no fault of their own. They are His children too."

"So, let me understand. You see Indians who aren't Christians as children who have yet to grow into their full-civilized form?" Duncan asked, light gleaming dangerously in his eyes.

Reverend Dalhousie turned to Papa again. "I am only saying there are men of the church — family men — who could do the wonderful work the bishop began here far better than I."

"I don't think —" I began, but Duncan Kilgour spoke over me.

"Wonderful work? Bishop Gaskell has little education and arrived here with his own garbled interpretation of the Bible, from what I've seen and heard. He then *proceeded to bully all and sundry with the sensitivity of an ox. Communities everywhere in this country are being ministered by so-called men of God – educated in a quick few months in some stuffy English seminary and sent here to teach the savages. How many months did it take you to become a minister? Two? Three?"*

Reverend Dalhousie rose to his feet. "I am an ordained minister, Sir. As long as I remain here, I will never lag in my religious duties."

Kilgour smiled sweetly at him. "Of that I'm sure, Reverend."

"Thank you for the tea, Miss Alexander. I apologize for interrupting your busy evening. Good night." Robert Dalhousie bowed stiffly and left.

When the door closed behind him, I cried, "That was uncalled for, Mr. Kilgour! He was our guest, not yours, and you were extremely rude to him – to all of us!"

"Beatrice," Papa said, "discussions like this are often heated. Don't be hasty in blaming Duncan. Testing a new minister is not a bad thing. Dalhousie is a man of conviction, but like so many men from the Old Country, sadly naïve about the people he has determined to save."

"He is a good man, Papa."

"Oh, I don't doubt that. And as long as he teaches goodness to all peoples, no one will fault him." He eased Grandmother gently from her chair. Duncan tried to help, but Papa waved him away. Together the invalids helped each other out of the room. Dilly followed, concern on her young face.

Kilgour sat back in his chair. "You realize, Miss Alexander, that Dalhousie was including your family when he said many of his parishioners are half-breeds. With no idea, of course, that it is the worst of insults. Many of these hastily educated clergy are dangerously ignorant." Seeing the look on my face, he added, "He would do well to learn about his flock before he tries to change them into his own image."

I pushed the last piece of greased paper into its pan and covered everything with clean towels. Was I ready for my morning baking? I cast around for something to organize. I couldn't think. The air was dense and close; black shadows fluttered nearby.

Did Robert Dalhousie see me only as a half-breed? Was he just like those girls in Upper Canada? Did he perceive me as part savage? I tried hard to take a deep breath. Was I tainted by my Indian blood? I couldn't breathe. Why was the floor moving under my feet? I couldn't stop myself from sliding to one side. Fingers wrapped around my upper arm and lowered me onto a chair, then pushed my head toward my knees.

When the buzzing in my ears settled, I sat up and tried to draw a deep breath, but I could make only pathetic gasping sounds.

On his knees in front of me, Duncan Kilgour muttered, "I'm so sorry, Beatrice."

I looked at him. "You are an opinionated pompous agitator with no feelings for anyone else. I hate you. You have ruined everything."

He rose and left the house without speaking another word. I slowly caught my breath. In a daze of misery, I tidied the kitchen and went up to bed, the candle casting long, ominous shadows ahead of me.

———

Escape from the shadows wouldn't come through sleep. I lay awake, the hours slowly ticking by. Duncan Kilgour had been educated by an aunt who was, from what I'd read in the newspapers and periodicals my great-aunt sent us, a bluestocking and a freethinker. I'd read that both were held in disdain by many critics for their intellectual pursuits and their determination to change society the way Dickens tried to with his novels. Kilgour had been all over the world in the last few years. What had he seen that made him so sure of himself? What had he read? I envied him his passion and certainty — yes, even his education by a woman whom, I reluctantly admitted, I would like to have known. He would be tested often in life about his freethinking views, of that I was sure.

I sat up. I wasn't actually agreeing with the man, was I? Was he right about Robert and others like him? No. He had to be wrong. Robert Dalhousie was a good man. Duncan Kilgour was a troublemaker.

Confused and deeply saddened, I took my diary, my pen and ink, and crept downstairs, opened the harpsichord, and played softly so as not to disturb the others. Nôhkom and Papa were used to my practicing at odd hours, but Ivy always protested.

I played "Drive the Cold Winter Away," a lively tune the girls will perform on Christmas Eve. I hoped it would cheer me. But I couldn't give it the lilting melody it called for. When I came to the third verse . . .

'Tis ill for a mind to anger inclined
To think of small injuries now;
If wrath be to seek do not lend her thy cheek
Nor let her inhabit thy brow.

. . . *I could go no further. The evening started out with such pleasure. Now, all celebration, all hope for a happy Christmas, was gone.*

As I write this, I realize I must face things as they are. In one respect, Kilgour was right. Reverend Dalhousie thinks of my family and me as converted heathens. I am sure he is sincere in his desire to be a good minister, but he appears to carry the seed of bigotry toward Indians and our country-born Scots deep inside him, like so many new British do. Perhaps that will change as he gets to know my grandmother's people at St. Anthony's and here in the settlement of St. Cuthbert's.

There is no hope of ever becoming something other than what I am. Nothing will change. I am destined to live with my father and his shrewish wife until I, too, am old and gray. I will remain alone. This is my future. This is what I must accept.

The little voice in my head scoffs at me: How will you perform your duties at church in good spirit? How will you continue with the choir, singing praises you don't feel, celebrating a feast you are no longer part of, all the while knowing the shadows are sliding closer?

Note to myself: Accept the way things are, Beatrice. Don't ask for more.

16

CASS

Beatrice Alexander and I looked at each other in wonder. I could see she was upset. As her figure shifted in the dim light, about to fade, I called out, "Don't give up, Beatrice! Be strong!" There was a wavering blackness all around her. In seconds, she vanished under it.

When I turned to go to my bedroom to see if the diary might be there, Daisy met me on the stairs. For a brief moment, I wondered how she'd gone back in time. . . .

"I heard you playing music," she said. "You woke me up! Who were you talking to?"

"Oh, go back to bed, you little troll."

As I pushed past her, she said, "You're crazy, you know! Mom says so! And you know what? I think you were sleepwalking like some freaked-out zombie!" She followed me down the hall.

I spun around. "Go. Back. To. Bed."

"I can't sleep. I feel sick."

"Great. I'll get the blame for that too. Just go to bed, Daisy!"

Fat tears rolled down her face. "But I do – I *do* feel sick." And to prove it, she threw up on the rug, just missing my feet.

I ran to get Jean, who lurched out of bed, shrieked, and woke up Dad. They both dashed up and down the hallway, bringing buckets, cloths, towels, and rug shampoo for the brand-new hall runner. Daisy stood there, shaking and whimpering.

"I told you she'd catch Cassandra's flu!" Jean shouted at Dad. "I told you!"

Dad, hair on end, handed me a hot facecloth and ordered me take Daisy to our room and clean her up. The hallway was smelling utterly foul, so I was happy to do it.

After I wiped her pasty face and changed her pj's, I said, "If you feel like barfing again, use this." I handed her a wastebasket with a garbage-bag liner.

"I don't feel like doing it anymore. I ate too much popcorn watching that stupid movie tonight at Tracy's stupid birthday party. Her mom gave us lumpy poisoned cookies and made us drink sickening herbal tea. I hate Tracy. And her mom."

"How much popcorn and how many of those poisoned cookies did you eat?"

"I don't know. Lots." Her cheeks were bright pink.

"You'll survive." I sat on the end of her bed. "I threw up once at a sleepover. Popcorn covered in Parmesan cheese. I kept eating it. I can't stand Parmesan anymore."

She let out a soft burp. "This popcorn was that

double-caramel kind you buy at the mall in the city. All sticky and sugary and buttery. And the cookies were double-double chocolate chip. The other girls were being mean to me, so I just ate."

She looked so pathetic, I patted her foot under the covers. "Sorry. I'm sure talking about food probably makes you feel worse."

She gave me a tremulous smile. "It's okay. I feel a lot better now." Her mouth drooped. "Nobody at school likes me. They used to!"

No wonder, with that constant scowl, those long braids sprouting out the sides of her head, and those oversized glasses that looked like they'd come from a Salvation Army bin. *How could Jean let the kid go around like that?* For one second, I felt sorry for the little twerp.

"Look, Daisy, if you'd just try and –"

"How are you, sweetie?" Jean cried as she rushed in. "You come on back to our room, love. You don't need to be here." She gave me a fierce look.

"It's not my fault. I have strep, not stomach flu. The kid ate too much junk today at the birthday party, that's all."

Jean peppered Daisy with questions, threatening to call Tracy's mother.

"Maybe all this could wait until tomorrow," I suggested. "She's pretty tired."

Jean looked at me, then sighed. "Come on, Daisy. Bed."

"But I want to stay in my own room!" Daisy wailed. "With Cass."

"No! You might get her throat!" She dragged the kid out.

"And I'd like to throw myself on yours with my bare hands!" I said to the closed door.

17

BEATRICE

I woke up with a piercing headache. Grandmother was sitting in her chair, looking at me from under the ruffled edge of her cap.

"How did you get out of bed?" I asked. "And you're dressed!"

She smiled. "My son asked Duncan to help me this morning. You were up late with your music, and he knew you would be tired."

"That man came into this room? Got you up? Dressed you?"

She nodded. I hadn't heard a thing. He saw me sleeping in my nightclothes. My face grew hot with embarrassment.

"He gave me porridge with sugar, as I like it," nôhkom said. "And cream from his own cows. Did you know he built his barn right next to his house and put his chickens in there? They are still sitting. He got that idea from others at the forks up the river who don't speak English like you or me. He is a smart boy, that Duncan."

"He is a cruel, coarse, vile man," I said, dressing quickly in the cold.

"He makes me laugh. He's a good thinker, that Duncan."

I sighed. "Nôhkom, how can you remain so cheerful alone in this room all day?"

"I am old. I have my memories. I live with my family – and with my husband, again and again in my thoughts. I have many years to see and feel once more. And I am not always alone. My son comes to visit me every day."

"Papa comes up every day now? I-I didn't realize. . . ."

"Little Minty or Duncan helps him. Sometimes all three are here to see me." She chuckled. "We tell stories."

"And Ivy?"

"She does not come."

"Do you mind that Papa married her, Grandmother?"

"I only care that my son is not happy. But you are home again and –"

"There's more unhappiness," I said.

She shook her head. "Now that you are back, he is getting stronger. I see that."

"Do you think he loves her?"

"What is sâkihitowin?" She put her hand over her heart. "It is what is in here. He is my only son. He is my heart – nitêh. And a good man. Like Duncan. Go along – you have much to do today."

Why did she keep talking about Duncan as if he were a sainted man? I kissed her and she held me tight.

"I wish I could sit here all day with you, nôhkom, listening to some of your stories. I promised Ivy I would get the rabbit pies and my cakes made early." I pinned my hair into a loose knot.

"She is always upset, that one," she scoffed. "You have all day to bake. It will help you move away from your anger."

"What anger?"

"Go, ôhômisîsis, with your big owl eyes, and make things for celebrating makosêwi-kîsikâw. I always liked English Christmas with your mother. I miss my son's wife. I loved her with my whole heart."

Tears burned my eyes. I left the room quickly.

When I pushed open the kitchen door, Ivy sneered, "Is this what you call getting up early? I have things to do!"

Papa was at the table eating his porridge, looking as if he'd been hounded since he sat down.

"I wasn't aware I was stopping you, Ivy," I said briskly. She sucked in a sharp breath. "But I did tell you I would do all the cooking today," I added.

"I heated the outside oven and in here, too, Miss Beatrice," Dilly said quietly.

I smiled my thanks, pulled on my pinafore, and gathered bowls, pots of rendered fat, pale winter butter deepened with carrot juice, and flour. I would make the rabbit pies first, then the cakes, and finally the shortbread in the lower stages of the ovens' heat.

Ivy hissed at Papa, "Do you see how she talks to me? And what good will she be in the kitchen! She can make a half-decent bannock, but can she bake a rabbit pie?"

He sighed. "She made all our meals after Anne died. Go and have a rest, Ivy."

It was as if the name Anne set her off even more. "A rest? Who will do a cleaning of the house today? Not her or that

Indian she's taken as her personal maid, that's certain!"

She was talking as if Dilly weren't in the room! "Ivy —"

Dilly spoke up, "I milked the cows, Missus. And dusted the rooms up and down." She gave me a small nod. She understood.

"You are an excellent helper, Dilly," I said.

Papa hid a smile in a large spoonful of porridge as Ivy flounced from the room.

I poured myself a mug of tea and cut a slice of bannock to chew on while I worked.

"Can I light a fire in your study first, Papa?"

"No, lass, I can do that. Duncan raised the wood-box, so I can reach it easily."

Mr. Kilgour seemed to do a lot around here. Didn't he have his own farm to tend to? I only hoped he had the good sense to stay away from me today.

It was already hot in the kitchen. The windows were frosted, letting in a smooth white light. Working and chatting with Dilly was the only way to stop Kilgour from pushing into my thoughts.

The pastry was on the rabbit pies, and I was telling Dilly how to determine when they were done, when Ivy walked in, her eyes scanning the clutter.

"I will need some eggs, please, Ivy," I said. "It's time to make the cakes."

She looked at Papa. He looked back with a steady eye. She opened one of the long cupboards, reached into a crock, and put six dull brown eggs into a shallow bowl. I needed more, but I could make do with those.

"Thank you, Ivy," I said.

"I know Gordon enjoys a slice of cake, though I don't eat it myself," she said.

As she walked toward the kitchen table, I caught a gleam in her eye just before she tripped. The soft-shelled eggs splattered onto the floor.

Papa called out, "Ivy! Wait, Beatrice. All is not lost. Don't move —"

But Ivy wasn't finished. She lost her footing and scuffled through the eggs, grinding them into the floorboards. "Oh, bless me, look what I've done. And that was the last of my eggs!" She turned to Papa with stricken eyes, then turned her back on him and smiled at me.

18

~

CASS

When I woke up, it was still dark. Beatrice's diary lay on the table beside the dwindling firelight. I quickly pushed the heavy covers back – maybe now I'd find out why she was so sad.

Should I write a journal too? But what if Daisy found it? She'd give it to Jean, and Jean would give it to Dad, and Dad would march me off to a shrink. Beatrice didn't understand what was happening to her and was clearly emotionally fragile. It scared me. If I suddenly wrote to her, it might tip her into a shadow so black she couldn't get out. Yet, I couldn't risk losing touch with her. . . .

I focused on the new entries she'd made to her diary. When they put one over on Ivy with the jar of filched apples, I laughed. Except for Ivy, everyone seemed in tune after that, and I realized Beatrice and Duncan were beginning to like each other. I was rooting for them. But hope ended when Reverend Dalhousie showed up and caused quite an upset. Or rather, Duncan did!

I couldn't get a fix on him. Like Beatrice, I wondered

why he'd come to stay near his mother. He clearly didn't like her much. It was as if he hardly knew her. And he definitely had some strong opinions – and a big mouth – about Robert and the Church!

I fell asleep wondering what would happen next.

When I woke up on Friday, I felt much better. I still had a week of antibiotics, but couldn't take another day hanging around the house. Besides, it was the last day of school, and I needed stuff from my locker. I bumped into Daisy and Jean on my way out of the bathroom.

Daisy looked better, but Jean said, "Holidays start tomorrow, so I'll keep her home." She stroked Daisy's tangled hair.

After the warmth of my bed for three days, the cold hit me hard, even with my ski jacket on. I was glad the bus came quickly. Martin's new girlfriend was on it. She swung her hair over one shoulder and stared right through me. Fine. Like I cared. Martin didn't get on at his stop, and I was relieved. I heard a few girls whispering – *bus, crazy, loser* – but I ignored them.

I got through the first few classes, but was exhausted by the time the principal came on the intercom just before the lunch bell. When he said we could all go home, everyone cheered. I had just pushed my way to my locker when Martin tapped me on the shoulder.

"You look better."

"I feel better."

"Sorry I didn't get back to your place. I had to work. Can you come to Pelly's on Sunday afternoon to plan this assignment? I gotta work tomorrow again. We can go online to do our research. I could pick you up around one and –"

Tricia the Bus Girl came up behind Martin and wedged herself between us, shoving me with her elbow. "Hi, Martin."

"This is Cass, Tricia. We're working on an English project over the holidays."

"You were the one who was so mean to Marty on the bus that day," she said.

I rolled my eyes. "Who isn't? Everyone is mean to Marty. I even wrote a song once called 'Let's All Be Mean to Marty 'Cause He's So Easy to Be Mean To.'"

Martin glared at me. "Now who's being mean?"

"I wouldn't go that far," I muttered.

He turned to her and said, "Cass and I have to talk, okay, Tricia? I'll – uh – be right with you."

A friend of hers appeared and looked me up and down with a dead cold stare. Martin looked trapped. I shrugged and walked away.

I was about to push the metal lever for the outside door when he came running up behind me. "So, you okay for Sunday? One o'clock?" His eyes were so dark, his shirt so white. "I'll pick you up, okay? We need to get this sorted –"

The two girls were halfway down the hall watching us, so I threw my arms around him. "Of course I'll come! I'll be ready at one on Sunday. See you then!"

I grabbed a seat on the school bus. *Why did I act so juvenile?* With luck, Martin would just laugh it off. At worst, he'd cancel Sunday.

Kids poured out of the school in waves, some getting into cars, others hopping on buses. I spotted Martin's watch cap and Tricia's long hair in the crowd and braced myself. But they walked past the bus, followed by the other girl, who was holding hands with a tall skinny boy. They stopped at a truck with PELLY'S FAMOUS DOGS AND FRIES, WE DELIVER on it. Martin climbed into the driver's seat. Tricia, blonde hair flying in the brisk wind, let the other two climb in the narrow backseat, then got in beside Martin.

As the bus trundled forward, I gazed out the window. I felt stupid, embarrassed, and utterly alone.

19

BEATRICE

I left the destroyed eggs where they were and went straight to the outside oven. The pies were golden and bubbly. I brought them inside and told Dilly not to leave the kitchen until I returned. Papa was staring at Ivy, a rigid set to his jaw, while she fussed over the ruined eggs with a wet cloth. I went straight to the front door, pulled on my moccasins, coat, hat, scarf, and mittens, and slammed the door behind me.

Thankfully Minty was feeding the animals. Between us, we soon hooked Tupper to the carriole. I clicked my tongue and we were off, in the opposite direction to the church. The track was tamped solid. Halfway to my destination, the sun's warmth on my bonnet made my neck and shoulders relax a little. The sky was a startling blue, without a cloud; the river crisscrossed with snowshoe and dogsled trails; the shoreline etched in crisp bright light.

An unwavering line of smoke rose from the Comper farmhouse chimney. In the yard, the old barn stood sharply against the blue backdrop. I could see a large new shed attached to the back of the small whitewashed house.

I reined Tupper in, surprised to see the back door covered with a painting of a great blue heron knee-deep in marsh grass. The bird looked like it would spread its huge wings and fly away if I came too close. Beside the shed, four large sled dogs lay gazing impassively at me with triangular eyes. I knocked on the heron's head. There was no response.

"Hello?" I called.

I opened the door and stepped into a spacious room. Someone had replaced the walls and upper loft with log supports. It reminded me of army barracks. Against the far wall stood two neatly made beds. There was also a stone hearth, with two horsehair parlor chairs and a small table for each. Beside me was a makeshift kitchen. A pot of something gamey simmered on the Carron stove. Beside it, a wooden ledge held plates, utensils, and a huge cast-iron frying pan.

A painter's easel and a table covered with jars of paint, brushes, cleaning spirits, and pencils stood in the middle of the room. Paintings were stacked three and four deep on the floor. I wandered around them in wonderment. Was this Duncan Kilgour's work? Surely not Minty's! I took in colorful maps on thick paper; birds and animals surrounded by trees and terrain; portraits on stretched canvases and smooth boards of local men, women, and children of the parish in their distinctive blend of English and Indian clothing, working in autumn fields; others of Swampy Cree people in traditional dress, of Ojibway men in a birch canoe skimming along the river, and of Rupert's Landers riding horses during a hunting expedition, their energy rippling across the canvases.

An unfinished work rested on the easel. It was of Minty, crouched over an empty trap. Nearby a wily rabbit sat behind a tree, watching. It made me smile. All the paintings were signed D.A.K. I wondered what the A stood for.

As I stumbled forward a few steps, the door banged open behind me. Duncan Kilgour said, "When there was no answer, you should have called for me outside. You have no business in here."

"You walk into my house whenever you please!" At that, he smiled. "I came on a mission. I'm not leaving until it's accomplished."

"And what's your mission, Miss Alexander? Have you come to add something to last night's war of words – like, perhaps I should burn in the caverns of hell?"

Frustrating stupid man made me want to smile.

"Your mother deliberately dropped the last six of her preserved eggs on the floor, rather than let me have them. She claims they were her last. You promised to give me some if she did not honor her promise. Even three would lighten the cakes. I don't want my friend's precious gift of fruit ruined by your mother's deliberate and willful . . ."

"Then, Miss Alexander, you shall have eggs."

"Thank you, Mr. Kilgour." I wouldn't give him the satisfaction of mentioning the paintings, however.

"Come! Let me show you something!" I was sure he was about to guide me to his work, but he turned to the door.

"I've been admiring your paintings," I heard myself saying and could have strangled myself with my mittened hand. "I can't imagine how you . . ." I waved one arm at them.

He looked nothing like an artist. His arms were crossed over a coat of dull white wool, with horizontal bands of color. His leather leggings were covered in flecks of hay, his moccasins filthy. He smelled of barn and fresh air.

"Aah. You can't understand how a lout like me could actually create something?"

"They are beautiful," I said quietly.

He shrugged. "Some might agree. To me, they're a record."

"A record? For what purpose?"

"Perhaps simply that I, Duncan Kilgour, once existed."

He turned and walked out of the house, leaving the door open.

20

CASS

I woke up late Sunday morning to find Daisy back in her own bed. Winter Break started the next day. I knew she'd spend the holidays hanging around the house and bugging me. Even worse, I suddenly remembered that tonight was Jean's Christmas party. My spirits dropped into the gray zone.

Yesterday Jean had made dips, sausage rolls, and samosas, with Dad helping in that aimless unhelpful way of his. I'd been banned from the kitchen.

"I don't want your germs on my food," she'd said, as if I were a plague ship passing through. "Better safe than sorry."

"And I'm not sorry to be set free," I replied lightly.

She frowned at Dad, but he was leaning over some ham slices, trying to roll them in cheese or the other way around, I couldn't tell, but they bristled with toothpicks.

Christmas was less than a week away, but there were no decorations up yet, except a glittery gold wreath with a sagging red bow that Jean had hung on the front door.

Dad and I had five huge boxes of Christmas stuff somewhere. *Would he even think to put out his Santa collection, or the set of snow houses for the mantel that Mom had collected over the years?* Not likely.

I looked at my bedside clock. Eleven-fifteen. Martin was picking me up at one. I was surprised he hadn't called to cancel. I had a shower and tied my mass of red hair back with an elastic, hoping to control it a bit. Even so, as it dried, I could feel the front bit springing free and dangling in wisps around my face. I hoped Dad had ordered the flatiron I wanted for Christmas, so I could straighten it when I went out. It would be nice, just once, not to look like I'd put my finger in a light socket. Dad always said I looked magnificently Celtic; I always said I looked like a patient from a Victorian madhouse.

Mom's hair had been a pale gold, cut in short wispy spikes; her neck long and slender, like a child's. Sometimes she'd acted more like a kid than I did. She could be embarrassing at times, but that was Mom and I loved her for it.

Most of the time.

"You goin' out?" Daisy asked, sitting up and rubbing her eyes.

"As it happens," I snapped, irritated by my own thoughts. At least Mom laughed a lot. Unlike Jean, who never laughed.

Daisy pouted. "Oh. I thought maybe we could play cards or something."

Not on her life. "Did your mom send you back here last night?"

"No. I heard them arguing again, so I waited 'til they were asleep and snuck back." She yawned.

"They've been arguing? Really? Like shouting?"

"Just kind of back-and-forth growling. They do it a lot. They think I'm asleep."

"What were they arguing about last night?"

"What do you think? You!" The new open-faced Daisy vanished and the narrow-eyed one returned. "Mom said last night that you are working on her last good nerve and that your dad has to read you the riot act, whatever that is. Jonathan said she shouldn't let you push her buttons. You know, Cass, you *should* change!"

"*He* said I should change?"

"No. *I* said that. Why can't you be nice to Mom? Why are you so mean to us?" Her mouth was wobbling.

I sighed. *This is what I get for being nice to the kid the night she was sick?*

"Daisy. Think about it. Your mom hasn't let me be part of anything since the words Just Married were painted on the back window of her car. You've been the kid from hell since the get-go. You lie about me, like the school bus thing, and make me look bad. Why should I be nice to you? Or her?"

She flopped back onto her pillow and hid her face with her hands. "Go away. I was going to tell you a secret and now I'm not." Her nails were bitten so badly, her fingertips looked like the stubs of half-worn pencil erasers. She was a mess.

A twinge of guilt made me say, "I don't care about any

secret, okay? But you and I don't have to hate each other. We could come to an arrangement. Like mild disdain."

"I don't know what 'disdain' means."

She looked so pathetically interested, I couldn't tell her the truth. "It means . . . er . . . polite. You know, trying to get along – that's what I think, anyway."

She nodded thoughtfully. "I'm tired of being mad," she said. "It makes me feel crazy all the time. I had a couple of best friends at school, but they don't want to know me anymore. Tracy *had* to ask me to her party 'cause I'm always invited. But no one wanted me there."

I checked my watch. "Look, I gotta go. We can talk more about this later, okay? Someone's picking me up in a few minutes." I gathered my folder and books together.

"Who?" she asked.

"Martin Pelly, if you must know, and because you and I seem to be okay at the moment, it might be nice not to get all snide about it."

I could see she was torn. This wasn't going to be easy for either of us.

She said, in a low voice, "So, what's going on with you? Like when I saw you looking at an invisible book . . . and then downstairs the other night, before I threw up, you were just standing there. I thought I heard music, but it wasn't our piano. Was it a tape? And why do you look weird sometimes – like you're seeing something I can't? You look like our old dog did when he just stared in the air and moved his head back and forth."

"He was probably checking out fleas flying around his head," I said, laughing it off. "I think I was having fevers at night and half-awake dreams. Not anymore, though."

"So you're okay now?"

"As your mom would say, I'm right as rain."

"What does that actually mean? How can rain be right?"

"I have no idea. So maybe we'll play a game tonight," I said. "I know one you'd like, I bet. Called Yahtzee. It's in the cupboard, if you want to get it out and read the rules. My mom and I used to play it all the time. It's fun."

"Tomorrow, okay? It's the Christmas party tonight, remember?"

"Oh, yeah. That. Not sure if I can make it."

"You'd better!" she said. "There's a surprise. A really stupid one."

"Really? Like I care?" But I couldn't help wondering what it was.

"I don't have any Christmas presents for my mom or Jonathan yet," she said. "Do you?"

That shook me. I should have phoned Aunt Blair about shopping. "No. I don't, actually."

She brightened. "We could go to Selkirk and buy something. Together!"

"Yeah, okay. Tomorrow. Maybe Martin will drive us to Aunt Blair's if I beg."

She hesitated. "Your aunt – the one Mom doesn't like?"

"Just because your mom doesn't like her doesn't mean you don't have to."

"Okay. I'll make a list today."

"Sounds good!" I said and headed out the door.

The kid and I had actually talked like two human beings. *How long would that last?* Probably as long as it took Jean to set us against each other again.

I wondered if Martin would let me hang around at his place long enough to miss most of the party. Dad would be beyond upset if I didn't show at all – and he *had* sort of stuck up for me in their fight last night. Maybe the party wouldn't happen if I just didn't think about it. I touched the pearl star inside my sweater pocket. I could wish on a star.

Jean was standing at the stove, staring at a teakettle sending out small puffs of steam. She looked exhausted. I put on my down jacket and grabbed a muffin out of the freezer and nuked it.

She poured water into the Santa-head pot. "Where are you going?"

"Out."

"Don't be gone all afternoon, okay? I could do with some help with the party."

"Your party, not mine," I said. "Wine and cheese parties were never allowed in our house. Mom said she'd rather go camping in the Interlake for a week in the rain with the sky full of mosquitoes than go to one wine and cheese party."

"It isn't a wine and cheese party. It's a Christmas gathering," Jean snapped.

"Are you serving wine?"

"Of course."

"And cheese?"

She stared at me.

I smiled.

"Well, as it turns out, your mom isn't here to argue the point, is she?" Her eyes widened. "Oh, Cassandra . . . I'm sorry. . . ."

I threw the muffin on the counter and shouted, "But that means *you're* here, doesn't it? And you will never take her place – not with me and not with Dad. Not ever."

I ran out the front door just as Martin's truck rolled up. It was warm inside and smelled of vinegar and fries, but it didn't comfort me. I felt like my hair was on fire.

He looked at me. "Jeez, you okay?"

"As I'll ever be," I said.

He put the truck silently in gear, and we took off in a spin of wheels through newly fallen snow.

21

BEATRICE

*K*ilgour's broad shed held three fat cows, four waddling geese, and one white gander that strutted and pecked around the feet of the docile cows. A tabby cat sat licking her paws near a dish of yellow cream. In a far corner lay two pigs on a clean bed of straw. In another, right against the house, was a tall wide cage of narrow strips of wood that held open nesting boxes and plump black-and-gray hens.

"Goodness," I said, "what a menagerie. And how portly they all are."

"If you want them to feed you, you keep them warm and feed them well in return."

"Nôhkom says your hens are still laying. That's amazing to me."

He nodded. "Not as well as in summer, but enough. I've convinced a few of the farmers to try putting their hens near their houses. I got the idea from a Russian family I met in my travels in Ontario. They have a huge barn attached right to their house. It made perfect sense to me. We've started a farmers' meeting here once a month to talk over such ideas."

"Fresh eggs," I said. "Why doesn't your mother use fresh?"

He shrugged. "I give them to her, of course. She insists on salt storing them so they last longer. She is very frugal, as you can tell from her larder. As your father has a stone house and so few animals in the barn to keep it warm enough, he can't really have laying hens in winter."

He opened the slatted door and took down a small hanging birch basket, tossed in a handful of clean straw, then went from hen to hen, gently moving them aside as they murmured and clucked.

He held up the basket. "Nine. Will that do? I can collect more tomorrow. I promised Mistress Cochrane a few for her sick boy."

"But I can't take them out of the mouths of sick children!"

"There will be enough. How many cakes are you making?" he asked.

"One large and two smaller. I know! I will cut up the large cake, and you can pass on portions to the more needy families from you and Minty –"

"I'll say they are from you. Only right and proper."

I pulled off a mitten. The pinkish brown eggs, stuck with wisps of soft gray feathers, were warm to my fingertips. A sudden surge of happiness made my hand tremble. For just one moment, I wondered, What happened to the happy girl I once was? How did I lose her? I took the basket, thanked him, and made straight for my little carriole.

"If you wait, Miss Alexander," he called, "I'll follow. I just saddled my horse when I saw you stealing into my house."

I swung around, but he was walking toward the big barn across the yard, chuckling. I can't help smiling as I write this. No one has teased me since I was a child. How many other times in the past few weeks has he done this and I misunderstood?

He led a chestnut mare from the barn and swung up into the saddle. I climbed into the carriole, tucking the eggs beside me. Tupper trotted happily after the other horse. The sun was warm on my shoulders. For the first time in weeks, I heard sparrows chipping in nearby bushes.

Halfway to Old Maples, Duncan Kilgour reined his horse and pointed at a track that led to the river. "Would you like to see an idea of your father's? One he could not make himself, but one I've just finished?"

I nodded. The track moved side to side like a ribbon, and we wound our way down to the river. Ahead lay a solid stretch of undulating snow, right up to the rock-hard yellow suds from the falls a quarter of a mile away. I could hear the faint rush of water in the distance. A hundred feet out from shore, I knew there was a small grass island, and between this and us sat a little hut.

"Come! Take a look."

I wanted to tell Papa about it, so I followed. Inside the tiny shack were two rough benches, a buffalo robe thrown over each. Fishing lines hung on the walls. In the middle of the thick ice floor was a rough-cut hole, partially frozen over. A hatchet lay beside it.

"Minty and I catch fish every time we're here," he said, standing close to me. "Your father was right about this spot being a sweet one. I'll give some whitefish and pickerel to you soon." He smiled warmly.

I stepped back from him. "I'm sure my father would enjoy that," I said.

He nodded. "I didn't send any to your house before you came home. Mother wouldn't have them. She hates fish — even though she comes from a fishing village, or perhaps because of it." He smiled again. "Now you can cook it for your papa. I've smuggled smoked gold-eye to him and kôhkom a few times. Minty does it the Indian way. And even he is fed to the back teeth with fish. We give a lot away and the remainder to the dogs."

"Don't forget to bring the boy for Christmas dinner, Mr. Kilgour. There will be lots of meat then."

He looked at me. "He'd rather eat at home. He is shy."

"The world is changing. Minty must be more social. I will expect both of you."

He sketched an exaggerated bow. "Yes, okiskinwahamâkêw."

Remembering his harsh words to me last night, I snapped, "You call me teacher as if it is an insult. I must get going. My ovens will be eating wood for no good purpose."

"My mother will also be smoldering." He laughed, perhaps more at me than at his little joke. "I'll cut more wood for you later. I'm looking forward to cake and shortbread."

"If I ever get to it," I said. "I've got choir practice tonight. I didn't expect to stop and waste time like this." I turned and walked out of the hut toward the hill.

"Beatrice!" I glared back at him. "Miss Alexander," he added, dropping his hands at his sides as if in defeat. "I am sorry I upset you last night. I can be too aggressive in my views, I know that. To hurt you was not my intention, but hurt you I did. I am a rat, but a humbled, pathetic, whimpering rat." He put one hand on his heart, trying to look pitiable.

Despite his gross exaggerations, or perhaps because of them, though I knew he was sincere, I said, "Must you always play the buffoon? I have no time for this!"

I gathered my skirts together and plowed my way back up to where Tupper and my carriole waited. I was checking the eggs were still intact when something hit me from behind, spraying the carriole with snow. I whirled around.

Duncan Kilgour was laughing so hard, he was holding his sides. Then he pulled off his fur hat and flapped it at me. "Your face . . ." he sputtered, then let out a loud guffaw.

I was taught by one of the supreme snowball makers – my papa – so mine was in hand and quickly packed before Kilgour even noticed. It hit him square between the eyes. He fell like a toppling tree, straight onto his back, where he lay still.

"That should teach you!" I cried.

He didn't move.

I called again.

He lay as still as a dead fish.

"Mr. Kilgour?"

No movement.

"Duncan Kilgour, don't play the fool." One of his legs twitched, then went still.

Had I knocked him out with one round? The top of the snow was warmed from the sun, so it was easy to pack into a hard ball. To be fair, Duncan had packed his lightly, so it easily broke against me.

There was a red welt on his forehead. He didn't seem to be breathing. With growing fear, I leaned closer. "Mr. Kilgour? Duncan?" His laughing eyes popped open and his arms and legs moved in a swishing motion, creating a snow angel. His beard and wild hair were floured with white. I kicked him in the side with my useless moccasins. His hand snaked out, grabbed my foot, and I landed sideways in the snow. He was laughing with such abandon that I finally gave in and joined him in the whole ridiculousness of it all.

"Look up at the sky, Beatrice!" he cried. "It's the color of sapphires!"

I lay back in the snow. Not a cloud to be seen. The sky was a jewel of perfect clarity. I made a snow angel to commemorate its beauty.

A shadow fell over me. Duncan held one hand out to help me up. At that same moment, my spirit girl appeared beside him, wearing a red hat, mittens, and a dark green coat of shiny material. She was smiling as if she knew something I didn't.

Before Duncan moved in front of her, I waved. And she waved right back.

22

CASS

Thick lazy snowflakes continued to fall, white butterflies whisking past the truck, making everything a muted white, green, and brown blur. Martin's wipers thunked back and forth.

"So what happened?" He was looking straight ahead.

"Not a good morning in my house, that's all."

"That happens."

I took a deep breath. "Outside looks like one of those watercolor Christmas cards my mom liked to send – all misty and soft."

I must have sounded shaky, because he said, "Not looking forward to this Christmas, huh?"

That was so totally connected to how I felt, I was stunned into silence. He parked in front of Pelly's and put his arm along the back of the seat. "Big fight with Jean?"

"Something like that. I'm okay."

He nodded, and we walked toward the restaurant.

"Aren't we going over to your place?" I looked toward the blue house with its screened veranda tucked behind a row of pines, about a hundred feet away.

"I always check in at lunch when my parents are away."

The restaurant was half full. Four young women were serving behind the wide counter. The place was covered with blinking, red-nosed, Santa-laughing, elf-grinning, silver-tasseled, Happy-Christmasy kitsch.

A couple of boys from our homeroom were standing at the counter, salting their fries – preppy types from the new development, dressed in expensive ski jackets and designer jeans.

"Hey, Martin," called the taller one, "you hanging out with that crazy girl from school? I was on that bus. Gus made us push it out. I ruined a new pair of shoes. Be careful, that stunned chick might decide you're going to run over Robin Hood and his trusty steed with that wiener truck of yours! You could end up bouncing down the bank straight into the river!"

"Robin Hood? How'd you come up with Robin Hood?" his friend asked.

The tall jerk ignored him. "Hey, it's Cass, right? You on dope or something, Cass?"

"You're the only dope I've ever seen around here lately!" I said.

His friend punched his arm and laughed. With a sneer, Tall Jerk started putting ketchup on his hot dog.

So the school was still talking about it. I felt sick. Martin took my elbow and steered me toward the tables on the other side of the room. "Don't pay them any attention. They're bottom-feeders. I gotta check in with Donna. I'll find you a place to sit."

"Hey, there, Martin!" an old man called from one of the booths whose window faced the parking lot. He was small and wiry with thick white hair. In the booth with him were two other men and a plump woman, her straight gray hair caught up in a barrette. They were drinking coffee and sharing big Styrofoam tubs of fries. They waved us over.

The snow was falling so thick now, you could hardly see the cars outside.

"That's my great-aunt Betty," Martin said, moving me toward the table. "The guy talking is her boyfriend, Walter. He owns a market farm. Won't sell it, even though his family wants big bucks off land developers. They're with their usual Sunday morning guys. We call them the Grease Monkeys – but never to their faces – because they're all wrinkled and they eat tubs and tubs of fries."

"Hi, Auntie Betty, Walter, Ted, Bill. This is Cass."

Bill, saggy-eyed and heavy-jawed, said, "You're getting to be quite the lad there, Martin. Didn't I just see you with another girl last week at that corner table?" He waited for a reaction, like all tattletales do.

"Don't tease him, Bill," said Martin's aunt, but she was smiling. She blinked at me with interest.

"Cass is my project partner in English class," Martin explained.

I waved one arm like a windshield wiper. "Hi. That's me. Project partner."

"Well, she's an angel, this one, ain't she?" said the one called Ted, who had wild eyebrows and a "ski" nose. "All that fluffy red hair like a halo floatin' in the air, eyes as blue as blue."

"Sit down, you two!" Walter ordered. "We got plenty of chips." He slid over in the booth, shoving Bill along with him. The table was piled with mitts, hats, and scarves, all smelling of damp wool.

"We're not staying," said Martin. "School stuff to do. Just checking in with Donna."

Bill looked at me closely. "Aren't you the gal whose dad married Jean Dennett? Didn't your mom –" Walter nudged him. "Yeah, well, I met your dad a while back. Nice fella. Glad to hear about him and Jean. She's good people, is Jean. Worked hard on her dad's farm, I'll say that for her. Ex-husband weren't worth half of her. A mean drunk."

My jaw dropped. "Really?"

"She could've been in the symphony or taught music in a big school," Walter said, "but her dad needed her after her mom died. So she came back from Winnipeg and worked for him. Then she met that Sean. Glad she got out of that mess."

Martin's great-aunt nodded. "Yep. She's well away from there, all right."

It was like hearing about someone I didn't even know. *Her husband was a drunk? Had he been mean to Daisy, too?* I couldn't take it in.

Martin caught sight of a small woman behind the

cash counter with a red poinsettia stuck into the base of her ponytail. "Be right back. Sorry, Cass."

His aunt waved him away. "She'll stay here 'til you're done, Martin."

"I'm fine," I said, squeezing in next to Betty.

"Haven't seen you in Pelly's before, Cass," Betty said. "But I've been to your place a few times. You were at school, though." She looked at me hard. "I met your Mom, Fiona, at the WI. I liked her a lot. She was funny."

"Yeah, she was. But I don't remember you."

The creeps took a table way on the other side of the room. I breathed easier.

"Fiona and I had lunch a few times," she said. "We hit it off. But then she got really sick again. Last time I saw her . . . let's see . . . was when three of us brought some meals over for you and your dad. That's right. You were there, but you were focused on your mom. I wish I got to know Fiona better. I helped out with her care with the WI near the end, but there was no time for small talk, you know?"

"Well, Jean is glad Mom's not around anymore." I tried to make it sound light, but failed.

The men sipped their coffee and fidgeted. Then Bill said he had to get going, followed by Ted. Walter stayed. He picked up a crumpled newspaper and looked at it intently.

Betty didn't comment on Jean. "I know your house, well," she said. "I used to play there when I was little. My mom was old Bart Andrews's housekeeper. I was glad to hear your mom and dad were fixing it up. Man, that house was filled with weird vibes sometimes. I felt it even as a kid. Did some research on it when I got older."

I sat forward. "You did? Ever hear of an Alexander family living there?"

"I did. The book I read about the area indicated that Gordon Alexander was an important local builder before he got hurt in an accident. About 1920, there was a fire in the rectory where the records were kept, and a lot of the really old papers were lost, including most of the Alexander family records. The files about the building of the church were kept, though, in the church office. His accident is mentioned in there."

Walter put down his paper. "My family's been here since 1840. Most of our records came through that fire. I got them all photocopied, but my family doesn't seem interested. They only want to sell the place off." He sounded more hurt than angry.

"What did you finally learn about the Alexander family?" I asked Betty.

Martin came back and sat beside Walter. "I got staffing problems again."

His great-aunt held up her hand. "He had a wife from England," she said to me.

"Anne Alexander?" I prompted.

"Could be. I'd have to check that. Gordon's mother was a Swampy Cree woman named Aggathas who married a Scot named Alexander. I speak that Cree dialect pretty well. My own grandmother came from Norway House. I lived with her for a long time when I was a kid, 'cause I was sick a lot. The name Aggathas probably comes from the Swampy Cree for *âkathâs*, which means 'English,' maybe because she married a man who spoke English."

"And her son had a daughter?" I asked.

"Yes. Gordon and his wife had one daughter, but the wife died young. I think the child's name was Beatrice."

"Wow," I whispered.

"The person who wrote this book claimed that the Gordon Alexander who lived at Old Maples probably was the same Gordon Alexander who became one of the first members of the Council of Assiniboia, set up to control the whole Red River settlement at the forks. This fellow was what they now call an Anglo or English Métis, but the thing is, his wife was still alive in the 1860s."

I blurted out, "I can explain – it was his second wife. Her name was Ivy. His first wife was Anne. She was English and died about 1849. Later on, he married Ivy Comper. She was Scottish, and after her first husband died in Scotland – his last name was Kilgour – she married a farmer from here called Comper. She already had a son, Duncan, in Scotland, who came here when he was older. I wish I knew what happened to him because –"

They were all staring at me. *Oh, oh. Too much information.* Martin's frown was deep. I was sure my face matched the color of my hair. "Sorry. Don't know what I'm saying. I can't prove any of it. I was sick and had some weird dreams. I'm getting them all mixed up with the real history of the house. I'm sorry. . . . I-I'd really like to see that book, though."

Martin snorted. Walter retreated behind his newspaper again.

"Cass, did you read anything about the house before the dreams?" Betty asked.

"No."

"Comper," she mused. "Not a common name hereabouts. They may have been an early family who died out. Could check the church records. Maybe they survived the fire."

Walter said, "One of my long-ago aunts married a Comper. My great-great-aunt Marianna, but she and her family went off to Portage La Prairie at some point. Other Compers are probably in the old burial site down by the river – under bushes and trees roots. There was a log church there, I'm told."

"Really?" Betty said. "I didn't know that, and I've lived around here as long as you. But my family records went up in smoke, like so many others. No wonder we can't find some relatives."

Walter shrugged. "I can show you where the site is in the spring."

"That would be great. I bet Anne Alexander is buried there," I said.

"The Comper farm . . . ," Betty said thoughtfully. "I wonder where that was."

Martin cleared his throat. "Listen, Aunt Betty, you should know that Cass –"

"I worked it out on the way here," I said, leaning forward. "I think it was right where that old feed store is."

"That section belonged to another family for years," Betty mused. "Cochranes. *Mmm.* Not to say a female Comper didn't married a Cochrane and the name ended with her. Have to check out land deeds."

Martin was staring at her. "Aunt Betty, you're not really going to check out someone's dreams, are you?"

"Why not? I've tried to tell you about the traditions of the people we come from, but you don't listen. Dreams are important, Martin."

I said, "Sometimes in that house, I feel like one part of me is here *now* and another is in 1856. I can almost feel what it was like back then. I guess that's why I dream about it." No point in mentioning a diary I couldn't produce as proof.

"The mid-1800s was a complicated time in this settlement," said Betty. "All made difficult by mixed heritages, country marriages, children from two cultures, and so many English coming in. A lot of the Company men in the big settlement deserted their country wives and brought over British women as their 'real' wives. Many of the native wives were forced to find their way back to their families or find another man willing to take them and their English Métis children in. Otherwise, they faced a pretty harsh life."

"I bet," I said.

She smiled at me. "So don't you worry what other people think, Cass. You know what you know." A knot loosened in my gut. She believed me!

Martin narrowed his eyes. "Auntie Betty, Cass doesn't actually know any of –"

I bristled. "Excuse me, but I think you should just –"

"You know, thinking about it, what bothers me is how many of the older families in this area still deny having native blood," Betty said.

"I thought people were sort of proud of that these days," I said.

"*Mmm*. Younger ones, maybe."

Martin frowned. "I've never given it any thought. Who even knows who's got native blood or not? I only know I do because of you, Auntie Betty."

She shrugged. "After the Riel Rebellion, many powerful English Métis quietly moved into white society, as if their ancestors never existed."

Walter nodded. "My whole family avoided mention of it for years, until one of my grandsons applied for Métis status. Got me to do it, too. That kid appreciates the land."

I had a pretty good idea who'd be inheriting Walter's farm. I wondered if his grandson would sell it.

"Anyway, Martin," Betty said gently, "what Cass saw in her dreams might be important. Her spirit may be moving through time."

He rolled his eyes. "Auntie Betty! You take the spiritual part of your aboriginal DNA way too seriously. Cass is pulling your leg. She does that. Talk at school is she played a trick on the bus driver that could've caused an accident."

I sat up with a jolt. "I did not! I would never do that!"

His aunt said, "So that's what those boys were teasing you about. What happened?"

My heart was pounding. "I fell asleep on the way home 'cause I was feeling sick. I had a dream. It got mixed up with being on the bus. I called out, and Gus put on the brakes. The bus stopped in a snowbank." I told her the rest.

"And everyone is saying you did it just to make trouble –" Martin said.

Walter said, "Hey, hey, enough of that."

"I didn't say I believe it," Martin said. "I said there's *talk* that she made it up."

Walter shook his head. "That don't make it better, son."

"And it's really you fudging over the fact that you *do* believe it!" I said.

I stood up. "Nice meeting you, Walter. Thank you for telling me all this, Miss Pelly. And thank you for believing me. Please don't tell Jean. I haven't said anything to her because she would only –"

"I understand."

"I don't feel like working, Martin. Don't bother driving me home. I'll walk."

As I strode away, I heard his aunt say, "Martin. What's *with* you? Anyone with any sense can see the girl . . ."

I didn't hear the rest. My bottom lip was trembling, and if I went back to say more, I knew I'd just cry. I ran out into the snow. I was sure his aunt would make Martin follow, so I took the footpath down along the riverbank that eventually comes out at the road.

The snow wasn't deep under the trees by the river. As I ran along the path, I heard a truck grind out of the parking lot. Martin was waiting at the road, leaning against the driver's door, exhaust hanging like a white cloud in the cold still air. I walked right past.

"Come back, Cass. Have something to eat. We'll talk."

"No."

"If you don't, Aunt Betty will never let up on me. Please? With mustard and relish on it? Best hot dogs in the world. And those creeps have gone."

"That leaves just one then!"

"Look, Cass, Betty believes you and that's good enough for me. I'm sorry. I really am. But you do have quite a mouth on you sometimes."

"I'd never do anything to deliberately distract a bus driver with kids on board!"

"I know that. Come back. Please? With vinegar and salt on it?"

If I went home now, I'd have to help Jean with her stupid party. I climbed into the passenger's side. The silence in the car was like damp smog. The afternoon sun was going down behind the curtain of snow. We met up with Betty and Walter getting into their truck. His aunt stood at the open door on the driver's side, snowflakes tumbling over her woolly tam.

"Good for you, Martin," she said. Then she took my arm and whispered, "Don't be afraid. There's a reason for everything. You'll figure it out. I'm sorry if I sound like some kind of phony wisewoman, but it's truly what

I believe. I've lived a long life, Cass. I've seen many things that don't make sense, and then something happens and it all fits together." She laughed. "Come on, Walter, let's get you home."

Inside Pelly's, Martin went straight to an empty table that said STAFF ONLY. The place was hopping, country Christmas music throbbing through the air. Lots of greetings, laughter, and noise. The woman with the poinsettia in her hair called, "We could use some help here, Martin!"

"Yeah, okay."

"Just for half an hour," the woman said. "I need you on the grill, Martin. Racine hasn't shown. She's fired for sure." She looked at me. "You can pitch in, too, can't you? I pay ten bucks an hour."

"I've never worked in a restaurant," I said.

"We'll just have you clear and wipe tables." She took my arm, dragged me into the kitchen, and gave me quick instructions. "Pile what you can on a tray, wash tables, check seats for grease, wipe them if they need it, dry them really well, come back, sort in marked bins, throw away, go back, repeat. Change the water with that mixture over there regularly. Oh, and make sure all the ketchup, salt, and vinegars don't run out."

She was a terrifyingly organized person. Martin gave me a thumbs-up and ran over to wash his hands at the sink. I grabbed a cloth and trays and took off.

The rush finally slowed down around six-thirty. I was so hungry, it felt like my stomach was folded in half. Martin came out of the back room smelling of grilled bread and grease. He put down a tray loaded with food, and we sat across from each other in the staff booth. He shoved a vanilla milk shake toward me. I wolfed down a hot dog – loaded – half a dozen onion rings, and a small order of fries.

"I don't eat this stuff much anymore," Martin said, "but when I work the grill, I get hungry for it."

"Are you a good cook?" My hands smelled of vinegar.

"Not bad. Tom Harrow's the best."

"The guy with the tattoos, the blue scarf on his head, and all those earrings?"

"Yeah." He looked out the window. The lights were now on in the parking lot. "Listen, can I ask you a question?"

I sighed. "I was telling the truth about my dreams, okay? Only what I didn't say was that, a lot of the time, I'm awake when it happens. Laugh. I don't care."

"That's what I was going to ask. So . . . you think your place is haunted, right?"

"Haunted? It's more like she's actually living there. If I tell you everything, you'll think I'm nuts."

"I know you're not nuts. Not entirely." He smiled, showing the gap in his teeth.

So I told him everything.

When I finished, he leaned over the table, his arms stretched out, hands almost touching mine. "So you are seeing the ghost of Beatrice and some of the people she knew. So, why, when I asked you if you heard music, you laughed it off?"

"I thought you wouldn't believe me. I'm reading her diary. *As she writes it*. Laugh that off! The thing that scares me is, she must have died young."

"Why?"

"Because that's how I see her – young."

"But she sees you, too, right? *You're* not dead."

"She died over a hundred and fifty years ago, Martin. She *is* dead."

"But it doesn't mean she died young. You said she's writing the diary as you read it. Maybe she goes on writing in that diary for forty more years."

"I never thought of that." Tears threatened.

He slid one hand forward and grasped my fingers. A shadow fell over us. It was Blondie, wearing tight jeans and fat furry boots, her silky hair flowing down the front of her blue parka. I pulled away first. Martin left his hand where it was.

Tricia said, "So what's with you two? Are you going out, or what?" Her face was tight. I felt sorry for her.

"No," I said.

"Yes," said Martin.

"Well, which is it? Never mind. I can take a hint. She's weird, you know, Marty. Everyone says so," she said and walked out of the restaurant.

I could see the manager, Donna, watching us out of the corner of her eye.

"Why did you say that?" I asked Martin.

"Don't worry, I'm not jumping the gun. I just don't like her much. She kept calling me Marty even when I told her not to. So you were a good – what I mean is . . ."

"A good excuse to dump her?"

He grinned. "Shouldn't we get to the schoolwork discussion?"

"I'm too tired. My dad and Jean are having a party tonight, and my dad made me promise to be there. I don't want to go, but –"

"Oh, yeah, Daisy mentioned that. What time does it start?"

I looked at the clock. "An hour ago?"

"You better get a move on."

Despite everything, the day had turned out to be a pretty good one after all. Maybe I should give in to Dad just this once. I grabbed my jacket. "You may as well come, too."

I didn't wait for an answer. I just walked out the back door and headed straight for the truck. As he leaned past me to open my door, he turned and smiled. My heart felt light for the first time in weeks.

23

BEATRICE

"*Are* you *seeing angels of your own?*" *Duncan Kilgour asked, looking at me sitting in the snow.* "*I've watched you — you are seeing something.*"

I dusted off my arms and hat. He pulled me up.

"*I must get those cakes in the ovens,*" *I said,* "*before your mother throws everything out.*"

He nodded, turned, and led the way to the carriole. As I followed him, I asked, "*You don't seem to know Ivy very well. Did you not grow up with her?*"

"*I was sent away as a child. I was told my mother could not support me,*" *he said.*

"*Did your father die?*"

"*Yes.*"

"*Was it sudden?*"

He looked at me. "*No, it was a long dissipated death, if you must know. My mother is a bitter woman. I came here to try and find out what happened to her and to see if we could one day be mother and son again.*"

I wanted to say, Well, let me know if you ever figure out your mother because I never will. *Perhaps my face said it for me.* "My papa has given her a good home" *was all I could think of.*

"I agree. Your father is a patient man. But you don't seem to be a patient young woman, Miss Alexander. You want my mother to see how good your father is to her and to change overnight. But you must give her time to mellow."

I let out an unladylike snort and pretended to cough. Only a man would think another man could change a quarrelsome and discontented woman. Ivy wouldn't mellow.

As I climbed into the carriole, he put out a hand. I waved it away, only to stumble and almost crush the precious eggs in their bed of straw. I settled in carefully and, as Tupper pulled the sleigh away, I heard the thud of horse's hooves, softened by snow, close behind. The spirit girl's face floated into my mind. Why did he ask me about angels? I could never tell him. He would think I was really an okîskwêw.

He left me at the house, calling, "I'll be back for some rabbit pie — don't eat it all!" *Although I tried not to, it made me smile as he spurred his horse down the road.*

The cakes were in their pans in minutes. Dilly, bless her, had kept the ovens stoked. The small Christmas pudding wouldn't have much time to ripen, so I added some of Papa's apple cider and placed it in a clean cloth in our old steamer. The kitchen grew warmer. My stepmother was nowhere to be seen, but Papa was there, repairing a moccasin. I slid two fluted rounds of shortbread marked with narrow triangles into the oven. More rounds waited their turn on the table.

Papa, Dilly, and I ate slices of the first rabbit pie for lunch, tender with rich gravy.

"I've missed your mother's cooking. You have her knack," Papa said, a spot of gravy on his contented face. Of course, Ivy chose that moment to walk into the kitchen. When I offered her some pie, she looked at it as if it were full of maggots and walked out again.

Papa shook his head, but neither of us had long to fret over Ivy, for there was a knock on the back door. When I opened it, three dark little faces stared at me from under bonnets covered in thick scarves. I'd forgotten all about the girls from Miss Cameron's school!

Each one carried a rolled cotton mattress of blue-and-white ticking and a deerskin mîwat to carry their belongings in. After introducing them to Papa, I sat them down and gave them each a portion of rabbit pie.

Caitrin, Dona, and Anna Grace were three of our pupils from northern posts. They looked remarkably like sisters, with their matching gray dresses, thick black hair in ribboned braids, and beaded moccasins.

After greeting them, Papa said to me, "Tonight is the party for the bishop and his wife, is it not?"

I stared at him. "I'd forgotten that as well! I'll take a basket of shortbread."

The girls helped me set the table for dinner in the dining room. Soon, they were talking quietly to Dilly. Afterward, I took them upstairs, where Dilly and I put their mattresses on the floor and covered them with quilts. As soon as they saw Grandmother, they clustered around her. She smiled happily, touching *each girl in turn, speaking in her soft singing birth language.*

Miss Cameron had made me promise to keep talking to the girls in English, as all the fathers wanted their daughters to fit into the settlement's British society, so I said in English, "This is my grandmother, Mrs. Alexander. You must help her when she asks."

Grandmother said in Cree, "We will do well. You must rest before dinner, Beatrice."

I lay down on my bed. Grandmother and the girls talked quietly by the fire.

"I don't think Ivy would welcome taking three of my pupils to the vicarage tonight," I said, "but perhaps . . ."

Nôhkom looked at me in amazement. "No, no! They will stay and keep me company. They can make me tea, and we will have our own party." The girls nodded vigorously. "My son's wife won't even notice they're here."

I smiled, closed my eyes, and fell instantly asleep. I was awakened by a gentle nudging. The Three Graces, as I now called the girls in my mind, crept back to Grandmother, who twitched her head toward them. They left the room in close single file.

I changed into my one good dress – a gown of dark green silk, with shiny black stripes and full sleeves. I sat close to nôhkom's knees, my skirt spread out, while she made two braids to loop around my ears before tucking them into the coiled knot on top of my head. When she was done, she kissed me with a loud smack. I placed the star pin at my throat and slipped on Mama's drop-pearl earrings.

"Pinch your cheeks, nôsisim, to give them color." I did as I was told.

The Three Graces appeared with a tray of food and gazed at me in wonderment. When I explained they were welcome to eat with the family, they sat on the floor around Grandmother. Given a choice, I would have done the same.

The dining-room table had been stripped and relaid in the kitchen by Ivy, who snapped, "No need to go to extremes and eat in that cold damp room just because we're going out of an evening. I sent those Indians upstairs to eat with the old woman. They don't belong at our table."

"Tonight," I said firmly, "they prefer to eat with my grandmother, but as daughters of respected Company families, they will sit with us whenever they wish."

Ivy glared at Papa, who said, "Beatrice is right. They come from good homes. All good people deserve our table." Ivy pinched her lips shut.

While Dilly served dinner, I threw on a coat, trudged to the oven outside, and, in its blast of fragrant warmth, pulled out three glistening brown cakes. As I carried them back to the house, the pans burning through my mittens, Kilgour appeared around the corner. He took one of them in his leather gloves, placed it on the table in the kitchen beside the remaining rabbit pie, and sniffed deeply. "Heavenly! Before I take off my coat and enjoy some of this, I have something for you."

He winked at Papa, then left the house. He returned carrying a tall graceful balsam tree in one hand and a bucket in the other, with slices of wood and a hammer inside. Behind him came Minty, hidden by a pile of freshly cut balsam boughs.

"We'll keep the tree's feet wet for you in the bucket," Kilgour explained, "and you can decorate it when you're ready. I will set it up for you, Miss Alexander, when you decide its location."

"Why have you brought that filthy thing into the house?" his mother protested.

"But I am thrilled with it, Ivy!" I cried. Without thinking, I gave Duncan Kilgour a hug and was enveloped in the scent of frosted pine needles by a strong arm dragging me closer. I stepped back quickly, tripping over my dress. He and Minty took the tree to the drawing room, which was cold – ideal to keep the cuttings fresh.

When Duncan returned, he removed his coat and fur hat. I noticed that his beard was trimmed and his hair slightly shorter. And clean. He wore striped woolen pants, a white shirt, plaid silk vest, and a heavy frock coat in black twill. However, on his feet were beaded knee-length moccasins.

That crafty grin of his was wide and challenging. "Am I proper enough for you, Miss Alexander?"

While Ivy scolded him for his Indian footwear, I busied myself cutting the pie. For once, I agreed with his mother. Didn't he own even one pair of decent boots? I ignored my inner voice, which suggested I was annoyed because he hadn't said how nice I looked.

Papa wore his gray frock coat and trousers, a vest with silver buttons, and a cotton shirt with a high-starched collar. A length of soft white silk around his neck was tied into a large floppy bow. Ivy was encased in a fussy purple taffeta dress. A small glittery brooch holding a tired feather adorned her coiled hair. Against her narrow chest rested a large cameo. Mama's cameo. My father was frowning at her, but she seemed determined not to look at him.

Ivy picked at her food, finally shoving it away. Minty, Duncan, and Dilly ate huge wedges of rabbit pie. I put out a plate of shortbread, which disappeared quickly. Then Minty went to the barn to hook up the horses. I put on a heavy green wool cape of my mother's and a dark green bonnet with a spray of grouse feathers on the side.

Minty brought the old sledge close to the house. It is used for hauling hay, but in the winter makes a most commodious box sleigh. Kilgour settled Papa under a buffalo robe, then fussed around his mother, the tightness on her face finally softening. He began to tuck a rug around me, but I told him I was fine.

He sat next to me. Heat radiated from him, and I felt sheltered and warm. We were off with a loud jingling of bells.

Just ahead, the vicarage appeared, its windows lit with tapers – a whimsical and pretty sight. A plain pine wreath adorned the front door.

When we knocked, the bishop, a self-important little man with unruly side whiskers, bounced up behind his wife, both crying greetings. Hovering in the background, his blond hair lifting in the breeze from the open door, was our official host, Reverend Dalhousie. I couldn't see his sister, Henrietta. They ushered us into a room full of awkward guests. Thanks to the Gaskells, our parish was not accustomed to formal social gatherings.

Mothers, eager to make an impression on the new minister – the most eligible bachelor in the village – had dressed their daughters carefully, many in their best summer gowns. A few girls were quite blue with cold, their shoulders covered only by fine wool or silk shawls with long fringes. Some mothers even *threw speculative glances at Duncan Kilgour, who was a lum-bering giant next to the elegant Reverend Dalhousie.*

"Here's our new choir mistress!" cried the bishop's wife, pulling me into the room as if I were an obstinate child. "I shall expect you all to be patient with her. I think Miss Alexander, although not quite as musical as I, will manage fairly well. In time." She looked at me doubtfully.

I heard Duncan Kilgour's low chuckle.

A voice called out, "Did you bring your fiddle, Duncan?"

"No," he called back, "it was made clear to me it would not be welcome."

A murmur ran through the crowd. The fellow who asked the question glowered at the bishop's wife, who was trying to remove the basket of shortbread from my hand. I pulled it back and gave it to Reverend Dalhousie. "Please add this to your table," I said.

He nodded and glanced toward a young woman languishing on a chaise longue. The bishop's wife patted his arm. "Poor Henrietta, not able to fulfill her duties again. Give the basket to one of those new servant girls and tell them to keep it back for me, Robert, dear. I do so love shortbread and will take it with me on my journey."

I bristled. "The girls are not servants, Mrs. Gaskell. They're my pupils. And I made the shortbread for the party. You are welcome to any that remain, I'm sure."

Two red spots appeared on her fleshy cheeks. She turned to Ivy and said, "You are to be congratulated for putting up with all of the disarray in your newly formed household, Mrs. Alexander. I thought Miss Alexander went to Upper

Canada to find a husband, but here she is back again, unmarried." She sighed. *"One has certain duties to one's husband's children. My stepchildren live far away, for which I am exceedingly thankful."*

"As they are, too, no doubt," I muttered to myself.

Duncan Kilgour took my arm and led the way to Henrietta's couch. She was dressed in deep rose, which exaggerated the paleness of her white blonde hair. A small pug-faced black-and-white spaniel lay on her lap.

Kilgour leaned over and said something to the woman. She laughed, covering her slightly protruding teeth with a small fan. He introduced me. She eyed me vaguely, before turning back to Kilgour. They chatted, while I stood there like an unwelcome third cousin. I hardly recognized this urbane man as the one I first met after returning home. Why did that irritate me so much?

I was pushing my way back through the throng when a voice beside me said, "I think Miss Dalhousie has made a conquest. That should make you happy, Miss Alexander!" The beastly woman was tracking me like a she-wolf.

Mrs. Gaskell continued, "Perhaps your brother will marry the vicar's sister, and they can find you a husband amongst his settlement friends." She took in a sharp breath. "I hear he goes to the forks often – to dances and card parties. Still, I suppose many young men sow their wild oats before they settle down. Miss Henrietta's rather pretty – and, of course, as British as he is – so I think her softer ways will tame him in time. I hope he has money for servants as she is quite hopeless about the house. What good she is to her brother, I cannot say. Why, I would imagine your own brother will —"

"He is not my brother, as you well know, Mrs. Gaskell," I said. "And I do not wish to hear malicious gossip about Miss Dalhousie. If you will excuse me." I took shelter beside Miss Cameron — who was looking fine in a brown dress trimmed with green braid — all the while wondering how many others thought I'd left the parish to find a husband.

Reverend Dalhousie joined us, no doubt seeking refuge from the anxious mothers and their shyly smirking daughters. As we chatted, I felt awkward, remembering the words spoken in our kitchen. When Miss Cameron moved to speak with someone, I was glad when a parishioner dragged him away.

Soon, two stout matrons took their places at either end of the tea table to pour. I ate three of my shortbread, so there would be less for the bishop's wife, and chatted with various people, but couldn't keep my attention from Kilgour. He was making a complete fool of himself, I decided, serving the vicar's sister with dainties and entertaining a group nearby with hilarious descriptions of his last hunting foray.

Papa was tucked in a corner, talking in earnest with three Company officers-turned-farmers. He looked very happy. Ivy stood alone near the fireplace, sipping tea. I lifted a plate of small cakes and offered them to her. She refused with a sniff, before saying in a satisfied tone, "It looks as if Henrietta Dalhousie and my Duncan have made a match. He seems quite smitten."

I murmured something about putting the plate back and stood at the tea table eating three more shortbread, despite the shadows gathering in on me from all corners of the room. Why did nothing ever change? Why couldn't I have found the

*strength to snub Robert Dalhousie? This was a man who
thought I was a half-breed, not a complete human being. Did
I look like a madwoman gobbling down my own biscuits to
keep Mrs. Gaskell from having any? An image of Dainty, our
mother pig, rose before me, and I almost burst into giggles.*

*The group around Kilgour was making such a disturbance
with hoots and clapping that Mrs. Gaskell had to bang the
dinner gong repeatedly to get everyone's attention. Robert
Dalhousie officially wished the bishop and his wife a fond
farewell, and the bishop offered, in return, a long and pompous
speech, while the last dregs of tea grew cold. At the end of his
oration, everyone bundled up for the short ride home.*

*Duncan moved away from the group around Henrietta,
his eyes searching the room. When they caught mine, time
seemed to stand still. He moved through the crowd and
looked down at me. "I think your papa has grown fatigued,
Beatrice. We should get him home."*

*I nodded, feeling something drop inside me. What had I
expected him to say? He reached up and, with his thumb,
wiped crumbs from the side of my mouth. For a moment,
the room vanished and the sounds of talking dimmed. He
turned and walked toward Papa. The rush of cold air from
the door as people said good night swirled around me.*

*I was speechless. He'd ignored me all evening and then
had the impudence to address me by my first name! And
he'd touched me in a way that would make anyone who
was watching think we were intimate. I turned away,
put on my cape and bonnet, and signaled to Minty, who
was in the kitchen.*

I didn't say good night to the bishop and his wife. Not that they noticed. But I embraced Miss Cameron and thanked Mr. Dalhousie for his hospitality, hoping he had not seen Kilgour's gesture to me.

To my surprise, he took me aside. "I was hoping to talk to you in a more private setting, Miss Alexander. But I have been so riddled with shame for my unthinking words that evening at your house, I felt I must speak before this evening was done. I fear that you think me a prejudiced dolt."

I held up a hand to protest.

He continued, "No, no. Please allow me to offer my most abject apologies and to tell you that, in my heart, I do not have the narrow-minded and bigoted thoughts I was accused of by Mr. Kilgour. I blush with shame to think that you might have misunderstood me. Please say you forgive me, Miss Alexander."

His apology was so gracious that I said, "Of course, I forgive you. Apology accepted."

"Then we are friends again?"

"Indeed we are, Reverend Dalhousie. Think no more about it."

He bowed. "I do not deserve such kindness. But I wonder if I might call on you tomorrow, Miss Alexander? I didn't have a chance to go over the Christmas service one last time with you, and I have something I wish to consult you about."

Duncan Kilgour pushed me in the small of my back to hurry me along. I stood fast and agreed to a late-morning visit with Robert Dalhousie just as Ivy and Papa interrupted with their own thanks. I rushed outside to climb aboard the sledge ahead of everyone else and sat right behind Minty. As I hoped, Papa sat next to me.

People called good night from all directions. Runnered carrioles, sleighs, and sledges left the vicarage one by one, horses puffing clouds of vapor, bells and harnesses ringing. The ride home was invigorating, the night air frigid and still. When we arrived, Kilgour helped Papa down, which gave me an opportunity to rush past him with a curt good night.

When I crept into my room, I was relieved to find the three girls and Grandmother asleep. I undressed quickly, climbed into the cold bed, and lay awake for a long time, my fingertips pressed against the side of my mouth.

Now, as the sun readies itself to lift the curtain of night, I will finish this entry and dress without disturbing nôhkom or the girls. I have slept very little. Only two good things came out of last evening. Robert Dalhousie and I are friends again. Perhaps "friends" is too strong a word, as we really know so little about each other. But it takes depth of character to apologize as nicely as he did. I noticed, when he touched my arm, his hand had been trembling slightly. Of course, I mustn't read too much into that. But at least he behaved like a gentleman should, unlike Duncan Kilgour, who has no sense of good manners. I can only hope no one noticed his behavior to me before we left. Ridiculous man!

The second good thing is that Papa enjoyed the time with his friends and looked better than I have seen him since my return.

Note to myself: For both those things, you must be content. Try not to care a fig for Duncan Kilgour's rash behavior!

24

CASS

As we drove along River Road, I was in the middle of telling Martin about how we could sneak out of the party early, when I saw something. "Stop!" I cried.

"What?"

"Just stop . . . STOP."

As soon as he pulled over, I jumped out and floundered through deep snow toward the river. "I saw her! With another person. Over there! By those trees!"

He caught up to me. "Saw who?"

I looked around. "*Her*. Beatrice Alexander. Walking. There! A man was with her. I know it was her." I bent over to catch my breath.

Martin stood quietly beside me.

"Okay. I'm nuts. She's not here. Let's go."

"You must have seen something, Cass. Your face lost all its blood. Hey! Look!" I looked. "Santa Claus. Heading toward your house. On skis!" A cross-country skier in a red hat was pumping his way down the middle of the river.

I picked up a handful of snow and threw it in Martin's face. He lunged at me and we fell together, half-buried in a snowbank.

"I hate you," I laughed, mashing snow into his collar.

He showered my face with more snow and tried to stand up, but I knocked him over. Just as he lunged again, I rolled over and tried to crawl away, but he grabbed my foot and pulled me back. I yanked my hat down over my ears to keep the snow out. He hauled me to my feet. I was debating whether to give him another shove when I turned and there was Beatrice. She was making a snow angel not far from us, swishing her arms, her moccasined feet moving back and forth. She stopped when she saw me, pure shock on her face.

"You're here!" I cried. "I didn't imagine you!"

A man, his back toward me, moved across my line of vision. When he turned to see what she was looking at, they both vanished.

Martin spoke in my ear. "Do you see her? Is she really there?"

I pointed, and he looked down. There was a perfect angel cut deep into the snow.

We were still talking about it when we drove up to the house. We agreed there were no footprints leading to or from the angel. It just appeared. He'd finally become a believer.

————

There was no parking space left in front of the house, so Martin pulled in by the barn and we walked across the road holding hands – it was nice. But *nice* ended at our gate.

The low bushes beside the house were covered in nets of twinkling lights, and a lit garland framed the door. I guess Jean got Dad to put them up. *Why didn't he wait for me?* We always put up decorations together. Always. We walked around the side of the house to find a lighted Santa grinning at us. It wasn't one of ours.

Inside, a person I didn't know, in a white apron and black dress, was working at a counter in the kitchen. We took our jackets and boots off. Our jeans were wet with snow. The place smelled of food, mulled wine, and coffee. Voices sounded in the main part of the house. Christmas music floated through the air.

"Are you Cassandra?" the woman asked. She looked me up and down. "I was told to tell you to go upstairs and change if and when you got home."

"Who are you?" I asked. *Change into what? Cinderella? An elf?*

"I'm Minna Stannard. Caterer and all-round helper."

"You don't need to help me with anything, thanks," I said, ignoring my wet knees.

She shrugged. "Just the messenger. Can you carry out some food?"

I took two plates. "Come on," I said to Martin. "May as well get this over with."

As soon as I said it, the door swung open. "Here you are," Dad said. "Got lots of schoolwork done, did you?"

Before I could answer, he rubbed his hands together and continued, "Good, good. Glad you're home. Everyone else has arrived. Jean thought of calling you, but didn't think you'd mind either way."

"Mind what? Missing out on decorating the house or just missing out?"

Dad's smile morphed into the stiff toothy one he puts on when he's uneasy. I handed him the plates of food and walked to the living room. It was crowded. Martin's aunt Betty waved from a distant corner. She looked nice all in gray, with a blue scarf around her neck. I could see Walter, beer in hand, talking to another old guy. The fire crackled and a CD choir sang "Do you see what I see?"

Yeah, I saw something all right – my aunt Blair in silky black slacks, high heels, and a white blouse with a high collar. She was also wearing Mom's black crystal earrings and choker. Her hair was piled on her head. She wiggled her fingers at me. I guess she didn't like the look on my face because she turned to Betty.

What the heck was she doing here? I headed toward her, only to stop halfway across the room. In front of the middle window stood a fake white Christmas tree, its branches decorated with blue-and-white bobbles and matching lights.

Daisy came over to me. "You guys put up a fake tree?" I asked.

She smiled at me, but when I didn't smile back, she looked at Jean, who was chatting to a small group of people. Jean wore a wine-red velvet skirt and matching

silk blouse. Her hair was pulled back with a glittery barrette. She looked like the nerdy teenager who never
knows what's in fashion.

"Oh, there you are, Cassandra!" she cried. "We
thought you'd left home! You missed out on the tree
hoisting and decorating. Couldn't wait all day, could
we?" She laughed and described how she and Daisy had
struggled to put all the fake white branches into the
metal trunk. A few people tittered, but most of Mom
and Dad's old friends looked uncomfortable.

"You didn't tell me you were putting a tree up today,"
I said stiffly.

"Well, it *is* a Christmas party, after all. But, as I say,
you weren't here."

"We always put up a *real* tree together." My voice
sounded strangled. Someone moved beside me. I smelled
my aunt's perfume, but I didn't look at her. I was too busy
looking at a young woman floating across the front of a
different tree – a dark green one beside the white monstrosity. It was Beatrice and she was looking right at me.

My heart lurched. I lifted my hand in greeting. I knew
I was being watched by some of the guests, but I didn't
care. I was sure I could smell real pine needles, along
with that cold snow odor that sweats off icy branches in
warm air.

Beatrice whispered, "What is upsetting you? Is it me?"
I shook my head. "No. It's her."

Beatrice's eyes followed mine. I saw Jean's white face
and a lot of others behind her.

Suddenly Dad said loudly to the room, "I wasn't home when the tree went up. Out getting more wine and mixer. No big deal."

That broke the spell. Beatrice disappeared. People started talking again, avoiding me. Aunt Blair took my arm in a gentle grip.

"It's okay, honey. Let it go."

I shrugged her off and said to Dad, "Yeah, no big deal . . . who cares, right? You, Mom, and me always put the lights up together. And the tree. With our special decorations. But Mom doesn't count anymore, does she? So . . . therefore . . . neither do I."

"Cass, Jean and Daisy did it as a surprise," Dad said quietly.

"No, no, you don't understand, Cassandra," Jean called out. "Your dad and I are going to make a big announcement tonight, and I want everything to be perfect, so –"

"Not a good time right now, Jean," Dad interrupted.

"But why not? Everyone we know is here. It will save on phone calls!" She cried, "Everyone! Jonathan and I are pregnant!"

There were mild oohs and aahs and some scattered clapping. I could hear Aunt Blair's sharp intake of breath. "Oh, God, not now," she whispered.

Dad gave Jean an exasperated look. "Cass, honey, I was going to tell you. . . ."

I pushed past him and stalked out of the room. Someone was following right behind. I pulled on my jacket and boots.

Aunt Blair said firmly, "Jon. Let her go. Just let her go. This is not the time."

Beside me, Martin was yanking his boots on. I banged the back door open. When I got to the road, I kept walking. Martin came crunching up behind me. He touched my shoulder, but I twisted away. Jean hated me – hated Mom – and she was getting even by having a kid with Dad. *Wasn't she too old to have a baby? Why didn't Dad buy a proper tree?* I asked him twice when I was sick, and he said he would. *What's the matter with him? What would Mom think? How could he have another kid at his age? What was Aunt Blair doing at the party? Was it because of the baby? Did she know about it? How?* A new baby would arrive soon, and Dad would love it, and . . . *our* Christmases – his, Mom's, and mine – were over. I stumbled on a ridge of snow and the shock of it forced out a loud sob.

"You're going the wrong way. Turn. Go to my truck. Your aunt's just left. She said to go to her place. Come on, Cass." Martin touched my arm.

I pulled away from him again, but I turned around anyway. I didn't know what else to do, where to go. When we walked past the house, I could see Dad's outline in the front glass door. He opened it when he saw us.

"Go away!" I shouted. "Don't talk to me. I don't want to hear you!"

Martin pointed at the truck. "I'm taking her to her aunt's place. She'll be okay."

Dad nodded and backed into the doorway, tripping

over the edge. Daisy was behind him and caught him before he fell. No Jean. Of course.

We were quiet until we pulled onto the highway.

Martin said, "Can I ask you something?" I shrugged. I was empty, exhausted. "Do you think your dad is happy with Jean?"

I rolled my eyes. "He married her, didn't he? If he's not happy, he has only himself to blame!"

The wind was blowing ground snow across the icy road in thin white curtains. Martin kept his eyes straight ahead, his face still.

I sighed. "Okay, I think he's happy sometimes."

"Are you and Daisy making things tense for them? I'm not accusing, okay? Just asking."

I was too tired to talk about Jean or Dad, so I didn't answer.

"And if you keep on at your dad, you might break it up, right?"

"Just be quiet, Martin, okay? You know nothing." I stared out the window.

We drove through the whiteness for a while. I suddenly realized that I was leaving Beatrice behind. *Would she be able to find me at Aunt Blair's?* I felt for the brooch through my jacket. Yes, it was still pinned in my pocket. *Surely she'd find me, wouldn't she?*

"So what was your dad like after your mom died?"

He wasn't going to give up. "He got up, he went to work, he came home, he went to bed. His eyes were dead – like no one was in there."

"And you?"

"I got up, went to school, came home, made dinner, went to bed. It was like a huge semi had crashed through our house, smashing half of it to bits. The way she left . . . it was . . . I was . . . there is no way to explain. Aunt Blair took me to her doctor after the funeral. He gave me something that helped me sleep, so I could at least get to school." I stared out the window again.

He put a hand over mine. "Sorry."

"Sometimes, at school, I heard kids talking about their makeup or their hot weekends, or griping about their parents, or crying over some guy or girl, all stupid superficial stuff. I just wanted to shout at them, 'Don't you get it? We're all going to die! Who cares about any of this crap! What's the point of *anything*?'"

"Still feel that way?"

"It got better. Then Dad married *her*. And she's done her best to – oh, just never mind, Martin."

"You clearly can't stand Jean."

I put my head against the backrest. "You think? She's uptight, jealous, bossy, and has absolutely no sense of humor. None. Zilch. My mom was all over the place, but she was easy to be around, and funny. Jean hates me. And my father just wants everything to be normal. . . ."

The sign for Jackson's Grange, a tiny hamlet between St. Cuthbert's and Selkirk, loomed up ahead. We pulled off, and a mile farther, came to a narrow stone house.

Beside it stood a brick building that had been a local tele-
phone station in the 1920s. My grandpa, Duncan Andrews,
bought it and turned it into an antique store in the early
1960s. Now it was my aunt's. People came from Winnipeg,
Selkirk, and as far as Brandon to buy stuff here.

Martin pulled into the driveway. "You aunt's just
getting out of her car. Maybe being at her place will give
you some space to think."

I smiled sadly. "Maybe thinking's the last thing I want
to do."

25

BEATRICE

I have found out that in her clear-out of the house when she married Papa, Ivy threw away all of my mother's hand-made Christmas decorations. I was not surprised, but angry even so. This morning, after milking the cows and cleaning the house, the girls and I opened the doors between the parlor and the dining room, lit the fire, and set out paper, paste, brushes, and paints.

As I organized a big pot of tea and a platter of scones for the girls in the kitchen, Ivy grumbled to Papa, "All this hullabaloo for Christmas! It's not right. It's not Godly!"

Papa said quietly, "Then just steer clear of it, Ivy, and all will be well."

She pulled herself up like an affronted hen and glared at me around her long beak. Soon after we began our work on the decorations, I saw her accusatory eye appear every so often around the parlor door.

I hoped Duncan Kilgour would stay away, but it wasn't

long before he was poking his nose in, too, acting as if nothing whatsoever was wrong. I couldn't confront him with the girls there, so I told him he could help nôhkom down to the dining room, instead of eating all my scones. Off he went.

The Three Graces and Dilly chatted brightly as they sifted through the bits and bobs in the box I keep under my bed. It was filled with beading supplies, porcupine quills, tiny pine cones, flattened and curled birch bark, leaves and flowers, pretty stones, and other things I'd collected on my summer and fall rambles.

"Look," cried Anna Grace in Cree. "Leather and bags of beads!"

Soon they were making tiny moccasins. Grandmother was tooth-biting simple designs on smooth pieces of pale birch bark lining, looping red wool through them as hangers. She said she learned it from a friend she once knew "up north." I fashioned paper-loop garlands and stars using precious silver tissue. As the morning wore on, our pile of little things to put on the tree grew and grew.

As we worked, Duncan wedged the balsam's trunk solidly into the wooden pail, using pieces of wood to hold it in place. Then he lay balsam boughs along the mantelpiece, tucking smaller pieces behind the long picture wires on the walls. All the while, he sang Christmas songs. He began with "The Contest of the Ivy and the Holly," looking toward the hall door now and again.

When he loudly intoned, "'Ivy hath chapped fingers, she caught them from the cold, So might they all have, aye, that with Ivy hold,'" I heard a gasp, and footsteps retreated quickly down the hall. Duncan chuckled and hummed a new tune.

Why did he come to Rupert's Land? He shows such clear disdain for his mother, but also a kind of amused pity. Not love. Why doesn't he go back to Scotland?

He stood far too close to me as we added the garland to the tree. I could feel the heat of his body. Then he made me irritable by devouring most of the scones.

Fortunately, it didn't take long to wind the garlands through the branches, but it took much longer to place each tiny decoration. Duncan watched benevolently from a chair by the stove, where I'd ordered him to sit. I found candle-holders with metal guards that Papa had made when I was a child, which somehow missed Ivy's sweep, and I tied them carefully to the tree. I placed small candles in each one, then commanded Duncan to tie a metal star to the highest branch.

"We can't light the candles yet," I said. "For these are all I have."

"I will make you more," he said.

I saw one of the girls elbow Dilly and smile, but one narrow-eyed glance from me stopped this silliness in its tracks. When I turned quickly to tidy our clutter, my little spirit girl moved across the room toward me. Her cloud of hair seemed to fill the room. She gazed at me sadly, almost desperately. I looked at the others. No one saw her.

She stood by our tree, looking intently at the shadow of a strange white one beside it. She looked so distressed, I walked right up to her. "What is upsetting you? Is it me?" I whispered.

My heart stopped when I saw us both reflected in the window. Her lips moved, but I could only catch the words

"It's her." And then she was gone. Who was she talking about? Her mother?

"What are you seeing out that window?" Duncan murmured behind me.

"I-I was thinking of my mother. I was thinking of Christmases past. I was thinking how long our winters are."

He looked at me carefully. "This is my second winter in the New World. I spent my first in Upper Canada. I hear the winters in Rupert's Land are even colder than in York. We must do something this year to brighten up –"

"The minister man is here. The young one," Dilly announced, returning from refilling the teapot in the kitchen.

I smoothed my apron. "Show him in, please, Dilly."

Duncan sat down and crossed his legs. Truly, his nerve is astounding at times!

"Mr. Kilgour," I said, "would you please help my grandmother to the kitchen? I'll give her some dinner there later. And I will receive Mr. Dalhousie in here alone."

The girls scuttled toward the door after putting some of the tattered tree branches onto the fire, where they fizzed and crackled. Kilgour fussed over nôhkom until the minister walked in.

"Dalhousie! Good to see you so soon," called Duncan. "How is your lovely sister this morning?"

I clenched my teeth.

"She is rather tired, but quite well, considering. The girls you sent, Miss Alexander, are being a great help to her."

"Duncan, Beatrice has asked us to leave," Grandmother said softly.

Duncan picked her up. "*Of course. Excuse us.*"

Grandmother frowned at me over his shoulder. She was trying to send me a message, but I couldn't work out what it was.

"Will you accept a cup of tea, Mr. Dalhousie?" I asked.

"Thank you, Miss Alexander." He took the cup.

"You said you had a hymn to add to my choir's list?"

"I've decided that learning a new piece would only put more pressure on you, Miss Alexander. We have more than enough music." He put his teacup aside. "I –" he cleared his throat, "I have another reason for coming here today."

"Oh, yes?"

He seemed reluctant to speak. "I've decided to remain in St. Cuthbert's just until spring. That should give the church authorities plenty of time to find a man who is right for the job."

Why was he telling me and not Papa, who was an elder of the church? "I'm sorry you'll be leaving. You will disappoint so many eager mamas." I laughed lightly, trying to imitate his sister, but failed miserably.

"I've been asked by an old friend to go to the wilderness, along the northwestern coast, thousands of miles from here. There I can practice true missionary work."

"But how will Henrietta take to the hard travel and remote land?"

He looked down at his hands. "If she had a kind companion, she would do well. As would I." He cleared his throat. "I rather hoped that might be you, Miss Alexander."

"Me? Why me? There are young women in the parish who'd suit the role much better than I. I would not be an easy companion."

"You do yourself an injustice, my dear. You have integrity and compassion. I will open a school there, and I want a wife from my own church – a servant of God, like myself, ready for hardship and challenge. One who would teach alongside me."

"You're asking me to come as your wife? But you hardly know me, Sir! To say nothing of your feelings for me."

"Surely, Beatrice – if I may call you that – a deeper affection will come to both of us in due course. I'm not wrong in thinking we like and admire each other?"

"I do like you . . . er, Robert . . . it's just . . ." But did I admire him?

"It would be a grand adventure in God's name for all three of us," he said, his eyes alight. Something gave me an inner warning, but I tried to ignore it.

I looked at my clenched hands. I was being offered an escape and was suddenly faced with a choice. A life-changing choice. But what about Grandmother? And Papa? Yes, Papa was physically stronger since my return, but . . .

My mind hurtled into the future. What if I suggested making Dilly responsible for Grandmother? That might work out well. And what about your confused faith – or lack of it? my small voice asked. Perhaps my faltering beliefs would solidify and strengthen by serving others. I could keep a journal describing our journey. Perhaps have it published one day. This might be my only chance to finally leave my shadows behind.

Duncan Kilgour's mocking smile floated across my inner vision. He would tease me mercilessly. But Duncan Kilgour didn't care two pins for me, any more than I – no, I wouldn't think about him. No doubt he would up and leave this village one day with a cheery wave, and I would be even more alone.

Robert Dalhousie broke into my tortured thoughts. "May I speak with your papa, Miss Alexander?" His thin face was guarded.

I knew I had to confront the reality of my situation then and there. I knew there was little real hope of ever taking nôhkom to the settlement to live. It was a young girl's romantic dream, nothing more. I would never have enough money to live an independent life – my own life.

As if someone else were speaking the words for me, I said, "I require time to sort out how my grandmother and Papa will be taken care of. For if I agree to your proposal, Sir, I will not return to my home for many years. If their future comfort is settled, then, yes, I will give you permission to speak with Papa."

He bowed slightly, then began to talk to me about his new mission with an enthusiasm that I wished he had injected into his proposal. I must confess, I barely heard a word about his future plans.

Before he left, he'd taken my hand. "I am sure your papa will not deny you this opportunity." His fingers were cool and dry. Was his smile just a little smug?

As the door closed behind him, my inner voice spoke up. Beatrice, Beatrice . . . what have you agreed to?

26

CASS

Aunt Blair was turning the key in the front door
when we climbed the front stairs. Once inside,
she threw her coat on an old wooden pew against the
wall. "Go into the living room, you two."

We tossed our jackets on top of hers. My old cat,
Tardy, wandered into the hall, his long tail twitching.
When he saw me, he leaped into my arms. I stroked his
fur, holding back tears. Aunt Blair's house always smelled
of sanded wood and varnish from her private work
space, beside the dining room. Tonight those odors
mingled with the scent of a balsam tree, covered in the
decorations that Blair had collected since she was a kid.
The living-room floor was layered in rugs, the couch and
chairs soft with down pillows. The walls were covered in
watercolors and sketches she couldn't or wouldn't sell.
Odd-shaped floor lamps with silk shades dotted the
room, casting pools of low light.

Aunt Blair clicked on the tree lights. I sat on the
couch, with Tardy on my lap. Martin stood, looking at

the tree. "My gran has decorations like these," he said.

Blair lit the fire. "One thing I can never pass up, Martin, is an old decoration. My dad made sure I always got first pick before he sold them." The phone rang in the kitchen. "That'll be Jonathan, Cass. I'll make some cocoa while I'm in there."

She headed down the hall. I silently thanked her for not asking me to answer it. But I still needed to know why she was at Jean's party.

When she returned, she threw me a mohair blanket. I tucked it around me, but couldn't stop shivering, even with Tardy's warmth against me. I sipped the cocoa she'd made. Martin looked relaxed.

"I told your dad to wait until later tomorrow before calling again," Aunt Blair said. "The shops in Selkirk are open early. I'm doing my final Christmas shopping and told him I'd take you along. He said to use the credit card he gave you last week – that you might like to buy yourself a nice outfit for Christmas Day. Look, you guys talk for a bit while I make up your bed in the spare room, Cass."

"Dad's just trying to make everything okay again," I muttered. "He likes things to be swept away fast. He's never figured out it just makes things worse."

"We'll talk later," she said as she left the room.

Martin moved over beside me. We stared at the fire.

"Maybe you should call your place and –"

"I feel stupid about what I did tonight, Martin, but not enough to say sorry to Jean, okay?"

"I wasn't going to say that. I –"

"I'm not sorry for what I said; I just feel stupid that I did it in front of all those people, especially about a tree." I gulped back the quaver in my voice. "Martin, Jean told *strangers* about this baby at the same time she told *me*. Dad was too much of a coward to tell me first. I can't go back there yet." I swallowed my tears.

He wrapped one hand around the back of my neck and gave it a gentle squeeze. "Maybe Jean will be over with an apology tomorrow."

"Yeah," I muttered, "and Santa's reindeers really can fly."

"What? You mean they can't?"

"Go home. You're as punch-drunk as me!" My stupid tears just wouldn't dry up. I pretended they weren't there.

He smiled. "I'll see you in the morning."

I climbed off the couch still wrapped in the soft blanket, swiped away the wet on my face, and followed him to the front door. He stepped out into the night.

Leaning on the door frame, I said, "Thanks, Martin, for being . . . you know, so great. I'm not sure why you bother, when you could get Tricia to go out with you again."

He tapped my temple with a fingertip, his face coming closer. "I like you. I like what's in there. Besides, you look so lost half the time; it gets to me."

"Glad I get to *somebody*. Mostly I don't even feel like I'm here, you know?"

"Oh, you're very here." He leaned closer, and I met him halfway. He tasted of cocoa and cinnamon. I wrapped my arms around his neck and leaned my cheek against his. "I know this baby thing is different than losing my mom, but Jean is using it to force me farther away from my dad."

He leaned back. "I don't know . . . I guess we all have to move away from our parents a bit. Maybe so we can find someone just for us. Let's face it, I've been hooked since I first saw that runny nose of yours in math class." I hugged him again.

A few minutes later, the twin beams of his truck swept the house, and I watched through the door window until the red taillights fluttered out of sight.

"He seems like a really nice kid," Blair said from a chair beside the fire.

She was holding a glass of wine. A plate of cheese and crackers was on the table. She'd changed into jeans, a black turtleneck, and a pair of fur-lined moccasins. I noticed for the first time how skinny she was, her face all hollows and angles.

I should have asked her if she was okay, but instead I said, "Why were you there tonight, anyway?"

"Your dad asked me to come. He said it would be good for all of us if we met halfway. Get rid of this tension between us. That it would be good for –"

"For me, right? For annoying, troublesome Cass? He used me as bait. And you didn't tell him to drop dead? You know who was behind it, don't you? Jean. She wants to get to know you so she can undercut me. And she wanted you to be there to hear all about their baby. To remind *you* that Mom is gone. I know you can't stand her. I know you think she was working on Dad even when Mom was sick."

She held up a hand. "Not going there, Cass. I was really emotional when Fiona died."

"But I heard what you said when Dad told you he was going to marry Jean."

It was last July. Dad had invited Aunt Blair for dinner. I was glad she came . . . at first. Aunt Blair and Jean sat side by side, not saying much, while Dad barbecued steaks and potatoes for all of us. After dessert, he'd lifted his wineglass and said, "Here's to my future wife, Jean. We hope to get married in a month. Lots of plans to make!"

Aunt Blair stared at him like she was stun-gunned. She didn't lift her glass, so Dad stood alone with his in the air.

"Daisy, go upstairs for a bit, okay?" Jean said. Daisy looked ready to argue, but Jean repeated, "Go upstairs, please."

Aunt Blair motioned for me to leave as well. I went to the kitchen, then crept back and stood outside the door.

". . . can't be serious!" I heard Dad say.

"It's been barely a year since Fiona died, Jon. Have you really thought this through?"

"Excuse me, I'm here, too," Jean said. "You're accusing us of having a relationship while Jon's wife was sick? That's simply not true."

"You were going out together almost as soon as she was gone," Blair said, "but I figured Jon couldn't cope without his wife and that you'd be there for him until his grieving was over. Mind you, I knew you were after him right from the time you first laid eyes on him. So did Fiona."

"What? She did not. That's ridiculous!" Dad cried.

"Maybe you didn't see it, but we did. Fiona thought it was funny and that Jean was pathetic. She said you were too stressed and clued out to notice, Jon. Well, I won't sit here and toast either of you. I don't want any part of this."

I ran down the hall and up the back stairs two at a time. When I opened my bedroom door, Daisy was sitting on my bed, looking around.

"Mom says we'll have to share this bedroom when they get married. I have way more stuff than you. I should have this room just for me."

I'd headed back down the front stairs and straight outside, just in time to see my aunt drive away. She hadn't even said good-bye. It was still light out, so I went for a long bike ride along the river, pedaling away from it all.

Now, in the glow of her Christmas lights, I said, "But you came to Dad and Jean's wedding. Why?"

"To be there for *you*. Also to remind them that Fiona was . . . I don't know . . . important to remember. Look, Cass, it wasn't an easy time for anyone. I can't say anything with certainty about what happened when your mom was sick. I'm still working through it all. I decided to go to the party tonight to see how things felt to me when you were all together."

I laughed. "Well, we didn't disappoint then, did we?"

She took a sip of wine. "I have to let it go. Accept things as they are, if I can't change them."

"Let it go? Accept things as they are? Did you swallow some of Jean's personal cliché pills? Next you'll be talking about closure!" I cried.

"Maybe I already am. Cass, I've spent the last two years in a sad dreary place. Fiona wasn't my identical twin, but she was my heart twin. I was the levelheaded sensible one; she was the fairy sprite. I thought she'd live forever – way past me – but that we'd be together until we were doddering old bats, no matter what. But she didn't stay, and when she left, she took away her bright light. I was left alone in the dark. Then I cut off contact with Jon. I stopped seeing Tom Hunt – the best relationship I'd ever been in. I started taking prescription pills to try and feel better. I worked in my shop all night sometimes."

Why didn't I know?

She took another sip. "But I've been for help and I'm coming out of it. I'm feeling more hopeful. Or, I was until tonight."

"So, you've had shadows all around you, too. . . ."

"Shadows? I guess I did. But all that time, I was being selfish, too. I left you on your own. For too long. Sure, you came over, we watched movies, we talked about books, schoolwork, and all kinds of stuff, but never about any of this. I knew you were suffering, but I couldn't step out of my own pit and help you. I'm sorry, Cassy."

"Don't feel guilty. You made things seem normal now and again for me. That's what I wanted. But I didn't know you were going through so much."

"How could you know? You were dealing with it too. But, after tonight, I feel you shouldn't be in that toxic environment – and yet I know I have no rights – I'm not your parent." Her voice shook. "So I guess what I'm trying to say is, if we both let your mom, Fiona, go a little, maybe we can accept that your dad has moved on and is trying to make a life –"

"For himself!" I cried. "Not for me! You saw Jean. She hates me." I stopped. "Wait. Daisy told me this morning that a secret was going to be announced at the party. So she knew Jean was expecting a kid. So did Dad! Why didn't he –"

"I don't know, honey. That surprises me. I think maybe he only found out ahead of the party, too."

It just came out. "I can't stay there anymore. Can I live here with you?"

She looked into her wineglass. "We both know what your dad would say to that."

"But if I got him to agree?"

"I don't know. It sounds like running away from the problem, Cass."

"But you just called it toxic there. Even for a while? Say, a year?"

"If your father agreed, of course I'd let you stay. But he won't."

"He might."

"Let's get through Christmas first, okay? But you have to promise, before any decisions are made, you will somehow make a kind of provisional peace with Jean."

"You know that's not going to happen."

"My one criteria for you moving in with me, Cass, would be that you don't leave that house hating Jean. Maybe family counseling would work. But that's the deal. Okay. *Bed*. I'm too tired to think anymore, and you're too emotional to see the sense in what I'm saying."

"So, in other words, you don't really want me here."

"Yes, Cass, I do."

I wasn't sure I believed her. We dragged our way upstairs, where there were two small bedrooms and a bathroom. We silently brushed our teeth together.

"'Night," I muttered.

As I was walking past her, she hugged me. "I love you so much, Cassy. I would do anything to make this better for you."

"I love you too," I whispered, hugging her back. I could feel her sharp shoulder blades under my hands. Maybe her shadows had been even worse than mine.

I ran to the spare room, changed into the pajamas I kept here, and climbed into bed. Tardy was lying on top of two hot-water bottles wrapped in fleece. I took one and hugged it.

—

I couldn't think about Jean and Dad anymore, or even whether or not Beatrice would find me here, so I thought about Martin. *What if, tomorrow, he acts distant and uneasy?* Maybe he was already regretting what he'd said. No more thinking. I fell asleep to Tardy's plump purring.

When I woke again, it was still dark. Suddenly Tardy leaped off the bed and ran into the hall with a Halloween-type hiss. Beatrice appeared in front of me, holding her journal. As I blinked up at her, she placed it on the bed and drifted back into the moon's pale light.

I turned on my lamp and read about her visit to the Comper farm. My heart stopped when she described making snow angels with Duncan and seeing me. Our timing was askew, but I knew for certain, now, that I really *had* seen her – and that I had also seen, twice briefly, the shadowy figure of Duncan Kilgour.

She called me her spirit girl. She was excited that we'd spoken – if only for a moment beside the Christmas trees. She knew I was unhappy, like her. And she'd more or less guessed the reason.

I read about the vicarage party and laughed at her wry humor, about Duncan's behavior to her, and, finally, Robert Dalhousie's marriage proposal. I lay back, wondering what it all meant. *Would it free her from Ivy and maybe even the shadows? Or would her leaving just make everything worse? Would my leaving Old Maples make things worse for me?*

Beatrice would finally have a great adventure to write about. *Is that what she really wanted? Didn't she notice how Duncan hung around her all the time? Didn't she take in how interesting and funny he was?* He was so much more attractive than stuffy old Robert. *And what did she want from me? Why were we seeing each other?* I stared at the pages long and hard.

I could feel the warmth of the diary cooling under my hands. In a desperate rush, I grabbed a pencil from a pot on the side table and wrote, *Wait. Don't rush. Think hard before marrying Robert Dalhousie. Be strong.* The pencil was slip-sliding over the page, leaving only faint marks. I pressed as hard as I could. *What about Duncan?* And I signed it *Cass*.

◦

27

BEATRICE

I stared at the closed door, uncertain what to do or think, my thoughts were in such turmoil. Robert had just left, believing we were promised to one another. I thought of Mr. Rochester's ardent proposal to Jane Eyre . . . how she heard him call to her across the moors after she ran away. But in my restricted life, there was no mad wife locked in a tower room, and I was not running broken-hearted from the man I loved. Writers of fiction create romance to stir lonely hearts. Like mine. However, one thing was clear to me – if I wanted to drive away the shadows and create a meaningful existence for myself, I must take the opportunity Robert offered.

I ran upstairs and wrote everything in my diary. But it did not help. I wanted so badly to share the burden of this decision with someone who would understand. Would my spirit girl understand? I closed my eyes and envisioned her clearly. She looked sleepy, and, when she saw me, she smiled and reached toward me. I held out my diary. When I opened my eyes again, it was still in my hands. How foolish I was!

Surely, I was losing touch with reality. Would I soon move into a strange imaginary world of my own? I placed my diary back in its secret spot, determined to do all the little daily things that would keep any kakêpâtis thoughts at bay, and walked firmly down each stair toward the kitchen. My decision was made: I would marry Robert Dalhousie and start a new life.

I prepared our midday meal of boiled bacon, cheese, and soda bread – nôhkom's favorite. I wondered if I should tell her about the proposal before I told Papa. Ivy was upstairs with one of her headaches. The fuss over the Christmas tree had clearly been too much for her. As long as she didn't burn it down, I didn't care. I looked at my beloved papa talking quietly to his mother in her language, while I stood at the edge of a great precipice, my heart pounding.

When the girls helped nôhkom upstairs to rest, I said quietly, "Papa. I have something to tell you," but at that moment, Duncan Kilgour walked in, carrying a mammoth frost-covered whitefish on a length of rope.

"Dinner, my lord, my lady! I caught it the second my bait dropped. Gutted and ready for the fire. Mother will only kill this magnificent fish a second time by cooking it. I beg you to prepare it, Miss Alexander!"

Why did sharp prickles of alarm go through me at the sight of him? I knew I must tell both of them quickly. Before I lost heart.

I opened my mouth, but the words that came out were "I must take some tea to Ivy – she is not well." I poured tea into a cup and stumbled to the door.

Ivy responded to my knock with a curt "Enter!" The room was as chilly as her greeting. "What do you want?" She sat by her stove wrapped in a quilt, her graying hair tangled on her shoulders.

"I brought you some tea, Ivy. Is there anything else you need? Perhaps more wood on the fire?"

"Is this some feeble attempt to make up for creating chaos in my house?"

"Not at all. Papa said you have a headache."

She took the tea and sipped it. "Pshaw! Cold." She held out the cup.

"I'll make a fresh pot."

"Don't bother." As I turned to go, a hand shot out and grabbed my arm in a tight grip. "Stay away from my son."

"Whatever do you mean?"

"Fluttering around Duncan with that butter-wouldn't-melt look. Undermining me. Stay away, I tell you!"

I pulled my arm back. "I don't want your son. I am already spoken for."

She let out a scornful laugh. "Who would marry you?"

I jumped straight into the yawning precipice. "I received a proposal of marriage from Reverend Dalhousie this very morning, as it happens."

"Don't lie to me! That man's as English as English can be and too full of himself to marry a half-breed."

"Nevertheless, he will speak to Papa soon."

"Then you must be forcing his hand somehow!" A light sparked in her eyes. "You're with child! That's it! Isn't it?"

"Don't be ridiculous, Ivy!"

She put her head back and called, "Gordon! Gordon!"

I ran down the stairs, followed by her shrill voice.

"What on earth has happened?" Papa said.

"I must speak to you, Father. Now. It is important."

"I'll go and see what's put her in such a dither," Duncan offered. "She won't stop."

"No!" I cried. "Your mother provoked me. She claims I have designs on you, Mr. Kilgour. . . ."

"Well, I can tell her that —"

I knew he was about to make fun. I held up one hand. "Stop! Please! Listen!"

"Out with it, my dear," Papa said, "or Ivy will be down here telling us herself."

I took a deep breath. "Robert Dalhousie has asked me to accompany him to his next posting. Out west. As his wife. Ivy has accused me of . . . seducing him into taking me along. It is a complete falsehood."

For a moment, no one moved.

"Have you accepted his proposal?" Papa asked.

I held my trembling hands firmly against my waist. "Only if you agree, Papa."

"I will not stay to supper," Duncan Kilgour said. "I will see you at rehearsal, Miss Alexander. Mr. Alexander, please do not allow my mother to make too big a fool of herself." He grabbed his coat and hat. The door banged shut behind him.

CASS

I was in the shower when Aunt Blair knocked. "Your dad just dropped off some clothes for you. The bag's on the floor out here. Martin's downstairs already."

By the time I brushed my teeth and got dressed, Martin was working on a pile of pancakes. He gave me a bright smile. He didn't *look* like he was thinking about how to tell me he wanted out.

I managed to choke down one bite. "Did Dad say anything?" I asked Blair.

"Only to call him when you're ready to come home. I told him you'd be here for a few days."

"Thanks." The next mouthful tasted better. I ate two pancakes. We were doing the dishes when the doorbell rang. My heart flip-flopped. *Please don't let it be Dad and Jean.*

Aunt Blair went to answer it, and, in the distance, I heard a whining voice. *Daisy? Were they all here?* Blair walked in with a flushed and swollen-eyed kid. No Dad. No Jean.

"She heard you were going shopping and told them you'd made plans with her for today. Jon's waiting outside for an answer."

"You promised, Cass," Daisy said with a sniff. "I got money I saved, and Jonathan says I can use your credit card too." She looked pathetic.

I swallowed down a flutter of panic. *How could I cope with Daisy around? How was I supposed to think and work things out?*

The kid had her hands folded under her chin like she was praying to me.

"I guess so," I said with a sigh.

She beamed and twirled in a circle, then ran outside to tell Dad. *What the heck was up with her?* She'd been the devil's spawn for three months. The news of the baby must have really affected her. She ran back in.

"Your dad says have a good day."

"Yeah. Sure. Thanks, Dad."

"We'll use my van," Blair said, "but I have to deliver some things on the way back."

Martin said, "How about you take Daisy, and we follow in my truck, Miss . . . er?"

"Call me Blair. 'Miss' sounds terribly old."

"Okay, we'll follow you, Blair. You can make your deliveries afterward that way."

"Sounds good, Martin. Come on, Daisy."

"But I want to go with you, Cass. You promised," Daisy moaned.

"Up to you, Cass," Blair said.

Half an hour later, we squeezed Daisy into the small back-seat and followed Blair's van along the road to Selkirk.

Daisy was quiet. Martin kept looking at me with a small frown. "So are you put off about what I said last night? About . . . you know?"

I could almost *hear* Daisy's ears prick up, so I answered carefully, "No. But I figured you might be sorry you ever said it."

He took my hand. I heard an intake of breath from behind us. Martin grinned and turned the radio on. "Jingle Bells" was playing. He sang over it, "Jingle Bells / Batman smells / Robin laid an egg / The batmobile lost a wheel / And the Joker got away, HEY!"

Then Daisy did a version from school about Santa smelling and reindeer running away. Martin topped that with a gruesome "Dashing through the snow / on a pair of broken skis / over the hills we go / crashing through the trees / the snow is turning red / I think I'm almost dead / they rushed me to the hospital / I almost lost my head! HEY!"

We made up more verses as we went along. When we pulled up in front of a row of craft and gift shops, my stomach hurt from laughing. We met up with Blair and cruised the shops. I picked out a china Santa for Jean that I knew she'd detest – his suit was flaming pink and a wobbly-legged fawn looked up at him with sickening adoration. One of Santa's eyes was off-center. Even better, it cost me three bucks. I looked at a pair of smooth oval green-stone earrings that Mom would have loved, so I bought them for her.

When Blair wandered off with Daisy to look for my gift next door, I picked out a dark green angora hat and scarf set for Daisy and some silver hoop earrings for Blair with a matching clip-on bracelet. Then I bought a black-and-yellow scarf for Martin. In the truck, Daisy showed me a holly-leaf crystal brooch for Jean, but was careful not to show me another small box she covered with her hand. I grinned inside. Jean would hate that hideous pin. *Would she wear it Christmas Day to please Daisy? Would she put my Santa gift on display? Doubters.* I had a prick of guilt about the pink china Santa, but it didn't last long.

Martin and I picked car stuff for our dads. I didn't get the usual Terry's Chocolate Orange for the toe of my father's stocking. There were no traditions for us left, so why bother?

I walked with Martin toward the truck as Aunt Blair dragged Daisy into a toy store. "You two go on ahead and find some lunch," she called. "I'll take Daisy to the tea shop down the street when we're done. I'll meet you back here at one."

The sun was shining, and, despite the wind, the inside of the truck was warm. "You want to go to the tea place with them?" Martin asked.

"No. I'm up to here with crowds. Let's eat in the truck. There must be a competitor you want to check out?"

We took off, stopping at a chip shop that featured double dogs. We shared fries and analyzed the cheap oil on them.

"My parents don't want me to run the restaurant," Martin told me. "They say it's just long hours, hard work, and worry. They want me to do what I want."

"And that is?"

"Well, I hope to run the restaurant, actually."

I laughed.

"Or," he continued, "a trendy one in Winnipeg. I'm going to chef school after grade twelve. Apprentice at a good restaurant. Work here on weekends. My mom and dad think I'll be a painter or a poet or an actor."

I pushed him. "They wouldn't want that. No money in it."

He slicked a strand of hair behind my ear. "You want to be rich one day?"

"No. Just happy. I learned when Mom died how fast things can go wrong. Money can't change that." *Or buy a whole new day,* I thought. *Or alter something you did that you regret . . . but I won't go there. Not today.*

His fingers twirled my hair. "So what's with Daisy? It's like she hangs on your every word. I thought you two hated each other."

I shrugged, not moving my head in case he stopped. "She's such a sad case, that kid. Those glasses are hideous. Her hair looks like a Victorian doll's wig – stuck on her head like it doesn't belong to her."

I glanced over his shoulder and saw a couple of stores

that made me sit up. I put my hand on his arm. "I have the best idea!"

He smiled and leaned closer. "*Mmm.* Me, too." I decided his idea was better . . . for now.

A few minutes later, someone rapped on the window. We both jumped back. Staring up at us was my unlovely stepsister, her huge glasses shining with interest.

"Where's Blair?" I asked, rolling down the window.

She pointed at the idling van two cars down. "We're going to deliver stuff to people who bought from Blair's store."

"You can't. Wait here." I got out of the truck and ran over to the van. "We're going to spend more time in town, then take Daisy back to your place, if that's okay."

"Good idea," Aunt Blair said. "I suspect your parents need a day alone."

"Yeah, so Jean can lecture Dad on how I can't be allowed to put that toothpaste back in the tube." She looked puzzled. I added, "Never mind. See you at your place. We'll be back by dinner."

When she drove off, I grabbed Daisy's hand and marched her toward the little shops on the other side of the road.

29

BEATRICE

*P*apa *groped for his crutches. "Come to my study, Beatrice."*

We'd just closed the door behind us when Ivy pushed it open. She looked like a madwoman, with her thin wild hair, staring eyes, and red blotchy skin.

"This daughter of yours has fallen with child and claims she is going to marry that upstart of a minister, who is no better than he should be! She doesn't even deny it! You must cast her out, Gordon!"

"I have been home less than a month, Papa," I said firmly. "I hardly know the man!"

"She's lying!" Ivy spat out. "All those choir practices – home late afterward! Why else would a man of his back-ground ask to marry her – a wanton half-breed."

Papa stamped his crutches on the floor. "Ivy! Be quiet!"

"Listen to me, Gordon! I am telling you, she is –"

"You've taken too much laudanum again, Ivy. I have warned you how it twists your mind. Robert Dalhousie asked my daughter to marry him because he knows she will make the best of wives. Unlike you, who spreads poison like

a ripe plague through this household. If you do not stop these slanderous lies, I will send you to your son's farm for good and shun you forever!"

Ivy backed against the door. "You would send me away? Duncan would not allow you. . . ."

Papa moved quickly toward her, sticks banging the floor. "Don't test me, Ivy."

She covered her face with her hands. "How can you speak to me this way? You know I love you, Gordon. You know I do."

His face softened. "Yes, I know you do, my dear."

She left the room quietly, head down.

Had I heard right? Ivy actually loved my father? *And though he didn't reply in kind, his anger had left as quickly as it came.*

"Papa, I don't understand," I said.

He lowered himself onto the leather chair beside his desk. "I don't expect you to, Beatrice. Sit down." He looked out the window into the snow-glazed afternoon light, which glanced off the smooth planes of his face.

"Ivy told me all about her life shortly after we buried Farmer Comper. She came to St. Cuthbert's after meeting him at a friend's house in Scotland. His country marriage had ended with the death of his Cree wife. Ivy was a widow and had been housekeeper to a bishop, who'd recently died. She was living with friends who could no longer keep her. Duncan had lived away from her for years with her aunt. She was destitute.

Comper was looking for a wife. She really had no choice but to accept him."

"Why was she so poor? Couldn't she, too, have lived with her aunt?"

He shook his head. "Ivy came from a family of modest merchants in Edinburgh. She was engaged to marry the oldest son of a rich merchant. A feather in the family's cap – a dull man, she said, but one who could offer her lifelong security. But then she fell in love with his younger brother. They eloped. Both families disowned them."

"I can't imagine Ivy running away with a lover."

"I have a daguerreotype of her." He opened a drawer and handed me a yellowing picture of a girl my age. She was thin, with soft eyes and a hopeful smile.

"You see. She was rather pretty. She fell with child almost immediately, only to find that her young husband's financial support had been taken away, not only because of her, but because of his enormous debts. She soon realized he was an addicted gambler when intoxicated and a repentant wretch when sober. They traveled around the country, Ivy taking on any work she could find and her husband gambling away what little they had, until he died a drawn-out painful death. She was left destitute. Fortunately, she was able to take on the housekeeper's position at the bishopric when Duncan was five. He was sent to his great-aunt's, with the agreement that Ivy would ask for nothing and give up all maternal rights."

"How sad. For both her and for her son," I murmured. No wonder the two were so awkward with each other.

"The aunt ran a private school in the country. She was everything Ivy was not. One of the new intellectual women – a freethinker, as Kilgour calls them – interested in science and nature and in using one's reason to decide what the world offers, rather than accepting old ideas. She was also possibly a deist – a believer in a divine being, but not in the authority of organized churches. The aunt taught Duncan art, music, and books. Ivy feels he has been terribly corrupted. But from what I know of the fellow, I believe he is open-minded and one who tries to see both sides of an issue. In any case, when his great-aunt died, she left everything to him. He used it to travel the world, having no idea where his mother was by then.

"Soon after Comper died, Duncan returned to Scotland. Fortunately, Ivy had kept in touch with old friends, and that's how he discovered where she was – here in Rupert's Land. He came all this way to find her."

"When she first came to Farmer Comper's farm, there were children to look after, weren't there?" I asked. "Minty and his older brother."

"The older boy died just after Ivy and Comper married. That left only Minty."

"Papa, when Minty and Ivy are together, she either ignores him or issues orders. It's as if they hardly know each other. He must have been a wee boy when she came here. Doesn't she care for him at all?"

"I asked her about that. She sent Minty to live with his mother's family at the Indian town, St. Anthony's, soon after his brother died. When Josiah Comper died, she brought

Minty back to help with the farm. She told me he is not her son, so she feels little affection for him. Despite all this, Minty's a good lad."

"Why did you marry her, Papa?"

He smiled. "She started out as my housekeeper. I was lonely; she was company. One day, she told me about her hard life and her bitter marriage to Comper. When I first suggested that we wed, she refused. But when I pressed her, she admitted she was ashamed of her two previous marriages. I felt sorry for her, Bea. I also liked her – she was different before we married."

"She was in love," I said.

"Perhaps. Or perhaps I was the first man in her life to be kind. Her father was a tyrant, her first husband a wastrel, and Comper a silent, harsh man. I could see, soon after we wed, that she was hoarding food. I tried to understand why and let it go at that. She and I were quietly content until my accident, and then –"

"And then I returned home and sparked fierce jealousy. But it's more than that, Papa. When I got back, nôhkom's body was covered in open sores! She had been dreadfully neglected."

He pressed fingertips to his temples. "I know this now. I truly thought my mama was simply growing old. I saw her as often as I could manage, and not once did she ever complain to me. But then, I was injured," he gave me a rueful smile, "and wallowing in self-pity. I trusted Ivy to care for my mother. God forgive me."

"I won't leave you or nôhkom to this woman. I'll tell Robert I can't marry him."

Papa covered my hands with his. "No. You must make a life for yourself, child. I am getting stronger every day. I'll make sure my mother is cared for. She won't suffer again. Duncan has already offered to hire a nurse to take the burden off you."

"He did? When?"

"Just a few days ago. I meant to tell you. He also arranged to have a new doctor from the settlement come and see me. He believes I could benefit from his opinion."

"What will you do about Ivy?"

"I offered Ivy a home with a healthy husband and a good yearly income. She found herself with a crippled man who was suddenly unable to work. To be fair, she has rarely complained. Yes, she is possessive and neurotic. She's as crippled as I am, but in a different way. I was too sick to fight her when she tried to keep me from my work on behalf of the local farmers. I will insist my friends visit me again. If marrying young Dalhousie is what you truly wish in your heart, then you must marry him. But tell me one thing, my dear."

I answered before he spoke it, "I do not love Robert, Papa. Not yet."

"Do you think you could love him, lass?"

"He is a rather distant man, Papa, but good. We will get along fine, I think."

"Is it only me and kôhkom you're worried about?" he asked.

"Who else would there be?"

He smiled. "I will give Dalhousie my permission, but think carefully on it first, my dear. I would hate to see you burdened by a loveless marriage. It's painful to lose someone you love, yet I thank God every day for those years with my Anne. Ivy has never known that kind of love – where you breathe easier knowing your cherished one is in the next room." He shook his head. "I'll miss you, but I want you to be happy."

I hugged him. "Nôhkom will advise me."

He shook his head. "Make this decision on your own, child. Then tell her. Do not burden her unnecessarily. You may change your mind for other reasons."

I left the room, wondering what he meant by not burdening nôhkom unnecessarily. Except for my worries about her and Papa, what could possibly make me change my mind? His words about my mother have gladdened my heart. I am thankful they found years of true affection together. Will Robert Dalhousie and I ever love the way my parents once loved?

30

CASS

The sun was sinking in a dark blue sky when we got back to Aunt Blair's. As soon as we parked, Daisy leaped out and ran in the front door. We were just in time to see the look on Blair's face when Daisy cried, "So, whaddya think? It's Cass's Christmas present to me – and Jonathan's too!"

She danced around the kitchen. Her hair swung easily, smooth and shiny, cut just below her ears, curving higher at the back. Soft bangs covered her wide forehead. The glasses we chose together were rimless, with cherry red arms.

Blair stumbled out, "Wow. Gorgeous, Daisy! Cass? Was this okayed by her mom?"

"No. But the kid really needed it. 'In for a penny, in for a pound,' as Jean would say!"

"I figure a pound of something will hit the fan when she goes home," Blair said.

Daisy laughed, put her arm up around my shoulders, and posed, one hip out. "It's two against one. But we'll win. Because Mom can't take this present back to the store!"

Martin said brightly, "All we need right now is for your dad to show up."

The doorbell rang. "Are you psychic, Martin?" Aunt Blair walked calmly to answer it.

We could hear Dad's voice. Daisy made a dash for the kitchen door, but I grabbed her. "Let me tell him first. He'll go nuts."

She grinned up at me. "I think seeing me will make him happy. He agreed to this, right?"

I let her go, took a deep breath, and followed, passing Blair coming back to the kitchen. All she said was "Oh, boy . . ."

When I got to the living room, Daisy's arms were wrapped around Dad's waist. "Oh, thank you, Jonathan! I know it's not Christmas yet, but Cass said I should have it done today. It's the best Christmas present ever, in my whole entire life!"

He held her at arm's length. She gazed up at him, her face flushed with joy. He pulled her close again and glared at me over her head. "I'm glad you love it, Daisy. You look really wonderful. Would you mind going to the kitchen with the others? I'd like to talk to Cass, okay?"

"Sure!" She sashayed out of the room, touching her hair carefully all over.

"Sit. Down." I sat. "What the devil are you playing at? Why would you do something as important as this without consulting the child's mother?"

"Because *the child's mother* isn't seeing her. Daisy's going to be thirteen soon. Kids are making fun of her,

Dad. Jean just sees you. Soon it will be all about the new baby. I thought the two of them were working together against me, but I realize Daisy has been trying to get Jean's attention all this time."

"You worked that out on your own, did you, Doctor Shrink? You can wipe that smile off your face. You are coming back with me, and you are going to explain to Jean why you did this."

"Okay. I wouldn't leave Daisy to take the heat alone."

"*Your* heat, Cass." He stared me down, but I didn't blink.

Blair and Martin were trying to keep a conversation going in the next room, but now and again I could hear a pine needle drop.

"I just don't understand what has come over you, Cass," Dad finally said. "I know you miss your mom. I know Jean is not a substitute. But your mom would have –"

"She had a name, Dad. It was Fiona. And she was *your wife*. Not just *my mom*."

"Do you really think it doesn't hurt me to say her name? Do you think I avoid saying it because of Jean? Do you have any idea how much I miss your . . . Fiona? But she is gone, Cass. . . ." The skin under his eyes looked bruised.

"And now you have a new life and a new baby coming. Does it matter what I do?"

"Are you still depressed, Cass? Is that it? Do you need to go back on the meds the doctor gave you after your – Fiona – died? I know your grades haven't fallen yet, but –"

"You think I'm acting out because of depression? Isn't that what Jean calls it, Dad? Acting out? You think this thing with Daisy is some kind of payback on Jean?"

"Isn't it? Jean's been finding you, everything, so difficult."

"It's all Jean, Jean, Jean. Have you listened to Jean, Dad? She speaks at me, as if I'm a stranger – no, a roomful of strangers. She *announces* things to me. She *proposes* things to me. She throws *clichés* at me. She never *talks* to *me*. She didn't want one thing from our old life in our own living room. And that's the point, isn't it? It's *her* home. I don't belong there."

"You belong where I am, Cass. I know Jean can be awkward at times, but she's shy in many ways."

I laughed. "Shy? You're kidding, right? A shy person who announces to a roomful of people at the same time she tells her clued-out stepdaughter – who didn't even get a say in choosing a Christmas tree, by the way – that she is expecting your baby?"

He could hardly drag out his next words. "She didn't tell me about the baby until just before the party. She took a home test while I was out. She'd been suspicious for a while, but . . . She would have told you if you were home on time. As for putting up the tree – well, isn't that just a little trite considering a baby is on the way, a baby that will be your half-sibling? I want you to be happy for us."

"First off, Jean lied about the test," I said. "She told Daisy about it the day before yesterday. Daisy said she knew a huge secret. I bet Jean's known for ages."

His eyes widened. He knew I was telling the truth.

"How can I be happy for you, Dad? You're married to a person who talks to me like I'm your distant relative visiting *her* home and she's waiting for me to leave. And where do you fit in her house, Dad? She told Daisy about the baby before she told you! Where's your favorite chair Mom bought you? In the old barn, right?"

"And so to get even for all of this, you took that twelve-year-old out and bought her an expensive pair of glasses and a haircut on *my* credit card, so that she is almost unrecognizable. I'm surprised you didn't get her a nose ring or a tongue stud."

"You didn't look very closely at her, did you, Dad?"

"You didn't!"

I shouted, "Of course I didn't! Who do you think I am? Jean's version of a head case who would put a ring in a twelve-year-old's nose?"

A small voice came from the kitchen door. "You and Cass didn't plan this, did you, Jonathan? I thought it was your idea to give me a makeover."

I would have laughed at Daisy calling it a makeover, but her look of sad awareness wasn't the least bit funny.

31

BEATRICE

Just before I left for choir practice, I opened my journal to make a short entry and found scribbled words on the last page that were not mine. My spirit girl wrote them! Her name is Cass. She told me to think hard about marrying Robert Dalhousie. And to be strong. Just as nôhkom's spirit told her to be strong. Then she printed in bold letters WHAT ABOUT DUNCAN? What on this earth did she mean by that?

I closed the diary and stared out the window. How could she write in my diary without nôhkom seeing her? I knew everyone in our village. Cass didn't live in St. Cuthbert's. She was a figment of my imagination. Why would she tell me to wait? Did I, in fact, at some point put the wide-looped handwriting on the page myself – under some mad delusion I was a girl called Cass? I hid the diary immediately.

Little did I realize that I would see her again so soon.

As I pulled on my second-best wool dress to wear to church, frost glistened in the corners of the bedchamber. I added more wood to Grandmother's small hearth and left her dozing in its warmth.

It was bitterly cold outside, and the hard snow crunched under Tupper's hooves. The harness bells clacked with cold. He wore a heavy blanket, and another one lay in the carriole to cover him when we arrived. The church bell bonged deeply over the farms, calling the choir to practice. Despite the cold, my hands were damp in their fur-lined pouches. I was uncertain how to greet Robert. Would Duncan Kilgour make things worse by saying something tactless or spiteful? I decided I would act as if nothing was agreed between Robert and me. And I would ignore Kilgour.

Earlier at dinner, Papa, Ivy, and I had eaten my fish-and-potato dish with little appetite. Ivy sat rigid at the table, throwing pleading looks at Papa, who spoke to the girls and me, but not to her. The girls had great helpings. I was pleased to see Dilly blooming under her friendship with the Three Graces.

Note to myself: You must tutor both Dilly and Minty after Christmas, right up until you leave, and then ask Miss Cameron to take Dilly into the school a few days a week.

If Robert followed through with his plans, we could be gone by spring. That thought set up a heavy banging in my chest, and I could not eat another mouthful.

I knew Duncan Kilgour was angry with his mother over the upset, but as he didn't care two pins for me or my feelings, why would he miss his fish dinner this evening? I recalled the contraction in his eyes when I told him about my impending engagement. Did he think I was doing the wrong thing, leaving nôhkom and Papa? Did he dislike Robert that much?

Then it came to me. Of course! Henrietta would be leaving with Robert and me! Duncan had probably run off to do his own proposing before she could get away. But she had to be five years older than him at least!

A shadow drew one wing across my vision, but I swept it away. What did it matter what Duncan Kilgour said or did? He didn't see me as anything but a silly young woman, easy to make fun of.

The Three Graces were already at the church, having traveled with Minty in the sledge to visit with their schoolmates before practice began. As I hitched Tupper to a post in the church's open stable, the moon's light sheared off the rolling sheets of snow, throwing itself back into the air with a luminous glow.

When I opened the church door, a breath of tepid warmth fluttered over me. The sexton can never be convinced to use enough wood to make the small church truly comfortable. I could hear voices in the nave.

The door swung open behind me, and Robert Dalhousie entered, his fur hat low on his forehead. "Good evening, Miss Alexander."

He could have been addressing one of the choir members. I nodded back, suddenly irritated. Someone pushed through the door behind him. Duncan Kilgour beamed at me. Had he proposed to Henrietta? Had she said yes? I gave him a cold glare.

"Aah, Kilgour," Robert said. "Glad you could join us. Bitter cold night."

"I've heard the weather on the western seaboard is always milder than here," Kilgour said with a devilish smirk, banging his buffalo mitts together. "Positively balmy for a young married couple!"

Robert looked shocked. I'm sure I looked horrified. How dare he reveal what I told him about Robert's proposal?

"I saw your lovely sister this afternoon, while you were out, Reverend. She told me your plans." He tapped the side of his nose. "Mum's the word, eh?"

So he did go to her! He was acting just like a caricature of a jolly good fellow from Punch *magazine, and I wanted to punch him.*

He bustled us toward the choir stalls, talking all the while about the weather — how many families were suffering with coughs and chilblains and how many were losing animals to the cold and lack of decent fodder. "Minty and I will make our rounds tomorrow with a sledge of hay. The Goddsons are still enduring Angus's back problems, so we'll make sure we do some work there. And Will McKay's wife is frail after the last birth. Another sickly child. Minty goes by and milks their two old cows for them, but both beasts are drying up." He shook his head.

Duncan Kilgour is a good man, *my inner voice said.* You must admit that, Beatrice. *But an impossible one! I snapped back.*

I held up a deerskin bag and said to him, "Here are the cakes I promised you, Mr. Kilgour. Perhaps you and Minty could give them to the families you talked about."

Robert, smiling his minister's smile, said, "Most Christian of you, Miss Alexander."

Duncan looked at him with amusement. Oh, why couldn't Robert, just once, be less of a dry stick! I turned away and got busy assembling the singers. My girls went through their songs quickly. The members of the church choir murmured appreciatively when they were done, and the girls, sitting in the front pews, puffed up with pride.

The church choir did quite well, except for the usual problems – the sexton's wife's booming tone that lagged one breath behind everyone else and Miss Stiles's overwrought nasal warbling. Small bursts of laughter broke out behind me, but my quick glare silenced them. I couldn't help being grateful for Duncan's rich deep voice, which added depth to the sparse bass section. More than once, he winked at me, which both irritated me and made me hide a smile.

Robert sat by the pianist, head on one side, lips pursed. When everyone made ready to leave, he took me aside. "I will speak to your father soon. But I don't feel quite prepared yet as I have Christmas Eve service tomorrow."

"Yes, of course, Robert," I said. "Perhaps Christmas Day?" For some reason, it seemed vitally important to have the announcement over with.

He looked startled. "No, no, that would be most inappropriate. It is a sacred day, after all. The church will be terribly busy. I don't know how I would. . . ."

Duncan was talking loudly to someone behind us. I flushed, hoping he didn't hear Robert's fussing, and then something – like a sudden warning from my spirit girl – made me say, curtly, "Of course. I didn't mean here at the church, Mr. Dalhousie. I meant at dinner, at my father's house later. But you are quite right. It might be better to wait until after Christmas to approach Papa."

I thought he might try to reassure me, but he looked relieved. "I agree, my dear. Best do it with dignity and restraint."

"Of course, Robert. It's not as if we're eager lovers planning to elope, is it?"

"Yes . . . quite. We'll have the rest of our lives to –"

"Repent at leisure?" Duncan, who had slid in beside me, laughed good-naturedly.

Robert looked like he'd been slapped by a challenger's glove. "I don't find that even vaguely amusing, Kilgour. I take deep offense at the insult to Miss Alexander."

People were staring, conversations dying.

I held up one hand. "Don't dignify his thoughtless comment by arguing it! I must go. I'll see you tomorrow at service, Reverend," I said loudly. "Good night."

He nodded, his face rigid. Mrs. Wright, who ran the Ladies Auxiliary, hurried up with a look of intense interest to discuss something about the morning service. I took the opportunity to escape.

As I strode down the aisle, my spirit girl, Cass, moved toward me, her hair an aureole of light. I stopped in my tracks, and her face lit up. She said, in a hollow whisper, "Did you read it? What I wrote to you?"

"Yes, yes!" I whispered back. "But why, Cass?"

Her smile fell, concern creasing her forehead.

"Beatrice. Don't do it! You know you don't –" The shadow of another figure appeared behind her, and they both vanished.

I covered my mouth. Don't do it? Do what? Marry Robert? Why? The room slowly lurched around me. Dear heaven, don't let me faint again. I was becoming like one of those overwrought feeble women in shoddily written Gothic stories that fill so many quarterlies. A firm grip cupped my elbow. Duncan Kilgour half-lifted me toward the church exit.

"What are you doing, you silly girl? About to marry a young man who is already a dried-up old stick?"

He had read my very thoughts! Blood rushed into my head, and the dizziness passed. I put on my fur bonnet, tying it tightly as I pushed my way through the small crowd in the foyer. I ran to my carriole, yanking off Tupper's extra blanket. Our sledge, with Minty driving, was already turning onto the river road, the girls singing and laughing. A dogsled skimmed past me with a hiss of snow, the owner calling good night. I waved as if I didn't have a care in the world. Gossip would be all over the parish tomorrow – that Reverend Dalhousie, Mr. Kilgour, and I were having a dis-agreement. Would Robert change his mind about marrying me when he heard it?

"Beatrice!" Duncan called, running up behind me.

"Go away!" I could hear the tears in my throat. I climbed into the carriole, and Tupper moved forward.

"I'll only follow you home, Beatrice, if you don't give me an answer to my question!" he said over his horse's back.

"All right, here is my answer!" I cried, pulling the reins taut. "Because I have to get away from this staid, dull place before I go mad. Because it will be an adventure – something I long for. I don't wish to leave my father or my grandmother, but I must and I will. Your dreadful mother and you just make it that much easier to go!"

"Me? Why me?" he asked, bristling like a black bear, his huge fur hat adding to the likeness. "What the devil do you mean by that?"

"I mean you are the one person I will be glad to see the back of!" I shouted. I snapped the reins, and Tupper, anxious for his evening feed, took off at a brisk trot.

32

CASS

Dad called Daisy back into the room and said, "I told Cass to buy you a Christmas present that you'd like. And she decided this was it. She didn't check with me, however."

Daisy narrowed her eyes suspiciously.

He continued, "I didn't know what was planned *exactly*. But you certainly look . . . spectacular!"

She brightened.

"However," he added sternly, "we were just having a discussion about the fact that she didn't ask your mother's permission."

"Guess we better go tell Mom then, huh?"

He looked toward me. "Right."

"I'll come with you," I said. "I won't let you do it when it's my fault, Daisy."

She suddenly looked grown up. "Jonathan and me will calm Mom down first. Then you come in." She giggled. "Mom'll have a bird!"

"Or a baby," I muttered.

"Yeah," she said, glaring at Dad.

"You'll have a kid sister or brother to boss around. It might be fun," I added quickly.

She looked surprised. "Let's go, Jonathan. You come in half an hour, Cass."

From the doorway, Blair said, "Everything sorted?" She was looking at Dad.

I could feel the invisible wall drop between them.

Dad said stiffly, "As much as it can be. Did you know about this?"

She looked him straight in the eye. "What do you think? That I encouraged it? Maybe even suggested it?"

He flushed. "Of course not. I apologize."

"We need to talk soon, okay, Jon? No blame. Just talk. For their sake."

"You're right. Thanks for looking after them today."

"I'm staying at Aunt Blair's for a while, Dad," I said, just so he was clear.

"Okay. But only for a few days."

I shrugged.

"One thing at a time. We'll talk about it later," he said and left with Daisy.

It was almost dark when Martin and I drove slowly down River Road. Snow was falling heavily, filling in Dad's tire tracks. As we rumbled along, I saw the stone and wood bell tower of St. Cuthbert's Church, its low body crouching behind. This was where Beatrice had directed her choir practices – in the church her dad built. The snow on the trees sparkled like an old-fashioned Christmas card. As we were about to pass by, I could hear a bell ringing. A dark figure, clad in a long dress and bonnet, walked quickly toward the church. Lights inside blinked on and off.

"Turn here," I said. "I want to look in the church."

"Why?"

"Just do it, okay?"

Martin pulled up in front. "You can be sure the place is locked up tight, until the Christmas Eve service tomorrow."

I climbed out of the truck. "You never know. Stay here."

As I scuffed through powdered white, I saw the indent of two sets of footprints below a half-inch of snow. One led to a snowblower that stood by the steps, ready for clearing in the morning. The other went up the stairs. The person I saw walking toward the church would have left fresh prints. There were none.

I pulled hard, and one of the heavy doors screeched open. Warm air washed over me. I walked into the silent nave, my footsteps echoing. Everything smelled of mildew, candles, old books, and . . . pine? A dim light came on near the pulpit. A huge decorated tree stood in one corner, its lights blinking on and off. Then the tree lights went off and stayed off.

"Hello?" I called.

"We're closed until tomorrow, I'm afraid," a voice called back. A man with thinning hair, wearing jeans and a leather jacket, moved from behind the tree, holding an extension cord.

"My name is Cass Cullen. Are you the caretaker?"

"Vicar. William Chancel – no church puns required, thanks all the same!" He spoke with an English accent.

I laughed. "What *is* the part called the chancel, anyway?"

"It's where the choir sits. Excuse me, I'll be right with you." He disappeared again behind the tree.

"Hey! That's what I wanted to talk to someone about – the choir." Something caught my eye. I glanced to one side. *Beatrice!* Her hair was pulled up in a braided knot, a few wisps floating free. Her face looked thinner. So it *was* her walking toward the church a few minutes ago. Suddenly, I heard distant, muffled voices all around me.

I said to her, "Did you read it? Did you see it? What I wrote to you?"

"Yes, yes!" Her words were a far-off echo. "But why, Cass, why?" She knew my name!

"Beatrice. Don't do it! You know you don't love him!"

She looked so shocked, I stopped. *Who was I talking to?* She couldn't actually be there.

"Hey! Are you okay? Miss?" Reverend Chancel asked loudly.

I looked away, just as the tree lights came on. When I looked back, she was gone.

"Do you live around here?" the vicar asked. "Are you lost?"

"No. I live at Old Maples."

"Aah. Jean Dennett's new family. She's one of my regulars. Plays the organ."

I knew she went to church, but hadn't paid much attention to it. "I was wondering if –"

He put a hand firmly on my arm. "Before you begin, I have to ask a question. Did you see someone or something in the church just now? A person or persons?"

"Why? Did you see someone?"

"I wondered if you were talking to one of our resident ghosts?" The tree lights went out again. "Dang and blast!" He fiddled with the light cord. "I'm here tonight because the lights keep going out on the tree, and no one knows why. Our caretaker has given up. These lights could mess up our services tomorrow night and Christmas Day. We've had electricians out three times. They all say they're fine. Anyway, the last few days, when I was alone fiddling with them, I . . . well . . . I was sure I saw people who weren't really here. I tried to make contact with them, but no go. I saw – most clearly – a slim young woman in a long dress and shawl . . . and now and again, a few others flitting around. One was a rather faded man with a cleric's collar and surplice, like I wear on Sundays. Once I even heard a choir singing, but only in snatches of sound." He looked at me. "Oops. I sound a bit mad, don't I?"

So . . . he was seeing Robert and Beatrice! "Do you believe in ghosts?"

"I can't do otherwise in this place! At first I thought I was going bonkers. But I'm an Englishman, and if we didn't believe in spirits – ghosts – we would all be bats, as we seem to be teeming with them on our little island."

I smiled. "With ghosts? Or bats?"

He grinned back. "Both. I called the last minister, Reverend MacDonald, in Toronto – he's over ninety and still going strong – and he told me quite matter-of-factly that these spirits always appear at Christmas. He calls them Miss Alexander's Choir."

I stared at him. "Why does he call them that?"

"I have no idea. But apparently he's heard them singing many times."

I heard footsteps and expected to see Beatrice right behind me. It was Martin.

"Goodness, it's a drop-in center tonight," said the vicar. "I'm Reverend Chancel. It's Martin, right? You helped Betty Pelly set up the manger scene a few days ago."

"Yes. She and my grandma come here."

Reverend Chancel nodded. "Not your parents, though."

Martin shrugged. "No. I usually come at Christmas with my aunt and Gran."

"I was just about to tell Cass that the previous minister, here for almost seventy years, knows a lot about this area. Miss Alexander was English Métis. It's a fact that mostly English Métis, or Anglo-Métis as some call them, Scottish Métis really, lived here at one time. It was a unique community in the province's history for that reason. Most were retired Comany men. We know a Miss Alexander taught for a year at Miss Cameron's school. That's in the old school records."

"Really? And just for a year? What happened to her?" I asked. "Did she marry the young minister, Mr. Dalhousie?"

"I haven't been here long enough to know much about them. Most of the records for the period you talk about were lost in a fire. A real tragedy, that was. I'm not sure who served here after Bishop Gaskell of St. Cuthbert's and surrounding parishes left. Old Reverend MacDonald is writing down the stories he was told over the years."

"Could you ask him what else he knows about Beatrice Alexander? She was eighteen around 1856."

"I will. I'm sure she'll be in his notes. I suspect Reverend MacDonald has kept a lot to himself after he and the old church historian – dead now – had a flare-up or two! Even so, most of it is all hearsay as there is little documented proof. We have very few things from Miss Alexander's time."

Martin said, "Could we look at those notes sometime anyway?"

"Of course. But not until after Christmas. I've a lot going on. It's too bad we don't have more material. I'd love to know all about her."

"You mean letters or a personal diary, right?" I asked.

"Wouldn't that be amazing? But if one existed, it would have surfaced by now. I hear your step-mom, Jean, is gutting Old Maples inch by inch. Maybe she'll find a letter or two behind the skirting boards."

I tried to laugh. "Yeah. If only." We thanked him and left.

So, he had seen Beatrice too. And didn't seem bothered by it at all. He hadn't actually talked to her, though, or given her unsolicited advice like I just did! *Was I wrong telling Beatrice not to marry Robert Dalhousie?* I had no right to meddle in her life, even if it was over a hundred and fifty years ago. Duncan Kilgour didn't think Dalhousie was right for her either. Maybe he thought he was the better choice. I did! *He couldn't actually be interested in pale sickly Henrietta, could he? What did he really think of Beatrice?*

It was only later, when we pulled up in front of Old Maples, that I remembered I was about to face Jean's wrath. As we walked toward the door, Martin hummed the death march behind me.

33

BEATRICE

I was too busy the next morning to think about Cass's scribbled message, about seeing her in the church, or even about Robert Dalhousie or Duncan Kilgour.

Ivy was subdued in the kitchen as she prepared Papa's breakfast, but each malicious look she sent in my direction hit its mark. After Papa went to his study, she sat, hands in her lap, and did not move.

I sent the girls off to lay the cloths on the dining-room table and trestle tables set up for the youngest diners, so the fabrics would drop their creases. I also gave them a list of the guests; asked them to count knives, forks, and spoons; to put glasses on the table and cups on the sideboard; and showed them how to clean Mama's wedding silver. Two days ago, I'd made a centerpiece of pine boughs and curled pieces of birch bark in Mama's only silver bowl.

There was stuffing to make from dried chunks of bannock, corn bread, onions, and wild sage; there were carrots, turnips, and potatoes to scrub. I hated turnips, but could make them tolerable with cream and lump sugar. There was *also a sweet sauce to make for the pudding and a huge pan of sauce from dried high-bush cranberries.*

I prayed Duncan Kilgour would not show up today. Just thinking about him made me prickly and irritable. But what if he didn't deliver the goose for Christmas dinner tomorrow? That would be worse. A venison joint, cut in thick slices, sat on the counter ready to be larded. But it would not be enough on its own, and Papa needed all the money he would get from selling the few remaining large roasts. I could use two of the inevitably tough chickens in the icehouse, but they were only good for stewing. I almost growled with frustration.

That stupid overgrown boy, deliberately baiting Robert, and then harrying me all the way to my carriole. Now there is no goose to roast or fish to poach, and there are nineteen people to serve tomorrow. And to muddle things further, Papa has invited neighbors for a ceilidh afterward. What will Robert think of one of his church elders having a party of music and dance? If he opposes it, he is more like the bishop than I care to think about. Perhaps Robert will realize how a few social evenings can lighten a long winter. I can only hope.

I decided on a thick dried-pea soup for dinner, with a round of raisin bannock. Pushing damp hair away from my forehead, I was feeling harassed and anxious, but refused to acknowledge the smug smile on Ivy's face.

The door banged open and Duncan surged in, holding a huge plucked goose by its feet in one hand and another large whitefish in the other. If I wasn't still so furious, I might have hugged him. He was like a snowy messenger from heaven. His mother threw him a look of disgust and left the room.

"Merry Christmas to you, too, Mother!" he called as the door snapped shut.

I was trying to peel a waxed turnip, but it kept slipping out of my damp hands. Having him near reminded me of the argument last night.

"Here," he said, putting down the meat, "let me do that before you chop off a finger. Where are your girls?"

"Oh, just go away, you sihkosis!"

He bridled. "I speak a little Cree, you know. And I am not a weasel. I came bearing gifts. How can you still be mad at me? I should be the one who is hurt, not you."

"Don't be ridiculous. I am angry with you because you are a cîkahikanis! Hacking and breaking everything to pieces. You badger and push and –"

"Oh, I am a mistanask as well, am I? An animal of different coats with a hatchet in hand!"

I threw the turnip at him. He caught it and stood looking at me, bouncing it gently from hand to hand. I would not cry in front of him.

"Beatrice. I know I have no right to offer unwanted advice. But there are other ways to freedom than marriage to a dull man – someone you hardly know, to whom you have barely spoken." He shook his head. "Forgive my frankness."

Though he looked in earnest, I said, "But still you get your knife in, don't you? You understand very little about Robert. You don't know him as I do." But did I know him? No. I didn't. Yet, I could not retract my words.

"You're right, of course. Forgive me. I do not want us to fall out."

"When have we ever fallen in, Mr. Kilgour? I will forgive you if you promise never to interfere in my plans again."

We stood eye to eye, the silence between us charged with something that told me I could change everything in that one moment. But, just then, the girls bundled into the room with armloads of linen cloths and napkins.

"We can't work out which ones go on the tables," said Dilly. I explained again and off they went to try once more.

Duncan said, "The girls have become good friends. Come, Beatrice. Let's be friends, too. I'll be your kitchen slave for the day as penance for being such an overbearing okimâw. You be the boss and let me be the helper." With hands pressed around the turnip, he looked like a little boy caught stealing someone else's ball and asking to keep it.

I couldn't help but laugh. "You're just showing off now. You're making me an okîskwêw, Duncan Kilgour. Soon I will be completely crazy! Here is a knife. Cut the turnip in small pieces, so it will cook quickly in the morning."

As he chopped, he asked, "As long as we're using Cree words, where is kôhkom?"

"Upstairs. I asked her to come down, but she claims she'll only get in the way."

He left the room and returned carrying Grandmother, who was tittering like a little girl, one hand to her lips. He set her down and ordered her to drink tea and supervise.

"But I know little about the English Christmas my grand-daughter's mother used to make," she said, her eyes twinkling.

"Don't believe her," I said. "Nôhkom was married for thirty years to a Scottish gentleman of high regard. She has cooked many splendid meals taught to her by my mother's sister, Aunt Louisa, who visited us from Devon. Nôhkom is also a ruthless card player, thanks to Aunt Louisa."

Duncan laughed. "I must teach you a game called piquet, Aggathas."

"That would be good," Grandmother said, with an impish smile that meant she already knew the game, but would tease him by pretending not to.

A sudden pain pierced my heart, and I turned away from her merry little face. How could I tell her I would be leaving her soon, probably forever?

As they talked and teased each other, I concentrated on making everything perfect for the last Christmas dinner I would have in this house. Once, when I sighed with weariness, Duncan put his hand on my arm. But I moved away – I could not bear tenderness from him. If only . . .

By dinnertime, the tables were set, the food organized, and everyone but me had eaten their fill of pea soup. We set off for the church in the sledge. Ivy was bundled up against the cold, her rabbity nose twitching between the folds of her fur scarf. She sat beside Papa, her head down. He may have forgiven her, but he was still angry. I wondered if he'd caught the looks she'd cast my way during the day.

The church was chilly as we assembled the choir in the small vestry and awaited the vicar's presence. I greeted Miss Cameron. "All is ready for tomorrow's dinner, and Papa is looking forward to seeing you there."

She smiled. "I'm happy to be coming, Beatrice. I have made plenty of creamed squash and ginger cakes."

Robert Dalhousie welcomed the girls and the church choir. Although he smiled at me warmly, I responded with coolness. He frowned, and I felt a twinge of satisfaction.

When we filed through the nave, the little church was full. It smelled of wet fur, leather, and the lingering odor of barn animals that had been fed or milked before church. The dark narrow faces and smooth round visages of Ojibway and Cree were mixed with those with freckles and red-tinged hair from their Celtic ancestors.

Our congregation always sits quietly. Robert is not an inspiring speaker, but at least he doesn't bounce on his heels and shout like Bishop Gaskell did. Both choirs did me proud, and, on the way home, I hummed my favorite Christmas song under my breath. Soon the others sang the words, and even Duncan joined in on the seventh verse with great gusto:

This time of the year is spent in good cheer,
And neighbors together do meet
To sit by the fire, with friendly desire,
Each other in love to greet;
Old grudges forgot are put in the pot,
All sorrows aside they lay;
The old and the young doth carol this song
To drive the cold winter away.

Duncan said, "This is a bit of good advice, don't you agree, Mother? We have been fortunate to find each other again, and now you are married to a better man than ever could be found on earth! So let's put old grudges in the pot and lay aside all sorrows for one day!"

What old grudges? Was he referring to me and Ivy? Or himself and Ivy?

Ivy nodded, then turned toward my father. He put one arm around her waist and began to sing "O Holy Night." She leaned her head against his shoulder. The rest of us joined Papa, as Tupper and our ancient horse, Baxter, pulled us homeward through the cold winter night. For the first time in a long while, the shadows floated away, into the starry sky.

CASS

Martin tried to leave me at the door, but I dragged him inside. The kitchen was empty, but we heard voices down the hall. I decided bold was best, so I left him there with instructions, in case I needed a quick getaway, and walked straight to the living room. The blue lights on the powdery white tree winked smugly at me. *Did I really expect that monstrosity to be gone as a kind of peace offering?* Daisy waved. She looked so different with that cap of dark hair and the slim new glasses. I knew then my decision wasn't just about getting even with Jean.

Dad opened his mouth, but Jean touched his arm and said, "Sit down, Cassandra."

I was standing close to a chair. I sat on the arm, ready to take off. Jean cleared her throat. "When I saw Daisy, I was shocked, as you can imagine. I assumed it was done deliberately to hurt me. But Daisy assures me it was a gift from you and Jonathan and that this *gift* had been decided beforehand."

Dad and Daisy looked as if they had never told a fib in their lives. . . .

"So," she continued, "I feel it's better to light a candle than to curse the darkness. Therefore, I am going to –"

"Am I the darkness?" I interrupted, my voice tight.

"Cass . . . ," Dad warned.

"No. I want to know. Do you see me as the darkness?"

"Cass!"

"No, no, Jonathan, I think that's a fair question," Jean said. "Of course, you aren't the darkness, Cassan . . ." she glanced at Dad ". . . Cass. I meant that in this instance, I prefer to take the high road after last night's fiasco. I would like to have been consulted about this . . . uh . . . *gift* to Daisy, but after hearing her explanation, I don't believe much harm has been done." She gave Daisy a small smile. "But you must realize, Cass, that Daisy is my daughter, and I need to know beforehand when things like this are done."

I shrugged, examining the hole in the toe of my brown sock.

Her voice grew hard. "You know, that shrug tells me you aren't really taking in what I am saying. And to get back to last night, it was embarrassing, to say the least. I had something exciting to tell everyone and you –"

I buttoned my jacket. I'd heard enough.

"Jean," Dad said, "you're okay with Daisy's early Christmas present, so let's leave it at that. We should have told Cass in private about the baby. She was shocked by the news. As was I. She knows that her mom and I tried for a second child, but . . ."

I lost it then. "Mom's name was Fiona! Why do you never say it in front of *her*? There isn't even *one* picture of Mom up in this house. Why is that, Dad?"

"Because things have changed, Cass. Accept it, honey."

I shouted, "Accept what? That our life before Jean means nothing? Accept that because Mom doesn't exist anymore in your life, I can't have her in mine? Accept that you can't even say her name for fear of hurting Jean? That everything Mom loved – our photo albums, her books, our Christmas stuff – are packed away somewhere in the barn? I had to put most of her antiques in Aunt Blair's basement just to keep them from being thrown out!"

"Cass. Stop!"

I pointed at Jean. "You've let her throw Mom away! Don't you get it, Dad? And soon she'll have your baby to coo over, and Mom will be pushed even farther back! Look at that fake tree. It's hideous. Everything in this house is Jean – there's no US here anymore, Dad!" My nose were running. I used my jacket sleeve to wipe it.

Daisy ran at the tree and, with a swing of her arm, knocked it sideways. It bounced right back, while plastic blue and silver bobbles bounced across the floor. The lights kept on blinking.

"I hate this stupid tree, Mom! I told you to wait for Cass! I told you she was nicer to me. Like a real sister. And, today, she did this great thing for me, and you just made it all stink again!" She grabbed one end of a branch and shook it hard. She looked like a mad little squirrel trying to destroy a robot tree. It was so comical, I laughed.

"Daisy! Stop it! What are you *doing*?" Jean cried. She pointed at me. "You think this is funny? I've tried to be nice to you, Cassandra. I've bent over backwards to be nice . . . but all I get back is sarcasm and nasty asides. Look at the havoc you're causing right now! I've had it up to here with you! You're like this brick wall I keep banging my head against!"

Dad said, "Jean! Please! This is getting way out of –"

"Well, the head can take a break! The wall is leaving!" I shouted. "I'm going to live with Blair." I ran out.

Daisy followed, hot on my heels. Martin must've heard because the truck was warmed up and ready to go.

"Daisy, go back in the house," I said as she ran after me, struggling into Dad's ski jacket. Snow sparkled around her, landing like crystals on her dark hair.

"No! I want to go with you. I can't stand Mom anymore. I won't go back!"

Dad opened the front door. "Daisy! Your mother says to get in here now!"

"I'm going with Cass!" She snuck under my arm, climbed into the truck, and fell into the backseat.

"Just go, Martin," I said, as Dad slid down the front walk in his slippers.

"No. I won't," Martin replied firmly.

I glared at him, locked my door, and put on my seat belt.

Dad's face hovered outside my window. I rolled it

down a few inches. Great puffs of vapor hung in the air as he spoke. "Come back. We'll calm down and sort this out." He was shivering.

"I've told Daisy to go back in, but I'm not coming. Not tonight, Dad. I can't." I was surprised to hear how calm I sounded.

"And I'm not going back in either!" Daisy said, her arms wrapped tightly around Dad's huge jacket.

"I think you should, Daisy. This'll only make your mom more angry at me," I said.

"I don't want her to be mad at you at all!"

"So go inside. Please?"

"Yes, Daisy, come inside. You've had enough, sweetie," Dad said. "You can go to your room, watch TV, and I'll bring you up something to eat. We'll talk."

She pushed out her lips to think. "Okay . . . but I'm not talking to Mom!"

"Not if you don't want to. But you might want to," Dad said.

"I won't!"

"Fine. Look, Cass, I don't like you running away like this all the time. Blair does not have the right to fill your head with stuff. You can't live with her. She isn't your . . ." He stopped.

"My mother? No, but she's Mom's twin sister. And she hasn't filled my head with anything. It's just too . . . toxic in your house, Dad. I can't think."

Martin spoke up. "Maybe let things cool for a day or so. If that's okay, Mr. Cullen."

Dad sighed. "Okay. One more night at Blair's. Then we work this out, Cass. You're not going to live away from me. I need you with me. We're a family."

He looked so upset, I almost gave in. But I said, "Whether I like it or not?"

"I want you to really think about what you just said to Jean and to me and consider carefully what you are going to say next. I don't want her upset this badly again, Cass, with the baby and all."

I looked him straight in the eye. "I *will* think about it. But, Dad, if Jean isn't willing to let Mom come back into that house somehow, nothing is going to work between us. Or between me and you. You and Jean also have to talk."

He swallowed hard. "You're right. I've been hoping . . . yeah . . . okay. I'll see you around lunchtime tomorrow. Come on, Daisy."

As she crawled out from the seat behind me, she whispered, "He called me sweetie!"

I watched them walk to the house, Dad's arm around her shoulders. "Well, there's one thing more or less fixed. Daisy and Dad are in sync."

"Thanks to you," Martin said, putting the truck in gear.

"Yeah, but everything else is like Humpty Dumpty, isn't it? Can't put it together again."

I looked back at the house. A small figure in a long dress and dark coat strode up the walkway, followed by other fluttery figures. I knew who it was. Like me, Beatrice was busy messing up her life. It hurt to think she wasn't somewhere on this frozen earth right now. I wanted to talk to her – *really* talk to her. I hated leaving that house.

The moon was high. Snowflakes sprinkled down, shining and flashing like tiny stars. The church lights were off, and Reverend Chancel's car was gone. The long driveways of the new houses along the road were covered in freshly pressed tire tracks, the houses glowing with colored lights and winking wreaths.

"Every year, a week before Christmas, Mom, Dad, and I would go out after supper to see the city lights in Selkirk," I said to Martin. "We'd drive slowly up and down the streets. Most houses were pretty sedate. We liked the crazy ones. Ours was always covered with Santa and Rudolph heads and big snowmen with lights inside. And Mom always put these crumbling red cellophane wreaths in every window, with an orange light in each one. . . ."

"Everything has changed for you," Martin said. "It's been really hard, I can see that."

"But?"

"No buts, Cass. I have both parents. Nothing has changed for me. My dad is nuts about my mom. He always says a man should love his wife a little more than she loves him. I think it's pretty equal in their case, but he's the kind of guy who brings her tea in bed every morning, you know? They argue, don't get me wrong, but I've had a great place to grow up in."

"They don't work in the restaurant? I haven't met them yet."

"No. They've been on holiday in Mexico. They go every year and leave the early Christmas rush to us. They'll be back bullying everyone in a few days." He grinned.

"So you're an only child like me?"

"No, I have two brothers. Only a year apart. Both are at university in Winnipeg. They live in residence. They'll be home a few days before Christmas."

"I'm sorry, Martin."

"For what?"

"I've been so focused on me, I've hardly got to know anything about you. I'm so selfish. I feel as if I'm ruining everything between us. I'll understand if you just, you know, want to dump me after this."

He pulled the truck over. The river was wide and white and shadowy blue, with dark cobalt stripes down its length from snowmobiles and skis. I leaned my forehead against the cold window. It was all so peaceful out there. *Why wasn't I?*

He tapped my shoulder. "Hey." I looked at him. "I saw what you did for Daisy. I know it was partly to get back at Jean, but it was mostly for Daisy. You were great with her today. That's building one bridge, anyway."

He leaned over and kissed me. I undid my seat belt and slid closer. We sat, heads together, looking at the Red River.

"So I'm not dumped?"

I heard his soft laugh above my head. "No. I'm like my dad. He says when he met my mom, he knew a good thing when he saw it. I see a good thing here, under all that sadness and anger."

"Aunt Blair will be wondering what happened," I said about ten minutes later.

Martin put the truck in gear. As I snapped my seat belt in place, I said, "I will take the bull by the horns tomorrow. Things can't keep going like this."

"Good idea. Tomorrow is the first day of the rest of your life."

"That which does not kill me will make me stronger," I cried.

"Yes! Take the bull by the horns," he shouted.

"Take my life in my own hands!" I yelled.

"Come hell or high water!"

"Come hell or high water, I'll crack the code of Jean Dennett!"

"You'll crack the nut!"

"I'll crack the whip!"

We were both screeching with laughter by then.

"Hey! We're cracking up!" I cried.

We sang a wildy varied "Jingle Bells" all the way back to Aunt Blair's.

35

BEATRICE

Christmas morning, I awoke weighed down by a gloom that was almost as bad as being engulfed by the shadows. Last night's momentary pleasure on the ride home was gone. Knowing this gray heaviness was due to my leaving home soon didn't ease the ache. I tried to imagine Penelope in her settlement home, opening the small portrait I'd painted of her, and Miss Cameron admiring her handkerchief, its border of fine cotton crochet, her initials satin-stitched in silk thread. But thinking of them only made me feel more dismal, for I'd be leaving them too, along with everyone and everything I had known my entire life.

Even if I stayed, I could never confide in either woman, for I am not really one of them, am I? How will I fit in with Robert's life in his new parish? Did he choose me because I am of mixed blood? Does he plan to use me as an interpreter or as an example of some kind? Is he unaware that Indians speak many different languages across this land? Can love grow in such arid soil?

I forced myself to get up and act as if nothing were wrong.

I settled nôhkom by the fire, trying hard to be bright and cheerful, but I was near tears the entire time. I gave each girl, including Dilly, a tiny deerskin bag in which to keep small treasures. Three of them, of course, were hastily prepared during the past few days, Grandmother doing most of the work. My contribution was beading their centers with flowers. In each one, I had put a penny. The girls were excited to receive them.

They gave Grandmother a bag of mint humbugs, which had been sent to Caitrin, one of the Three Graces, by her parents. Nôhkom was deeply touched and thanked them all equally, before sharing the treat. Flushed with excitement, they gave me a beaded and feather-tagged bookmark, with TEACHER carefully sewn in red. I thanked them with as much enthusiasm as I could muster.

Nôhkom opened the parcel I gave her, and she and all the girls exclaimed over the soft blue shawl I had secretly crocheted at school. Then the girls and I left her to stoke the ovens and the Carron stoves in the house. I would heat the stoves all day so the pipes winding throughout each room would keep our guests warm.

I set Ivy's and Papa's gifts beside their breakfast plates – a lace handkerchief for her, with the initials I.A., and a cherry wood pipe for Papa I bought while in Upper Canada. When they came down, Ivy was actually smiling! She handed Papa a thin parcel, and he put a small square box on the table for her. I served them venison sausage and bread.

"Happy Christmas, dearest girl," Papa said.

"Happy Christmas, Beatrice," Ivy said primly, eyeing her parcels with interest.

Papa pressed a paper-wrapped present into my hand. "From Ivy and me."

I took it and walked down the hall to the parlor. The doors between the two rooms were open, the tables set. In the glow of the fire, I saw my reflection in the dark window. A sad countenance stared back at me.

As I write, I ask myself: Will it be a brighter Christmas next year, when Robert and I celebrate our first Yule together in a faraway place? I try to imagine him preparing his sermon while I cook our breakfast. Of course, as his wife, I will be expected to attend church every Sunday. Why does this make me feel so sick at heart?

Earlier, when I'd sat down by the fire to open my present, I wished with all my heart that Mama was there to share the moment with me. Inside the paper wrapping was a book of sonnets by Elizabeth Barrett Browning. Last winter, my aunt had written to us about this book with great excitement. Papa must have ordered it months ago. I opened a page at random and the first words I saw were

How do I love thee? Let me count the ways.
I love thee to the depth and breadth and height
My soul can reach, when feeling out of sight
For the ends of Being and ideal Grace.

I closed the book quickly. Had the poet really felt this way about her husband? Would I ever have feelings like this for Robert Dalhousie? No. This kind of passion would never consume me. But if I didn't marry Robert, where would I *go? I couldn't stay here with Ivy. It would destroy any chance of peace or happiness. I heard Duncan Kilgour's voice say once again:* But there are other ways to freedom than marriage to a dull man – someone you hardly know.

He was right. I didn't know Robert. How could I live with a man who was a virtual stranger? A humorless, earnest man of God? And one with a sickly sister, whom I was being asked to look after! Is that what Robert really wanted from this marriage – a companion for his beloved sister? What did he really think of me – Beatrice Alexander?

"Oh, Cass," I cried. "Whoever you are, wherever you are, were you right in telling me not to commit to him? Tell me what to do!"

I looked up and saw a thin silhouette of her by the Yule tree. I was rising to speak to her when a small voice spoke behind me, "Miss?" I jumped. Dilly said, "The outside oven is ready, Miss. For the niska."

"What? Yes, of course."

No time to indulge in upset about another lost moment with my spirit girl. Our guests would be arriving following the afternoon service, and that goose needed to go into the oven. Thank goodness one of the older choir members agreed to lead the music for the later service.

Dilly, the Three Graces, and I worked for the next few hours, they with much chatting and laughing, I with grim determination. After the trussed goose was settled in the outside oven and the venison larded and tied to a spit, we went to church. Papa was too tired, after last night's festivities, to go, and Ivy chose to remain at Old Maples with him.

———

I was on the dais preparing my music sheets, when Robert arrived. He smiled, and I lifted my hand in greeting. Last night I'd put aside a scarf for him, which I had knit for Papa months ago. I tried to imagine myself giving it to Robert. Would he be pleased? Did he have a gift for me? How little we really knew each other. And, of course, I had no mother to guide me through a courtship, if that indeed was what this was.

This time, his smile held a flicker of warmth. Could we share a happy life together? Or, at least, a contented one? Is that what I wanted?

Soon I was distracted by the opening and shutting of the church doors and the bright chatter of my choir members.

Duncan appeared beside me. "I will not be singing in the later service."

"But why?" I asked. "You are one of our best singers."

"Am I?"

His teasing made me instantly testy. "Don't be coy. You know you are!"

He bowed slightly. "I am coming to the house to help you, Beatrice. I can't leave you with those children to set out that entire dinner. My mother will be no help at all. You're tired and strained. I see it in your eyes. Your papa will need help dressing. The fires need watching. No, Minty and I will be at your command all afternoon. No arguments!"

As he turned away, I wondered why Duncan was the only one who ever seemed to understand how I was feeling.

And why he always ruined any good intentions by teasing or ordering me about.

All went well with the service, and, back at home, the girls ran upstairs to tell nôhkom all about it. I wrestled the heavy venison roast on its spit toward the hearth's supports. Suddenly, the whole thing tipped upwards and almost knocked me into the fire. Ivy appeared beside me, and together we grappled it into place.

"Thank you, Ivy."

She wore a plain gray dress. Around her neck was a pretty necklace that had been my English grandmother's – given to her on her wedding day and to my mother on hers. The thin chain held a swallow in flight, with tiny gems for eyes, signifying affection from the giver. She pressed one hand against it.

"This was your papa's gift to me." It was said as a challenge.

"It's lovely and suits your dress well."

She looked startled. "Thank you for the lace handkerchief. I liked the way you did my initials."

I continued to work. "And I thank you for the book of poetry."

"Yes. Your papa chose it. I will make you some tea. You must be tired. And may I offer a jar of saskatoons for dinner this afternoon? And some pickled relish?"

"They would be most welcome. As would tea." I piled the plates with cake.

When I heard Ivy set the teapot down, I covered the cut fruitcake with a damp cloth. She sat at one end of the table, I at the other. We drank our tea in silence.

Finally, she cleared her throat. "I . . . I was wrong to accuse you of tricking Reverend Dalhousie into a marriage agreement,

Beatrice. I was not well that day, and the laudanum I took clouded my mind. I apologize."

No point in goading her with the fact that I knew why she was doing this. Humbling herself must be hard for her. "I accept your apology," I said, trying hard to mean it.

"Your papa loves you so much," she continued. Her expression was unguarded for the first time. "And . . . and I know he loved your mother just as much."

"Yes."

Looking thoughtful, she caught her top lip between her teeth. Then, to my surprise, she said, "I know he married me for convenience. But I loved him from the moment we met. Yes, you can stare, Beatrice. But it is the truth. I'm glad you are leaving us soon. Also the truth. It's hard for me to see how much your father loves you – for no other reason than you are his child – but it still pains me. I don't feel that same love when he looks at me. I never will. I only pray that he won't abandon me."

"But you have Duncan if, God forbid, anything should happen to Papa."

She looked to one side. "I don't imagine Duncan sees it that way. After all, I gave him up, didn't I? He doesn't know how it broke my heart to leave him. I had no choice! And suddenly, when I married Mr. Comper, I was told to raise two Indian boys that weren't mine. To feed and clothe them, all the while knowing I was betraying Duncan. It became too hard to bear. When the oldest one died, I sent Minty to his people in St. Anthony's. He was better off gone. My husband could be a violent man." I wondered why she was telling me this.

She sighed. "I was so happy when Duncan arrived from Scotland. Sadly, we have little to say to each other. He doesn't know me as I once was. And he will be leaving me soon."

"He will? When? Where is he going?"

"I don't know where. He told me yesterday. But when he is gone, if your papa abandons me, I will be utterly alone."

I was torn by shameful satisfaction and pity, but I said gently, "If you are a loving wife and care for Aggathas, you will gain my father's respect and affection."

"But not his love." She turned her cup around and around. "Never his love. That is why you must leave, don't you see?"

This was not the nasty, vicious Ivy I had come to know. This was a frightened Ivy. And one that gave me hope. Once I married Robert, I must trust that she and Papa would sort things out.

It was then that something struck me hard – Duncan was leaving.

I prayed he would wait until I left first. And when I had gone, would Ivy take care of nôhkom? Would she truly change? When I had gone . . . when I had gone . . . the words numbed me. Shadows swarmed inside my head.

I said firmly, "Ivy, my father chose to marry you. He will give you affection, care, and loyalty. But only if you earn it."

"How dare you speak to me this way! When I have unburdened myself to you. I knew it would be a mistake. I knew it!"

"Oh, Ivy! Why do you waste time showing how much you hate me? That only heightens Papa's scorn. Don't you see?"

Her eyes stared, then she burst into tears, her thin hands covering her face.

I couldn't make myself embrace her, so I patted her arm. "I'm sorry, Ivy. Please understand, I am trying to help."

She pulled herself together. "I am not one who cries. I will stop. You're right, of course. But I'm always afraid and I don't know why."

Like me, I thought. I wanted to tell her this, but instead I said, "Shall we call a truce? For Papa's sake?"

"Yes, for Gordon's sake. And mine. I am fair worn-out with it all."

"Good. Then let's prepare for our dinner party!"

As we organized the kitchen in subdued harmony, someone thumped on the back door. Dilly opened it. Duncan and Minty came in, carrying loads of wood. There were a number of brown-paper packages teetering on top of Duncan's pile. At the same time, the Three Graces walked in from the back rooms.

"Happy Christmas!" Duncan cried, putting down his burden and removing his hat.

We all stared like wâpitiy facing a raging fire. Duncan's hair had been cut, and his beard was gone. He looked so different, so young, his face now full of smooth angles.

The girls warbled back, "Happy Christmas!" and tittered behind their hands.

"Happy Christmas, Duncan," his mother said. "Why, don't you look handsome, my son!" She hugged him.

"Are you all right, Mother?"

She moved the presents to the table. "Of course. Why wouldn't I be?"

He looked at me. I raised my eyebrows and smiled. He dumped cut pine into the big wood-box.

Papa was urged from his study and settled in his favorite chair.

Duncan took off his heavy coat. Under it, he wore a dark woolen frock coat and trousers and a waistcoat over a white cambric shirt. And polished boots! He smelled of lavender, not a hint of barn. Was he planning on announcing his engagement to Henrietta tonight?

With great solemnity, he handed presents to each and every person. Except me. Fur mittens for the girls, a pretty fan for Ivy, and a beautiful painting of the river in autumn for Papa.

"We're Father Christmas's messengers," Duncan said. "We've delivered mittens and slippers to the children of the widows and also hay – and your cakes, Beatrice – to them and others. We're proud, but trying to be humble about it."

The girls laughed and told Minty how soft and well-stitched the mittens were. He smiled shyly.

"I have something for your grandmother," Duncan said. "May I take it up to her?" When I nodded, he added, "Perhaps you could bring her a cup of tea as well."

He lifted a large flat package and made for the door. There was no option but to follow, a cup of tea in one hand, a small plate of fruitcake in the other. Upstairs, he handed his present to nôhkom with a grand gesture. She must have been sleeping *for she looked confused at first, but when she recognized Duncan, she grinned.*

I needed to just get away from him. Cleaned up like this, with the tight black curls brushing his ears, he was too . . . it came to me with a jolt . . . compelling.

Grandmother opened her parcel and let out a cry of delight. I took in a sharp breath. It was a painting of me – in my best dress, my black hair coiled around my head, the star brooch pinned against a collar of the finest white lace. I didn't own such a collar. It was beautiful. My painted likeness looked at me with sadness and a half-smile. Is this how I looked to the world? To the artist? I felt for my little pin, but it was not there. Had I simply forgotten to put it on? I was sure I hadn't.

Grandmother said to Duncan, "It looks exactly like nôsisîs. When my ôhômisîsis is gone, it will bring me min-wêntamowin to look at it. Kinanâskomiṭin, Duncan!"

He bowed. "You're welcome. I'm glad it will bring you contentment."

My pin forgotten, I stared at nôhkom. "How long have you known I'm going away?"

She shrugged. "For almost as long as you. Do not worry, nôsisim. It is time for you to make your own home."

Duncan took a package out of his pocket and handed it to me. "I didn't forget you."

Inside was the beautiful lace collar from the painting. "The portrait is so lovely and this . . . this is most beauti-ful." My heart filled with joy and grief.

"I have nothing for you," I whispered. I could not look at him. For if I did, surely my heart would break.

36

CASS

Martin dropped me off at Aunt Blair's. She was sitting by the fire, reading. "Everything okay?"

I shrugged off my jacket. "No."

"Oh, dear. I was hoping . . . I just made tea, I'll get it. Why don't you go put your pj's on, and we'll relax, listen to some music, maybe talk, if you want to. I've got a casserole in the oven."

Did I want to talk? I ran upstairs, pulled on my pajamas, fleece housecoat, and thick socks. When I came back down, there was a comforter on the couch. I wrapped myself in it and took the mug of tea she handed me.

"So what happened?" Blair said.

I told her, trying hard to be fair, but knowing I was slanting it my way.

"You challenged her again," Blair said. "I know what she said was rather silly, but she was trying to be generous . . . in her own stilted way."

"Sounds as if you kind of like her now." I sounded sulky.

"Look, Cass, I don't like or dislike Jean. I had an opinion when your dad married her. I've let it go. I was judging her based on my feelings of loss. I don't *know* her."

"Well, I do."

"I want this to work for you. I hope you didn't talk about living with me yet."

"Why?"

"Okay. You did. I'm sure your dad was not thrilled with that."

"He's says we'll talk again, but basically, it's a no go. I didn't agree."

"I hope he doesn't think I put you up to this to cause more problems."

"I don't know what he thinks. He'll let me know, of course."

Blair slouched back in her chair and rested her head against its pillow. "Nothing is easy when someone so well-loved dies. Your dad was inconsolable. He's trying for a new, more hope-filled life. I can't blame him. I'm just glad I feel Fiona around me. I didn't for a long while. I'm sure you can feel her, too. That's a comfort, isn't it?"

I stared at her. "You can feel Mom? How?"

"I just sense her near. Sometimes I'm sure I can smell her favorite perfume, *Je Reviens*. Once I thought I heard her laugh, when I was singing. She always said I couldn't hold a tune."

"You're just imagining all that!"

She straightened up. "Don't you feel her? Are you upset I told you, Cass? Surely you, of all people –"

"I don't feel her, okay? And I don't feel her because she doesn't want me to. She wants to be near you because I broke my promise. . . ." There. It was finally out.

"What are you talking about, Cass? Fiona could never be mad at you. Not in a million years. What promise could you possibly have broken?" She pushed a box of tissues at me.

"The biggest one of my life. I –" My voice broke.

"What?"

Tears streamed down my face. I grabbed a handful of tissues and wiped them away. "I wasn't there!" I cried. "I went to the store to buy her some ginger ale and met a girl from school. We talked, and I felt free for the first time in ages. I didn't want to go back home – I didn't want to see Mom huddled under the covers, packed with hot-water bottles, hardly breathing. So I went for coffee with that girl, and we talked about music and movies, and it was fun. I stayed a long time. But when I got home, Mom was already gone! I promised to hold her hand when she went. I promised to say good-bye. You and Dad were both crying, so I couldn't tell you how I'd let her down. The stupid cans of ginger ale were still in my hands, and you guys are hugging me as if I'd done nothing wrong." I sobbed into my hands.

Blair hugged me. "Let it out, honey. Then I'm going to tell you something."

After a while, she left the room and came back with a hot cloth. I pressed it against my face. "Nothing you tell me will help. Nothing can."

She pushed back my hair. "Listen to me. Your mom would have completely understood what you did. She told me more than once that she hated you seeing her so sick. She often asked you to take more time for yourself, remember?"

I sniffed. "I *couldn't* take time out."

"She knew that. And you know what? I think she chose that time to die – so you wouldn't have to see it. She's with you. I know she's all around you."

"But I don't feel her," I whispered.

"Cass, have you ever thought that maybe *you* have been closing yourself off from *Fiona*? To punish yourself somehow? If you open yourself up to your mom, I know she'll come. I wish you'd told me this two years ago. No wonder you fight so hard for her around Jean. Guilt is a terrible responsibility. Especially when you did absolutely nothing wrong."

"Didn't I?"

"No. Your mom made the decision for both of you. She'd be extremely upset to think she only made things worse. Maybe you need to forgive her. Maybe you're mad at her for leaving you when you weren't there. God, I'm sounding like my own shrink now. . . ." She laughed, sadly.

I could feel the grayness lift a bit. We talked for a long time. About Mom. About Dad. And Jean. I told her about putting out Mom's things and Jean's reaction to it. She shook her head.

"Do you still think that Jean was after Dad, even when Mom was still here?" I asked. "You said that to Dad."

She looked uncomfortable. "I don't know anymore, honey. I was a wreck. He was a wreck. Jean always seemed to be around. I never really took to her, even when the local women would come and help out. There are some people you meet that you just fit with, you know? She and I don't fit. She's the exact opposite of your mom."

I nodded.

"But I have to admit, I wasn't fair to Jean. I didn't look at her as a good thing for your dad because it felt like she was taking my sister's place. I hated her for it. I don't anymore."

I told her what I'd found out about Jean's ex-husband. I didn't tell her about Beatrice. Not yet. Maybe one day. Martin knew. That's all that mattered.

"It's no wonder Jean's trying to control everything," she said. "Poor woman must be feeling pretty insecure. And if you're always talking about how much your parents loved each other . . ."

"I think Jean's just a bossy cow. She hates Mom."

"Don't hug this ideal vision of your parents' marriage too close to you, kiddo. Your mom wasn't an easy person to live with. You know that. She had her ups and downs and . . . well, your dad was always patient." I opened my mouth, but she shook her head. "They loved each other a lot, but your dad has never had anyone looking after *him*, has he? He's always looked after his older parents and then Fiona, keeping her on steady ground. She was a joy most of the time, but the down times were tough."

She was right. Mom had definitely been an up-and-down person. We used to argue, but we usually ended up laughing when it got out of hand because Mom's sense of the ridiculous always kicked in.

I smiled, remembering. "She called herself a Real Handful. She told me I was more sensible at thirteen than she was at thirty-five."

We talked about some of the crazy things she did, like making us all go vegan for weeks until Dad and I found her stash of pepperoni sticks behind all the veggies in the fridge.

Blair put her arm around me, and we laughed. Afterward, she said softly, "Yeah . . . Fiona wasn't easy to be around sometimes."

I nodded. "But I'd never tell Jean that!"

"Don't you think Jean offers your dad something he needs at this time in his life?"

"You make him sound senile, with a helpful nurse on hand."

She sighed. "Cass . . ."

"I don't know if she is what he needs. I only know I don't need her. We don't fit together and we never will. It's like she's a fish and I'm an apple; she's a tree and I'm a . . ."

"Wood-boring little insect?" she said. We both fell over laughing.

"Can I still stay with you if I want?" I asked. "If things . . . you know . . ."

"You don't ever have to ask me that again. That room upstairs is yours whenever you need it – if your dad agrees. All I ask is that you work out a deal with him that suits everyone, okay?"

"I'll have to think about that part," I said.

She left the room and came back with two bowls of lasagna. I noticed she didn't eat much either. "I'm wiped. Ready for bed?"

"I'm gonna stay down here for a bit."

She picked up the half-empty bowls and left. I snuggled back under the comforter and watched the flickering fire. For the first time in a long time, the air went deep into my lungs when I took a breath. I felt better about Mom and me, but I was so tired. . . .

I woke up in the dim light to find the diary lying open on the coffee table. The conversation between Beatrice and Ivy was riveting. I had a better idea now why Ivy ended up so damaged. *Maybe you should think about Jean's past life, too,* my inner voice said, but I ignored it. I read about Duncan Kilgour's arrival – the painting of Beatrice for her grandmother and the lace collar for Beatrice.

She thought she had put on the star brooch, only to find it missing from her dress later. Now I had it. Pinned to my pajama top. It was amazing that I was the one who found it in the old hearth. Wait! I knew why it wasn't on her dress! She'd been wrestling with the spit, which must have knocked against her collar. If she hadn't closed the clasp properly, the brooch probably flew into the hearth, landing on the tiny shelf where I found it. Then soot fell on it during the cooking of Christmas dinner, and no one found it.

It was obvious she was in love with Duncan and didn't know it. *Did she and Robert announce their engagement that night?* I eagerly turned the page. Nothing. All the rest of the pages were blank.

37

〜

CASS

I got dressed and made scrambled eggs, toast, and coffee for Blair and me. She came in just as the last piece of toast popped up.

"There was bacon in the fridge," she said, yawning. She was dressed for work, in jeans and an oversized plaid shirt.

"I'll make it next time. I called Martin. He's coming over to drive me to Dad's." I couldn't seem to call it home.

"Good," she said, pulling her hair into a ponytail with an elastic. "I sat in bed last night, making a decision, too. And then I acted on it."

"What was it?"

"I called my ex, Tom. We talked for an hour. He's moving back to Selkirk for a year to manage a friend's framing and art gallery. There's a small apartment above the shop, big enough for a studio. That way Tom can paint, but also make a living. He likes Winnipeg, but misses his friends here."

"Like you."

She grinned. "Yeah, like me. I told him I wasn't off my rocker anymore. He laughed."

I guess my fear showed on my face because she said, "This won't affect your being here, if that's what you're worried about, Cass. He knows about you. No . . . we'll take it one day at a time. I'll just be glad to see him again. I feel . . . ready."

I nodded, still feeling uneasy.

"I mean it, Cass. I'm not rushing into anything. It will all be fine. Okay?"

"Okay."

"Good. That's settled."

We ate our breakfast. I tried to enjoy it, but knew what lay ahead at Old Maples. When Martin knocked, I reluctantly got ready for the drive to the guillotine.

"Call if you need me," Blair said, making sure I had my cell phone.

Martin took my hand, and we headed to the truck. As we drove down River Road, the sun peeked over the line of trees across the river, spraying luminescent rays and throwing long shadows across the frozen white. A few cars lumbered past, the drivers wrapped in woolen hats and scarves.

Old Maples sat solidly under its heavy rounded cap of snow. It had once been Beatrice's beloved home. *Would it ever feel like mine again?* Maybe, one day, I'd live here with my own family, but for now it was Dad and Jean's. Not mine. Not Mom's. I left Martin listening to a CD and went in the back way to find Daisy sitting in the breakfast nook.

"Jonathan's still in bed. Mom's in the living room. She said if you came home early to go in there."

"I'll wait here until Dad gets up."

"No! You have to talk to Mom anyway, right? She wants to make things better." Her cheeks were bright red. "Please, Cass? Just go talk to her."

"Okay, okay!" I edged down the hall. Jean was curled up on the couch in front of a snapping fire, wearing a bathrobe and slippers. Her hair was held up by a big clip. She looked softer – tousled and tired. She gave me a sketch of a wave.

I didn't say hi. I was too busy staring at a huge balsam tree beside the fireplace, a pile of boxes in front of it. The room smelled of melted snow, balsam, and smoke. The fake tree was gone. For just one moment, I hoped to see Beatrice standing there.

"You okay, Cass?" Jean asked.

Cass? Wonders never cease.

"Your dad didn't like the blue-and-white twinkle tree any more than you did." She smiled. "It never really mattered to me what kind of tree we put up. We bought that hideous white thing when Daisy was small and used it for years, so I guess I put it up because it was something we always did. But I can see that you and your dad put great store in having a real tree."

"Are those boxes . . . ?"

"Yes. Your mom's – Fiona's – and your decorations. We found them in the barn. They're all here. But I haven't given up my tree altogether." She pointed to the dining room, where I could see blue lights flashing in a far corner.

I sat on the ledge of the fireplace and let the heat warm my back.

"Cass," she began, "I realize I've messed things up right from the get-go. Your dad tried to point this out to me time and again, but I just felt he didn't understand my position or your attitude to me. But when Daisy took your side and tried to leave last night, it really hit me: I've made a mess of everything. I talked to Daisy. She says you've only been responding to me like you have because I don't listen . . . because I'm someone with my own agenda."

I stared at my feet, not knowing how to react.

She went on, "I fought for everything I got in the way of concessions or support from my ex-husband. Then after marrying your dad, I was so busy putting forth my position, I forgot that you and he needed to have input into how your home was run. If I'd done one stitch in time, I could have saved nine. My little joke."

I tried to smile. "What *does* that mean, anyway?"

"It means if I was paying attention and fixed what was obviously becoming a problem right away, I could have kept us from making things worse for each other. When I made that announcement about the baby at the party, I think I was trying to avoid a clash between you and me by not telling you privately. Stupid, I know. I also knew your parents wanted another child after you and it didn't happen. I should have been more sensitive."

I shrugged. "It's done. No point in throwing the baby out with the bathwater."

She laughed softly. "Good one. But the dirty bath-water has to go, right?"

"Yeah. It does."

"It won't be easy, Cass. We've said some things to each other that will take time to heal. But from now on, we can maybe talk it over when stuff isn't working."

"I'd still like to stay at my aunt Blair's for a while. Come here weekends or something?"

She nodded slowly. "I'm not sure Jon will agree. He's got some issues with Blair."

"She's ready to sort all that out with him. She's a great person. The best. I want to spend time with her. And I think you, Dad . . . all of us . . . need some quiet time. I need to be by myself for a while. To think."

"I'm not trying to push you out of here, Cass. But you might feel more like coming home after you've been away for a bit."

"I have my own room there. . . ."

She stiffened, but then said, "I took away your room from you, didn't I? I wanted so hard to make this Daisy's home, too. I thought it would be good for you two to share a room and get to know each other. She was so lonely."

"You wanted me to share for her sake though."

"You're right. Daisy's dad has remarried. A woman with four kids. He's not interested in Daisy. I was all at sixes and sevens when we moved in here – full of anxieties. You see, I knew that if your mom . . . if Fiona hadn't died, I wouldn't have your dad in my life. Jon is the person I've waited for. You know, the one you hope will come one day. And even though I knew I was blowing it with you, I just kept on doing what I thought was right. But none of it was right. Was it?"

I didn't say anything. She smiled sadly.

"I know how much your dad loved Fiona. I think, because you look so much like her photographs, I felt threatened somehow. Jonathan adores you."

I was hearing an echo of Ivy's words to Beatrice. I knew it took guts to say it. "But he loves you, too." Surprisingly, my tongue did not fizzle into a burnt leaf.

She sighed. "Yes. He loves me, too. I know that. Just differently. So . . . I can only try, Cass. I'll make blunders again. But you must call me on them . . . if you can . . . by talking, not arguing."

"I'll try." I looked at her.

She was blinking hard.

"I think my being away for a while will help," I said.

"But you'll come back for weekends, right? Daisy would miss you if you didn't. She's turned into your biggest fan. So watch out, she'll be begging you for sleepovers at Blair's!"

For the first time, we smiled at each other.

38

CASS

"Your poor dad woke up this morning with a beast of a cold," Jean said. "I'll just go and make sure he's okay. And soften him up a little about your staying at Blair's – if you want."

I nodded. When she came out and signaled to me, I crept into their bedroom and perched on the end of the bed.

"Jean told me. So is this what you really want?" Dad asked. His hair was on end, his skin whiter than usual, the pale freckles splashed across his nose like bits of dark soot. He looked hot and irritable.

"Yes. Just for a while."

"You'll be here for Christmas Eve and Christmas Day, no arguments."

Had he actually accepted what Jean said? "Of course I will."

"And when I'm feeling better, Blair and I will talk."

"She didn't have anything to do with my decision, Dad. I asked her if I could stay. She never once hinted about my living there. And she won't do it unless you agree."

He snorted. "But I bet she said this place was not a good atmosphere for you."

I looked away.

He sighed. "She's probably right. But this is only temporary, Cass. We need to talk it all out. I want you home with us. But I don't want you to come home because I tell you to. I think you'll want to return once Jean and I settle things. There'll be big changes in this house."

"Like what?"

"I'll let you know. Get your things together. Jean can drive you."

"No, it's okay. Martin's waiting."

"That's another thing we need to do. Talk about Martin." He laughed when he saw my face. "Don't worry. I like the kid. But a talk is required."

I gave him a short hard hug. "I'll be here every weekend, Dad. I just –"

"I know, honey. I understand. Don't have to like it, though. I'll expect you here every Friday, and you'll go to school from here on Mondays. One month. Then we rehash this. I'll be checking up on you." He coughed and burrowed down under his blankets. "I'll have that Martin talk when I feel better. Meanwhile, just assume you've been given it."

I laughed, then went to my room to pack. Daisy was lying on her bed, her back to me. I could hear the odd sniff.

"I guess your mom told you what's happening." I zipped the bag shut and worked my way through the books I needed for the English poetry paper. Regular school stuff could be picked up another day. I zipped my laptop into its case.

Daisy didn't answer me, so I sat on the end of her bed cross-legged. "I just need some time away. I've been causing too much trouble in the house. I need breathing space. Dad's okay with it. I'll see you on the weekends."

"Yeah, but your stuff will disappear bit by bit, until all that's left is your bed and a few weekend clothes in the cupboard. I bet you're even taking your laptop, right?"

I glanced over at my pile of luggage. "I need it for schoolwork. You can come and visit me at Blair's. Martin and I could pick you up at school now and then, after Christmas. Take you over. Maybe have supper a few times in the holidays. We can all play Yahtzee."

She rolled over. Her eyes were red. "What about Christmas?"

"Are you kidding? Strict orders to be here."

She rubbed her eyes with her fingertips under her glasses. "Okay. Does Mom have Blair's phone number?"

"Yep. And I have a cell phone. I'll give you that number, too."

She nodded thoughtfully, taking the scrap of paper I handed her. "I guess that's okay."

After I'd climbed into the truck and Martin pulled away, I just couldn't make myself look back at the house.

When I hauled my stuff into Blair's, I stood in the hallway, suddenly shy and awkward. She gave me a big hug. "What's the deal you made with your dad?"

I gave her the short version. "I'll tell you more over lunch."

"Good. I hope the deal includes a family counselor. I know a good one."

"I'm thinking Dad'll decide if we need to rip our hearts out in front of someone."

She laughed. "Right. Hi, Martin. You can carry your stuff up to your room later, Cass. I've set lunch by the fire. Nicer there."

"Would it be okay if Daisy came over a few times for dinner? I told her we could play Yahtzee."

"She's welcome anytime. You decide when!" she said, heading for the kitchen.

Martin said, "Your aunt's a great person. Think your dad and her will be friends again?"

I smiled. "Anything's possible now."

39

CASS

Christmas turned out okay. Dad asked Blair for Christmas dinner, but she went to a friend's place. We were all a bit relieved, I think.

Dad was still thick with cold. He drank spiked coffee while we opened presents in the morning. As a token of our fledgling truce, I decided to give Jean the earrings I'd bought in Selkirk. She wore them all day. And no clichés flew. I'd left the pink Santa in my stuff at Blair's.

Jean wore Daisy's holly pin at dinner. Daisy was excited and out of control, of course, but we rode through it. I went to Martin's afterwards to visit with his family. His brothers teased him about me all night. It was fun.

I waited to hear from Beatrice, but nothing happened. On Boxing Day morning, I was getting ready to go back to Blair's when I tried touching the star brooch one more time. Still nothing.

Did Beatrice leave Old Maples suddenly? Did she marry Robert earlier than planned? What happened to Duncan? To

Beatrice's father? To Ivy? To her grandmother? What happened that Christmas Day in 1856?

How could it all just end like this? I'd learned so much about Beatrice through her journal, but what had she ever learned about me? Had I made any difference in her life? Why did she stop writing?

The more I thought about it, the crazier it seemed. *How could two people who lived a hundred and fifty years apart connect?* If only we could have really talked – just once. I had so many questions; I know she did, too.

Martin and I spent a lot of time together. It was fun working on our English project, and we got an *A*. His parents were great, and I saw quite a lot of his aunt Betty. I got to know his grandmother too. But every time he dropped me off at Aunt Blair's, I went right back to worrying about Beatrice, Duncan, and Robert.

I tried not to let my anxiety about the past get in the way of making things better with Jean. Dad was clearly happier now that she and I were trying to get along. She hardly ever slipped up and called me Cassandra anymore, and when she did, she'd laugh and say, "Oops! I'm in trouble!" I didn't roll my eyes. Not in front of her, anyway.

If we were totally honest, we'd have to admit we didn't really like or trust each other much, but we were trying. And if our feelings never went beyond a quiet truce, like Beatrice and Ivy's, that would be okay.

Was I feeling Mom around me? No. I tried talking into

the air sometimes, hoping she'd hear me, but it was harder than I realized bringing down the wall I'd put up between us. Maybe Blair just thought she felt Mom because she needed to feel her.

Daisy made new friends the first week back at school – two geeky girls, all grinning braces and spectacles, who hung out at Old Maples and played board games and Barbies and talked about boys for hours. But I had my own room to hang out in – at last.

Dad said he'd make changes in the house and he did. I suddenly got my room back when Jean had her small grand piano moved into the dining room. She'd have her music lessons there until they built an extension on the west side of the house that would also include a second-floor room for the baby.

One day, Jean called me at Blair's. I took the phone carefully. "The renovators got going on your fireplace today. Should be done by the weekend. But no live fires, Cass. Those old fireplaces worry me." I reluctantly agreed.

Aunt Blair gave me two old comfy chairs from her shop and an electric grate that glowed as if it were burning real coal. I could hardly wait to see what the fire-place looked like underneath its ugly painted wall box.

The following Friday, I went to Old Maples from school to find the renovator's truck outside. Two workers were having coffee with Jean. I waved at her and ran upstairs.

I stood in the doorway. There it was: Beatrice and her grandmother's fireplace, just as it appeared in my dream!

Made of limestone, its ancient slabs were dotted with tiny prehistoric water creatures. Around it was a set of narrow worn shelves. My heart sank. All the shelves were empty. No diary.

"So it's really over," I said to the quiet room, holding tight to the little star brooch. "You are really gone. And I'll never know what happened."

A small soft voice whispered, "Yes, my chick. She left us for a while. But she also remains here. Look to the small door below."

Over my shoulder, I caught a flash of bright old eyes and a pale bonnet surrounding a crumpled dark face. And then it was gone. But I could feel her presence close to me, watching and waiting.

I studied the fireplace. All I saw was the small stone structure, five plain shelves on either side, and a smoke-discolored mantel. *What did she mean,* Look to the small door below? Each set of narrow shelves ended with a deep baseboard. I kneeled down and pushed, but each board remained firm.

I sat back on my heels. Beatrice's grandmother had directed me here, so a cupboard or alcove had to be here somewhere. I examined one set of shelves close to the floor. Nothing. I looked at the other set and found a small hole in one board. I put my finger in and pulled. The board held fast. I braced my foot against the wall and pulled again.

The board came away with such force, it knocked me over. Rubbing my sore hand, I peered into the low rectangular space under it and pulled out a flat object.

Beneath a thick layer of dust was a leather-wrapped parcel with faded writing on it.

To Cass. Happy Christmas!

Shivers went from my knees straight up my body and into my arms. I opened the parcel carefully. Sitting on the floor, I began to read Beatrice's last entry.

40

BEATRICE

*F*lustered *by Duncan's gifts, I fled the room, exclaiming over my shoulder that there was still much to get ready. Once in the kitchen, I searched for my pin, remembering suddenly that I'd worn it to church. Did it fall off there? I scoured the house for it. When the girls asked me what was wrong, I told them and they helped me search. It was nowhere to be found. Even Ivy helped. I wondered briefly if she had taken it, but, for once, became certain she was innocent. If it was lost forever, surely this was a warning.*

I continued doggedly with dinner preparations, hoping they would help me stop thinking about Duncan and the lost pin. Before I knew it, the food was almost ready and our guests had arrived, greeted by Papa and Ivy. The girls were watching the guests crowd into the hallway. I was a bundle of nerves, hiding in the kitchen. For I had made a momentous decision. Would I back out at the last moment? Did I have the strength to speak up? To muddle me even more, Duncan came into the room to offer help after building up the fires.

"No, no, I am fine!" I said, my voice high and off-center as I struggled to lift the iron bar full of venison off the fire with Papa's old leather mitts.

He leaned over and, with towels around both hands, grabbed it from me. "I'll tend to this. You do something else."

I didn't argue. He carefully slid the slabs of venison onto a massive wooden board while I mashed the turnips. Then he carved the venison, the goose, the large whitefish, and the pickled buffalo tongue he'd also brought earlier. The room steamed with mouthwatering odors.

I tried to stay as far away from Duncan as I could, but I seemed to find him near me every time I turned around. We often touched without seeming to. He'd heard about my lost pin. "We will find it," he kept saying.

I was breathless with apprehension about seeing Robert and so upset about the pin that I begged Duncan not to talk of it again.

When I lined the dishes up on the table, the girls carried them out to the dining room. I tried to pull myself together. I had to carry out my final decision. Now. As Duncan and the girls headed out the door, loaded down with the final platters, I ordered Dilly to ask Reverend Dalhousie to come to the kitchen. Duncan's platter banged against the doorjamb, and I caught a glimpse of his startled look as the girls ushered him through.

I took off my apron. A few moments later, Robert, looking fresh in a new collar of untainted white – a present from his sister or a concerned woman of the parish? – edged through the door.

"Your little maid said you wished to speak to me. I'm sorry you have to spend so much time in the kitchen, but the table is groaning with your appetizing dishes."

I coughed lightly. "Yes. I do have something I wish to speak to you about, Reverend . . . Robert. A painful and difficult thing."

He nodded solemnly. "You've made a decision, and you have not chosen me."

I put my hand to my throat, feeling for the missing pin. "Whatever do you mean? Not chosen you? Who else would I—?"

He bowed slightly. "Forgive me for interrupting. Kilgour woke up my entire household this morning, banging on my door. He insisted on talking to me. He told me that I would destroy you if I married you, that he was not going to see you waste your life with someone who didn't love you with all his heart." He smiled a tight smile that did not reach his eyes.

"He didn't!"

"Do not be too hard on him. You were about to decline my proposal anyway, were you not? I wish only your happiness, Miss Alexander. Let it end here."

"You mean, you are not even a little bit upset?"

"As you have said, there is no love on either side. Nothing has been announced yet, so no one need know I asked. I wish you well, Beatrice. However, in retrospect, I think your decision is the right one. For I fear you may not have the . . . um . . . temperament for the arduous and selfless work of a minister's helpmate."

Not the temperament to be his helpmate? Not his wife, but his helper? Duncan Kilgour spent the morning manipulating my life, and now I was being chastised by this pompous preacher.

I cried, "Come! Let us eat our festive meal, Reverend. For it appears you have something to celebrate. Not having me as a wife!"

I marched out of the kitchen. I touched cheeks with Henrietta and Miss Cameron and welcomed their guest pupils. Duncan was already seated beside nôhkom at the long table. I commanded everyone to sit down in my best teacher's voice. And they quickly sat.

Duncan glanced at me, his face wary. Nôhkom smiled sweetly. Papa, always the genial host, was cheerfully chatting with Henrietta, who seemed quite animated, her dog's squashed little face peering over the tabletop with gluttonous eyes. Even Ivy didn't complain that I was acting as hostess. She smiled coyly at Papa from the other end of the table. I held my head high. Soon the food was passed around, for I insisted everyone in the house should be seated, including Dilly, who was bright cheeked and happy, wearing one of my old dresses.

Papa's apple cider was poured by Duncan. As he poured some into my glass, he leaned over me, as if about to say something, but I talked loudly to Papa and ignored him. I wanted this meal over with, so I could plead a headache when the after-dinner guests arrived. I was desperate to go to my room to vent my utter fury and mortification at Robert Dalhousie's and Duncan Kilgour's cruel behavior and to cry for my lost pin.

Duncan Kilgour kept trying to catch my eye. He looked worried. As well he should – bullying loudmouth that he was, slinking off to threaten Robert and turning him against me. Robert was talking to Miss Cameron, their heads together.

Perhaps I should change my mind. Robert was a decent, kind man, after all. And what happiness could I hope to find by remaining here? However, one could not turn down a marriage proposal only to ask for it back. Besides, he didn't want me! A wisp of shadow fluttered around my head.

It was a jolly dinner for everyone else, it seemed. Miss Cameron and Robert were conversing amiably, while the young people, shy at first, were soon chatting and laughing.

Papa talked to me about my new book of poems, admitting he'd read it before wrapping it for me. I smiled, but my smile felt frozen in place. As the girls cleared the table, Papa patted his stomach and Ivy giggled with delight.

The world had surely spun upside down.

When Dilly and the Three Graces entered the room with the pudding, sauce, and other sweets, Papa demanded the pudding be lit. Over its blue light of alcohol, Duncan gave me a bleak smile. I stared back, ice in my veins.

After the pudding and sweets were eaten, the tables were pushed back for music and dancing. Soon the other guests arrived – Mrs. McBride, her husband, James, and her three sons, carrying their violins; and a neighbor, Jacob MacFadden, and his family, who were also great friends of Papa's. Soon fiddles were tuning and people were dipping into the warm wassail bowl by the fire. Everyone demanded that Duncan and Minty bring out their fiddles as well.

Duncan laughed and said he'd fetch them from the kitchen. But he moved to stand beside me. "What is wrong? You look –"

"Go away!"

He took my arm and I shook him off. "What is it, Beatrice? Has Dalhousie said something?"

Papa and Ivy were staring at us.

"Go to the kitchen. Now!" I commanded.

He hesitated, then called out, "Even Beatrice wishes me
to play the fiddle. I'll grab yours, too, Minty!"

I followed him down the hall. When the door shut behind
us, I pushed him so hard he lost this balance and banged
against the table.

"How dare you interfere in my life! I was about to tell
Robert I could not marry him, but he told me you'd already
tried to force him to take back his proposal!"

"I did no such thing. I told him to think of you and not
his household needs. He needed testing!" Duncan was
looking haughty and hurt at the same time.

"So you decided to manipulate things in your usual
bullying way! Robert told me I did not have the temperament to be a minister's wife! You suggested that,
didn't you?"

He sat back on the edge of the table, arms folded. "So he
has been trying to figure out how to wheedle his way out of
it all along. You see? I warned you!"

"He's too much of a gentleman to do such a thing. I
turned him down!"

"Of course, he would have married you! He sees himself
as a man of honor. But I knew you were going to leave with
a man who didn't love you, just to spite me!"

"You? What makes you think you had anything to do
with my decision? You are an arrogant rooster!"

"What you're really angry about, Beatrice, is that you turned him down, only to find out that's exactly what he hoped you would do!" He laughed loudly.

"That is a lie!" I shouted, my ears roaring with rage.

"Think about this, Beatrice. I've saved you from going to church every Sunday to admire the dull droning sermons of a dull droning husband; from tending to his frivolous, sickly, hypochondriac sister; from tea at precisely four, rising at precisely six; and especially from books of carefully chosen anemic poetry. Now you are free to read dangerous novels, maybe even write a book of your own, and to enjoy musical evenings of quadrilles and Red River jigs." He nodded his head at the door, where the lilt of fiddles and violins playing their mix of Celtic and Indian tunes drifted in.

"I had already decided not to marry him, you buffoon!"

He put up his hands. "But how was I to know that, lass? All I knew was that I must warn him off. Don't you see? You would have withered away in that barren, stale life. And I would have wandered the world, grieving for you every day of mine."

I stared at him. "What?"

"I love you, Beatrice. Marry me."

"Don't you dare tease me! As if I would share my life with someone who wouldn't treat me as an equal. Who would always try to control me. I would wither and die in that life as well!"

He stood in front of me, saying softly, "Your decision not to go with Robert Dalhousie – I had nothing to do with it?"

"No."

His face came close to mine. I could feel his breath on my

cheek. "Nothing? Nothing at all? Be honest with me, Beatrice. Please."

I wavered. "No. Nothing. Oh, I don't know!"

He put his hands on my shoulders, and this time I didn't push him away. "You must know me well enough now, my dearest girl, to realize that a marriage between us would be one of equal companionship, interests, and great affection. I cannot promise to be an undemanding husband, and I would not expect you to be a timid and easily controlled wife. In fact, I demand that you be difficult and bossy!"

I looked up at him. His hair was wild from brushing his hands through it. His cheeks were flushed. "Yes, I think I know you well enough," I said.

He shook me gently. "Then you will marry me?"

I touched his warm face with the tips of my fingers. "Do you love me, Duncan Kilgour?"

"'How do I love thee? Let me count the ways.'" He grinned. "Yes, I got to read your father's gift to you as well. Do you want to see me wasting away for love?"

I laughed. "No. I suppose I will have to marry you. But for one thing."

"And what in heaven's good name is that?" he cried.

"Minty and Dilly must come with us wherever we go."

"Done!"

When Dilly danced into the room, humming the tune from "Strip the Willow," she found us lost in each other.

After composing ourselves, Duncan and I rather awkwardly announced our engagement to the group assembled in the parlor. Robert Dalhousie and his sister clapped hands, as *if delighted. The students shrieked, and Minty grinned. Papa pounded Duncan on the back. Nôhkom pressed her hands to her heart and smiled in a knowing way that made me laugh outright. Ivy didn't faint or shriek, but turned white, as if ready to oblige us with either at any moment. Fortunately, Papa wrapped one arm around her shoulders, so she pasted on a valiant smile.*

Later, when I was preparing pots of tea, Miss Cameron came to the kitchen. "I must congratulate you again," she said, pressing her cool lips to my cheek. "I am so happy for you. Duncan is a wonderful young man."

I blushed. "I do love him, it seems."

"That, my dear, has been obvious for some time. And I have news that I hope will make you happy for me. Mr. Dalhousie has quietly offered me his hand in marriage. I have accepted. We won't announce it until just before he leaves. My dear friend Miss Stiles will be happy to take over the school."

"Robert? He asked you? Already?" I blurted. "I mean, are you sure about this?"

"Lately I have found myself longing for change, Beatrice. Robert is a kind man. I think we will do well together. I would like a family. I'm older than him, but still young enough to have children." She smiled. "I'll learn to love Robert. He is all that is good. I do know he asked you first, Beatrice, and that you turned him down."

I embraced her and laughed. "It was mutual, I assure you. He told me I would not have made a good minister's wife, in any case. I'm sure he will soon love you as I do."

She touched my hand. "You are the lucky one, Beatrice. For you have already found love. I hope I will be as blessed."

We hugged, and I watched her leave with great sadness.

Soon Robert, his sister, Miss Cameron, and their girls left. The rest of us danced the evening away – to "Reel of Four," "Double Jig," "Rabbit Chase," "Tucker Circle," "Red River Jig," and "Drops of Brandy" – with Duncan and the other men taking turns fiddling until sweat poured down their faces. At midnight, our guests cheerfully prepared to make their way home.

After I tucked nôhkom into bed, and the girls struggled groggily to their pallets, Duncan and I sat in the parlor. We were reluctant to part.

"No sign of your little pin?" he asked, his thumb gently caressing my hand.

"No. Perhaps, one day, we'll stumble upon it," I said. "I hope it's in the church somewhere. I'm sure it can't be lost forever." He nodded and I said, "I wonder where we will be this time next year, Duncan?"

"Beatrice, I've been a traveler for a long while now. I will willingly settle here, if that is your wish." He clasped my hand firmly. "I only want to be with you. Where does not matter."

"I would love to see the things you've seen, Duncan. Go to some of the distant places you've traveled. But not until the spring has come to the river."

He pulled me gently toward him, "But we will marry before then?"

I leaned over and kissed him. "Oh, yes, we will marry before then!"

41

CASS

That's where it ended. But a paper pouch had been stuck to the inside of the back cover. In it was a thick photograph, browned with age, and a small envelope. In the lower left corner of the photo was written HUMPHREY LLOYD HIME, PHOTOGRAPHER, 1857. I sucked in a sharp breath.

The photograph showed a young woman with large eyes and wing-tipped eyebrows, wearing a creamy white dress and lace collar. She was seated in a chair, holding a bouquet of spring flowers. On her head, a ring of smaller flowers shone in her black hair like tiny stars. She wasn't able to smile because the exposures for photographs of that time took ages, but she radiated happiness. Behind her stood a young man with a barrel chest and a mop of dark curly hair, dressed in a formal suit. He was not smiling either, but the photographer had captured the humor in his eyes. One hand rested on the young woman's shoulder. I could see the toe of a polished boot. Beatrice's decision, no doubt!

I hungrily studied their faces, their clothes, every inch. Then I sat on the floor, hugging the picture. Finally, I turned it over and read To CASS, FROM BEATRICE. ON MY WEDDING DAY TO DUNCAN KILGOUR, APRIL 12TH, 1857. With trembling fingers, I opened the small envelope.

What can I say, my spirit girl, dearest child of my ancestors and future children, for I know from nôhkom that you are of my blood. She died three weeks after Christmas, and she returned to me in my dreams to tell me who you are. It's true that the soul is everlasting, Cass. When we die, we experience only a bodily death. Our spirits continue our passage.

I know the future holds many blessings and hardships for both of us. But I look eagerly toward every new day. I wish we had been able to know each other. We would have become the best of friends. But thank you, nitâniskocâpânis, for helping me.

Christmas Day was a happy one, despite the loss of my brooch. But then, like a flash of lightning, came the day when I suddenly knew, with a rush of joy, that it was you who found it. It is my gift for you to pass on to your children and their children. You gave me a greater gift by telling me to turn away from Robert Dalhousie and toward the one thing I've longed for since my mother died – a dear friend to whom I can say anything and still know I am loved . . . my husband, Duncan.

When you read this, I will be gone. I smile when I say this, for what I mean is, I will be gone from this parish – for Duncan, Minty, Dilly, and I will soon be off on great adventures together. Papa has insisted that we go. We will return one day, and I know from nôhkom that I will be blessed with three sons and one daughter, who will bear the child that leads through four generations to you. Of course, you will understand that I will also be gone from this earth when you read this. Do not grieve for me. For I have much to see and do before that time arrives!

My greatest wish would be to talk with you . . . to know more about you. I know so little, and yet you greatly affected my life. Perhaps that is the way it was meant to be. I hope, in some small way, I helped your sadness. I will always hold dear the vision of you when I first saw you, with your halo of red hair. My Christmas angel. How did this happen to us? We will meet again, I know. Be strong, nitâniskocâpâ-nis. With love and trust, Beatrice.

I saw something flicker at my window. The light outside dimmed, and the small smiling face of Beatrice's grandmother was reflected in the frost-swirled glass. She faded, and, as soon as she was gone, Mom's smiling face appeared and quickly faded. *Did I really see her?* I don't know. But I know, like Beatrice, she is with me now. Really with me.

CREE GLOSSARY

I want to extend my sincere thanks to two people who guided me through the compiling of this Cree Glossary:

Arok Wolvengrey – associate professor, linguistics coordinator, and head of the Department of Indian Languages, Literatures, and Linguistics, First Nations University of Canada. My heartfelt thanks for your help – and your patience and kindness.

Phillip Paynter – Swampy Cree elder and teacher, who hails from Norway House. Your knowledge of the Swampy Cree dialect was invaluable.

Most of the words in this glossary are Swampy Cree from the Norway House area in Manitoba, except (as said by Mr. Paynter) in the case of "badger," for example, for which no word exists in the dialect. As Beatrice's family lives in a community not far from the Red River settlement and the aboriginal parish of St. Anthony's, Cree words from different dialects would have been incorporated when necessary.

The glossary is alphabetized as per the conventions of the Cree Standard Roman Orthography (SRO): a, â, c, ê, h, i, î, k, m, n, o, ô, p, s, t, w, y, (th).

All spellings with short vowels (e.g., "a," "i," "o") precede their corresponding long vowels (e.g., "â," "ê," "î," "ô"). In other writing systems, particularly those used for eastern dialects of Ojibway, long vowels are often represented by double vowels. Phillip Paynter sent me his words using the double vowels, but I chose to use the SRO format for clarity and ease of understanding in the novel's text.

A further convention of the Cree SRO is to avoid all capitalization. This convention, however, is not necessarily unanimously accepted throughout Cree-speaking territory. I have used capitals only when the words are at the beginning of a sentence.

AUTHOR'S NOTE

It is obvious that my main character Beatrice would speak Cree, learned from her Swampy Cree grandmother. However, there would have been no Cree dictionary for her to refer to in order to *write* the language in her journal. She would, no doubt, have relied on phonetic spelling. I decided, once again, for clarity and ease of understanding, to stay with Arok Wolvengrey's spelling of the words. In the glossary, I have also used the double-vowel words Mr. Paynter gave me, and they are in brackets beside Mr. Wolvengrey's Cree SRO words. Any errors in this glossary are mine alone.

You will also notice that I leave out words like "my," "your," "their" before some Cree words. For example, *nitêh* is the Cree word for "my heart." The "my" is implied in the Cree word.

Although the general history for this area along Manitoba's Red River was researched with care – from the early settlement in what is now Winnipeg to Lower Fort Garry, about twenty miles away – the parish of St. Cuthbert's is entirely fictional, as are all the events and characters in the story.

âkathâs – English [Note: the name Aggathas probably came from this Cree word.]

âpihtawikosisânak – half-breeds or Métis

cakâstêsimowina (cahkaastesimowina) – shadows

cîkahikanis (ciikahikanis) – hatchet

ê-nôhtêhtâmoyân (enoohtetaamoyaan) – I am short of breath, feeling faint

ininiw – Cree, Cree man, Cree Indian, Indian

kakêpâtis – silly crazy

kinanâskomitin (kinanaskomitin) – thank you, I am grateful to you

kîhkwîsiw (kiihkwiisiw) – whiskey jack, Canada jay, gray jay

kôhkom (koohkom) – your grandmother

mac-âya (macaaya) – evil, nastiness

makosêwi-kîsikâw – Christmas, celebration

minwêntamowin (minwentamowin) – joy, contentment

mistanask – badger

mîkowâhp – wigwam

mîwat (miiwat) – packsack, backpack

nikâwiy – my mother

niska – goose

nitâniskocâpânis (nitaaniskotaapaan) – my great-great-granddaughter [Note: the extra diminutive suffix (*-is*) is not strictly necessary, but adds an element of endearment; without the diminutive, it would be nitâniskotâpân.]

nitêh – my heart

nôhkom (noohkom) – my grandmother

nôsisim (noosisim, noosim) – my grandchild

okimâw (okimaawiw) – head person, boss, king, leader

okiskinwahamâkêw (okiskinowahamaakew) – teacher, instructor

okîskwêw (kiiskwew) – crazy person

ôhômisîsis (oohoomisiisis) – little owl

sâkihitowin (saakihitowin) – love, mutual love, affection, charity

sihkosis – weasel [Note: sihkosiw and sihkos are also correct.]

sîwîhtâkan (siiwihtaakan) – salt

wâpitiy (waapitii) – white-tailed deer

winsikis – snakeroot [Note: there are a number of Cree words for this plant. The Cree name for Seneca in Saskatchewan and Manitoba is winsikis, while the pioneers called it rattlesnake root because it was considered an antidote for venomous snake bites.]

wîtisâna – (wiitisaana) his/her blood relatives, his/her siblings

"à la façon du pays" – in the manner of the country, commonly referring to a marriage between a white man and an aboriginal woman during the fur trade. The marriage was sealed by a simple ceremony of agreement between the two parties and an exchange of gifts.

Anglican Church Missionary Society (CMS) – a London-based arm of the Anglican Church that funded mission outposts in different parts of the world, including the Red River settlement. It stressed the themes of the Christian religion, education, and European farming methods to advocate Anglo-Christian principles and to encourage cultural changes within the aboriginal societies.

Carriole – a light open or covered sleigh or toboggan drawn by a single horse and sometimes dogs.

Carron stove – a type of stove made at the Carron Foundry in Falkirk, Scotland, exported to fur-trade posts in Canada. The most common was a rectangular firebox made up of cast-iron plates. These stoves were very practical as they could easily be taken apart and shipped.

Ceilidh – a party with folk music, dancing, and story-telling.

The Company – The fur trading company known as the Hudson's Bay Company (HBO) was commonly referred to by people in the Red River settlement as "The Honorable Company," or simply, "The Company."

Freethinkers – The Victorian freethinker movement was an ill-defined group made up not only of writers and intellectuals, but a growing number of working class who formed a more radical freethought movement. Freethought is a philosophical viewpoint that things, such as religion, should be formed on the basis of science, logic, and reason, and should not be influenced by authority, tradition, or any other doctrine. People who practice freethought are known as freethinkers.

The Interlake – the name given to a region in Manitoba, Canada, that lies roughly between Lake Winnipeg and Lake Manitoba and is made up of fourteen rural municipalities. It has a number of popular bathing, camping, and fishing areas.

Receipt – a recipe. Both "receipt" and "recipe" derive from Latin *recipere*, meaning to receive or take.

Rupert's Land – a territory in Canada (and a very small portion of the USA) purportedly owned by the

Hudson's Bay Company (HBO) between 1670 and 1870, although many aboriginal groups who had lived there for generations disputed the HBO's control of the area. Besides most of Saskatchewan, southern Alberta, southern Nunavut, and northern parts of Ontario and Quebec, it also included all of Manitoba.

Sexton – a church officer charged with the maintenance of the church's buildings and graveyard. In smaller Anglican churches, this office was often combined with that of the verger, who assisted in the organization of religious services and other "nonspeaking" duties.

The WI – The Women's Institute movement was started in Stoney Creek, Ontario, in 1914 by farm wife Adelaide Hoodless. After the death of her infant, Mrs. Hoodless launched a movement to create a support group that would help rural women by providing an organized source of support, education, and companionship. It is still active today in many rural communities.

Writer – an office clerk in the HBC, whose job was to keep accounts, write daily journals, and keep up with correspondence.

York boat – an inland freight boat used on larger waterways and lakes from about 1790 to the early 1870s. It was rowed by ten to twelve men and able to carry several tonnes of goods and provisions. York boats could be portaged by pulling them over log rollers on wide portage trails.